I0545725

THE DEVIL'S DIAMOND;

Or, the Fortunes of Richard of the Raven's Crest.

CHAPTER I.

INTRODUCES THE HERO.

THREE Spanish galleons were labouring heavily through the troubled waters of the Great Southern Ocean, laden with death and destruction to an innocent and happy people.

At the prow of the foremost, that which bore the flag of the commander—Francisco Pizarro—stood Richard of the Raven's Crest, gazing with a thoughtful and somewhat troubled mien towards the green slopes and wooded heights bordering the beautiful bay of St. Matthew, the place of their destination.

As he stood there, leaning in an easy, graceful attitude against the bulwark, his splendid form was exhibited to full advantage. He was but a boy in years—for scarce sixteen summers had flown over his head—but he had almost the stature of a man and the strength of a gladiator was in those rounded limbs, yet lithe and supple with the grace of youth.

The fiery blood of Richard Cœur de Lion, the hero King of England, coursed in his veins, and in every lineament of his handsome face—in every flash of his bright blue eye, Richard of the Raven's Crest showed that he was no unworthy descendant of the lion-hearted monarch.

"And this is the land," mused our hero, "which the dauntless Columbus discovered, and to which Amerigo Vespucci has given his name. It is, indeed, a new world, which the haughty Spaniard has dared so many perils to subdue. By St. George, a fair country, and well worth the winning, and yet my mind misgives me."

Richard had been so absorbed in his own reveries that he had not noticed the approach of a spare, slightly-built man, whose swarthy complexion, sharp regular features, and dark eyes, proclaimed him a Spaniard, while the long robe of coarse brown serge, girt at the middle with a cord upon which hung a rosary, told of his priestly profession. It was Vincent de Valverde, chaplain to Pizarro's expedition.

"Benedicite mi fili," said the low, deep voice of the Spanish priest. "Like a true son of holy Church, thou already longest to set foot on the land which the faithful are to wrest from the grasp of the heathen."

"I will not deny, padre mio," rejoined Richard, "that it well contents me to see the end of this long and toilsome journey; but——"

"But what, my son?" said the priest, regarding Richard with a searching, inquisitive look.

"I have misgivings, holy father, as to the justice of all this. Since we came in sight of yonder lovely land, the very aspect of which seems to breathe of peace, I have asked myself what right have we to carry desolation, fire, and sword into its midst."

"Go to!" exclaimed Valverde, while a faint flush of colour tinged for a moment his swarthy cheek. "Darest thou question the justice of aught our holy father, the Pope, hath sanctioned. Dios mio, I fear thou art little better than an infidel thyself, and yet thou claimest descent from Richard Plantagenet!"

"Ay, and let no man gainsay it," said our hero, haughtily.

"Be it so, my son," replied Valverde. "Then prove thyself worthy of the illustrious blood that courses in thy veins. When did Richard of the Lion Heart spare the heathen who polluted the Holy Sepulchre. They were dogs, and sons of dogs in his sight, and he struck, and spared not. Thou hast the thews and sinews of thy mighty ancestor. Few but Pizarro, our noble commander, could stand up against thee, boy though thou art in years. Prove, then, that thy heart is as strong as thy hand; and carry forward the work which our holy Church has set thee to do."

"Be it so, padre mio, replied Richard; "I was but thinking——"

"Thou art but a boy, Senor Richard," interrupted the priest, sternly "and it ill becomes thee to think when thou art told to act. Trust me, if the noble Pizarro heard thy heresy, he would show thee but scant patience——"

"What I have said to thee, padre mio," returned our hero, proudly, "I would say to Pizarro or any man. A Plantagenet fears not to speak his thoughts —ay, or to act upon them, should he think fit."

"Here, then, is thy opportunity," said Padre Valverde, with a malignant smile. "Here comes the noble Pizarro himself; speak thy rebellion into his ears, if thou darest."

Richard of the Raven's Crest turned suddenly, and found himself face to face with the great Spanish commander, and for a moment the two looked at each other without speaking.

This extraordinary man, whose name will live as long as the world has a history, was, at that time, in the prime of life—short in stature, sparely built, but of extraordinary strength and powers of endurance. His marvellous personal courage and his resolution, which only looked upon obstacles to his will as things to be conquered, had already made his name famous; and of all the men in the Spanish forces there was not one who would not have shuddered at the idea of thwarting his will.

"Who talks of rebellion?" said Pizarro, at last, in a singularly low, musical voice, contrasting strangely with the stern resolute expression of his features.

"That did I, noble Pizarro!" replied Valverde, with the same malignant scowl upon his face. "Senor Ricardo has thought fit to question the justice of our cause, though he knows well that our holy father, Pope Alexander, hath sanctioned and blessed it."

"Muerte de Dios!" exclaimed Pizarro, frowning until his heavy brows almost concealed his eyes. "What is this you say, Padre Valverde? Speak, Senor Richard of the Raven's Crest. Defend yourself!"

"There is no cause, noble Pizarro!" replied our hero, calmly. "I am English born, and free to think and act as I see fit."

"Thou art not!" returned the fiery Spaniard. "Thou art here serving under my banner, sworn to fight in the cause of holy Church, and for his sacred majesty, Charles of Castile. How then darest thou say that thou art free to act and think for thyself?"

"I am no subject of Charles of Castile," replied our hero, haughtily. "But what I have pledged myself to perform, that will I do. My gold has helped to equip the expedition, my sword shall defend it—but only when my conscience bids me strike. Senor Pizarro, you have your answer."

Pizarro flushed deep red, and his right hand

went to the hilt of his sword, but controlling himself by a strong effort, his brows unbent, and his features relaxed into a scornful smile.

"I was a fool," he said, "when I brought from Spain a meddlesome boy to mar my plans. I was a fool when I thought that, because thou hadst the strength and stature of a man, thou must needs have, also, a man's tried wisdom, and that because thy sword was sharp, thy wit must be as keen. But mark me, Richard of the Raven's Crest, I alone am master here; when I speak all must obey. Francisco Pizarro brooks no interference with his will."

And, without waiting to hear another word, the Spanish commander strode away, accompanied by Padre Valverde, leaving our hero undecided whether to follow and defy him, or wait the course of events.

He decided upon the latter, for, looking for a moment at the retreating figures of the Spanish commander and the priest, he turned, and, with a scornful smile, gazed again upon the fair land to which the heavy galleons were bearing them.

"Ay, Francisco Pizarro," he muttered half aloud, "thou art indeed a fool, if thou thinkest that thy overbearing Spanish pride can daunt one of my race. I have heard of the infamous cruelties which Pizarro's predecessor, Cortes, inflicted upon helpless women and children. Let me but see a sign that he intends to tread the same bloody path, and he shall find that he has no mean enemy to deal with in Richard of the Raven's Crest!"

CHAPTER II.

HOW THE EXPEDITION LANDED IN PERU—THE SECRET CONFERENCE—RICHARD OF THE RAVEN'S CREST CLAIMS HIS RIGHT—THE QUARREL—"ST. GEORGE FOR MERRIE ENGLAND!"—RICHARD OF THE RAVEN'S CREST DEFIES PIZARRO.

THAT same afternoon the Buen Esperanza, the San Michel and the San Josef ran into the Bay of St. Matthew, and in the universal joy at the safe arrival and in the bustle of the preparation for landing, both Pizarro and our hero forgot for the time the angry words which had passed between them.

Not so the crafty priest, Vincent de Valverde. With him to mistrust was to hate, and he saw already in young Richard of the Raven's Crest a possible formidable obstacle to the full accomplishment of his designs.

"Yes, I was too hasty," mused the priest; "I ought to have known better than to let that English boy so move me. We are too few in number to dispense as yet with the aid of his strong arm and that of his bull-dog follower, Hubert, the free lance. But once let our triumph be assured—once let our footing in Peru be certain—then, Richard of the Raven's Crest, look to yourself, and dread the vengeance of Valverde!"

While the crafty priest was thus communing with himself, our hero and his follower, Hubert, were holding deep and earnest converse upon the same subject.

"Trust me, Master Richard," said Hubert, a grizzled war-worn veteran of forty years, but still strong and sturdy as the oak which his native England bears—"trust me, these crafty Spaniards mean but this, that you and I shall serve their purpose until they can do without us, and then——"

"Ay, and then, good Hubert," said Richard, as the free lance paused.

"Why, and then we shall be thrown aside even as you would cast from you a broken sword or a dented morion. You know full well, Lord Richard, that it was not with my good will that you joined hand and glove with Pizarro."

"But his solemn promises, good Hubert!" said our hero. "His agreement that I should command one-third of the forces, and take a third share of the spoil, in consideration of the twenty thousand pesos I advanced towards the equipment at Seville!"

"Women's words—reeds—straws! Think ye that Pizarro will hold himself bound to aught that suits not his purpose, or to what your sharp sword cannot compel him?"

"I cannot think as thou would'st have me do, Hubert," said Richard. "Pizarro is a good soldier of tried courage, and has energy that nothing can daunt. Such a man could not break his plighted word."

"Green years, green wit—saving your presence, Lord Richard," said Hubert, bluntly; "if you will not take my counsel now. At least watch Pizarro, and, above all, the priest."

"That will I do for mine own sake and thine, good Hubert," returned Richard. "And now let us to our posts. Pizarro is about to land the forces, and we must not be laggards."

The bustle of preparation on all three galleons was now at its height. Men were hauling stores out of the holds, others were making ready the boats which each ship carried, whilst a third set were busily constructing a raft on which the few horses they possessed were to be floated to the shore.

Though there was so much apparent confusion, yet, in reality, the utmost order prevailed. To each body of men Pizarro had issued his orders, and they were obeyed as the commands of a leader who was at once feared and respected. Before the red glow of the sunset had faded from off the mighty empire which they had come to conquer, Pizarro's forces were all landed and encamped.

It was a strange weird sight, endowed with a picturesque beauty that was all its own. The white tents of the Spaniards lit up here and there with flashes of ruddy light from the watch-fires, the solemn grandeur of the vast waste of waters, whose ceaseless sound mingled with the murmuring of the night wind, fell like dreamy music on the listener's ear.

The click of the wine cup, the soft melodies of the guitar, as some player, with no unskilful hand, accompanied his voice in some gay song of love or war, and even the angry oaths of some losing gamester, broke out upon the silence of the night; but the quarrels were soon quelled, for Pizarro was a strict disciplinarian, and well those who served him knew it.

In one tent alone silence reigned, and that was where Richard of the Raven's Crest lay stretched upon his couch of sheep-skins, trying in vain to court that sleep which the restless thoughts within his mind drove far away.

The hours of the night-watch passed on one by one into the gulf of eternity; the revelling of the soldiery died away, and the whole camp seemed hushed into repose, when the curtain forming the entrance to the tent was slowly raised, and the form of a man came noiselessly in.

Richard was on his feet in an instant, and his right hand gripped the hilt of his sword.

"Stand!" he cried. "Who is it dares enter the tent of Richard of Raven's Crest, like a thief in the dead of the night?"

"Gra'mercy, Master Richard, but you keep good ward in the night-watches. 'Tis I, Hubert."

"Pardon, good friend," said Richard, with a laugh; "but in the dark 'tis hard to tell an honest man from a thief. What brings thee here? Had not their Spanish wine power to addle that thick head of thine?"

"I' faith, I have not tried," returned the free lance, bluntly. "I came but to see why you were not at the council."

"At the council! What council?" demanded our hero. "Thou must be dreaming, Hubert; there is none to-night. When I left Pizarro, he said that

HOGARTH HOUSE LIBRARY.

BOUVERIE STREET, FLEET STREET, E.C.

The following is a list of the REVISED EDITIONS of the Hogarth House Works, published in Volumes, bound in Illustrated Covers, also in Penny Weekly Numbers, all in print, and ready for immediate delivery:—

TOM WILDRAKE'S SCHOOLDAYS.

In Five Vols., price 1s. each; also complete in one Vol. as a Prize Edition, and handsomely bound in cloth and gold, price 5s. 6d.—This celebrated School Story was the first of its class ever issued in weekly numbers; and in the face of numerous imitators it still holds the foremost place. The story is a faithful narrative of the life of a high-spirited young Englishman at school—showing what he did and how he did it, and what he learnt and its influence on his after life. The story is carried on through Tom Wildrake's adventurous career, down to the time when he felt himself entitled to rest on the laurels he had so nobly won by his many brave deeds during the heartrending Indian Mutiny and in Australia and elsewhere.

YOUNG TOM'S ADVENTURES
In Europe, Asia, Africa, and America.

Complete, price 1s. 6d.—This is a sequel to "Young Tom's Schooldays," and narrates his hair-breadth escapes and adventures both with wild men and animals in the four quarters of the globe.

THE BOYS OF BIRCHAM SCHOOL.

Complete, price 1s. 6d.—This story claims to be the first school story that ever appeared in a periodical solely devoted to boys. For dramatic incident and genuine fun it has never yet been equalled.

CHARLIE AND TIM AT SCARUM SCHOOL.

Complete, price 1s.—This story of the life of two boys, who are sworn chums, at school, has always been a popular one with our young friends; showing, as it does, how a sincere friendship may be formed at school which may have lasting effects on our boys' after lives. Every schoolboy should read it.

CHARITY JOE; or, from Street Boy to Lord Mayor.

Complete, price 1s.—This is the true story of an outcast, who, by his honesty and indomitable will, rose to be the Chief Magnate of the First City in the World. His adventures at school, and, accompanied by his dog Toby, with a travelling showman, should be read by every lad who wishes to know what an English boy can do, no matter how humble his first start in life, or how great his temptations.

OUT ON THE WORLD.

Complete, price 1s.—This history goes direct to the heart of the reader, being a story of real life, depicting the troubles and trials of two children who were stolen from their home by gipsies. Little Jack's brave defence of his fellow-prisoner, Lilly—He shoots at Tinker Tom—They escape and tramp to London—Their adventures on the way; they join a troupe of tumblers and become street-players —They are recognised by the gipsies—The fair—The booth on fire; and, after many narrow escapes, they are captured by Tinker Tom, who cruelly ill-uses them—They are traced by the players to Tinker Tom's den—They are followed and risk their lives to save the children from a horrible death—The children are restored to their parents through the skill of the detective police, and well reward those who assisted them in the days of their adversity. This work is very graphically illustrated with numerous Wood Engravings.

YOUNG TOM'S SCHOOLDAYS.

Complete, price 1s. 6d.—This is the story of the life of Tom Wildrake's son at school; and, although complete in itself, should be read by everyone who has read "Tom Wildrake," as all the readers' old friends reappear in its pages.

RAGS AND RICHES:
A Story of Three Poor Boys.

Complete, price 1s.—The illustrations to this work are from the inimitable pencil of Phiz H K Browne, who did so much towards rendering popular many of the works of Charles Dickens. So faithfully is the story of these poor boys told, and so realistic are the scenes described, that it has been pronounced by competent critics the best story of London life published since "Oliver Twist."

FRANK FEARLESS;
Or, the Cruise of the Firebrand.

Complete, price 2s. 6d.—We doubt whether for fidelity of description and stirring incidents this magnificent sea story has been equalled since the days of Captain Marryat. The story of the misjudged hero's long and troubled conflict, not only with the pirates, but with his own mistaken countrymen, should be read by every true British boy who can lay its lessons to heart and profit by them.

MIDSHIPMAN TOM;
Or, the Cruise of the War Cloud.

Complete, price 2s.—This is the faithful narrative of the life of a Midshipman on board a Man-of-War, and shows the trials, temptations, and prizes incident to the career of a boy who wears the uniform of our gracious Queen at sea. Though strikingly sensational, the element of fun is not omitted.

BLACK-EYED SUSAN; or Pirates Ashore.

Complete, price 1s.—The pathetic and stirring story of William and Susan is here told in a way which is bound to enlist the sympathies of all who are possessed with a true Briton's love of adventures at sea.

THE BRIGANDS OF THE SEA;
Or, the Sailor Highwayman.

Complete, price 1s. 6d.—Money Marks, the hero of this most extraordinary romance of the sea, is no imaginary character, and nearly all the soul-stirring incidents herein described are founded on fact. The career of this world-famed highwayman of the sea is one of the most sensational narratives ever offered to the reading public. It is profusely illustrated by an eminent artist.

THE WAR CRUISE OF THE MOSCA;
Or, the Six Fighting Mids.

Complete, price 1s.—In this Stirring Story of the Sea, the talented author takes a wide departure from his school and military stories, and shows us that though he is familiar with the cavalry sabre, he can give us a vigorous and truthful account of the life of those whose lot it is to wield the sailor's cutlass, and fight their country's battles on the boundless deep.

FOR HONOUR; or, the Young Privateer.

Complete, price 1s. 6d.—This powerfully written story of the life of a Privateer during one of the most stirring periods of England's Naval History, is a marvellous combination of the sensational and the humorous. No British boy can read the sayings and doings of Monkey Jack and Crikey without a laugh, and no British boy can read the heroic actions of the young Privateer without feeling a thrill of exultation that he also belongs to that glorious Empire on whose domains the sun never sets.

ADRIFT ON THE SPANISH MAIN.

Complete, price 1s.—This Story of the old Buccaneers carries us back to the glorious days of good Queen Bess—the days when England settled for all time her right to the title of "Empress of the Seas."

ALL'S WELL.

Complete, price 1s.—The Story under the title of the above popular seaman's cry is full of pathos, sensation, and humour. In dramatic situations it is probably superior to any story of the sea ever written. With each copy is presented gratis a Magnificent Portrait of the greatest naval hero of modern days—Horatio, Lord Nelson.

SHEET-ANCHOR JACK.

Complete, price 1s.—A powerfully-written narrative of the life of a jolly jack tar "before the mast," and should be read by every true English boy.

THE PIRATE'S ISLE;
Or, the Wonders of the Deep.

Complete, price 1s.—This is a story of adventure, both on sea and land. Full of sensation, pathos, and fun.

THE BRITISH BOY SAILOR.

Complete, price 2s.—A faithful narrative of the life of a poor boy on board a British Man-of-War, during the glorious days of Nelson, showing what a British boy's pluck can do to raise himself superior to circumstances.

WILLIE GRAY;
Or, the Wreck of the Polar Star.

Complete, price 1s.—In this spirit-stirring story the entranced reader is carried into strange countries, and through strange perils by flood and field; but, from first to last, the interest is so well sustained that those who once take up the book are unable to lay it down until every line has been perused.

HOGARTH HOUSE, BOUVERIE ST., FLEET ST., LONDON, E.C.

THE DEVIL'S DIAMOND,

OR, THE FORTUNES OF
RICHARD OF THE RAVEN'S CREST

I. GOODING Sc:

THERE, IN THAT GLITTERING HEAP OF GOLD, WAS THE RANSOM OF A DOZEN EMPERORS.

he would seek his couch, for he was weary, and bade me do the same."

"There he lied, like a Spaniard," returned Hubert. "I saw with these eyes, Lord Richard, the messengers going between his tent and those of his brother and that wily snake, Valverde. There is something a-foot, but what, I know not; for though I heard them speaking, I never could learn more than half-a-dozen words of their cursed lingo."

Even while Hubert was speaking Richard of the Raven's Crest was donning such articles of his clothing and armour as he had thrown off when he laid himself upon his couch, and, buckling his sword to his belt, bade Hubert lead on.

"There may be nought in this, good Hubert, but keep thou watch outside Pizarro's tent, the while I enter, and if thou hearest me cry; 'St. George for merrie England!' out with thy sword and dash in."

"That will I, Lord Richard," replied Hubert, gravely; "it will be something new for the crafty Spaniards to learn that an English mastiff can keep watch as well as bite when needs must."

A sentinel was posted at the entrance to Pizarro's tent, but without deigning to answer his challenge, Richard of the Raven's Crest struck aside his levelled spear, and flinging up the curtain, strode into the tent.

A rude table had been set up in the centre of the tent, and covered with a flag. Round this were grouped Francisco Pizarro, his brother Ferdinand, (then second in command), Hernando Soto, his lieutenant, and the priest Valverde.

At the foot of the table were the two young Mexicans whom Pizarro had captured in his first expedition, and trained to act as interpreters; and a third figure, habited in garments of such quaint rich beauty, that Richard for the moment forgot all else as he gazed upon them.

The tunic which formed the young Peruvian's under garment was composed entirely of the skins of humming birds, so tastefully and artfully arranged that at the least movement of the wearer he seemed to be clothed with flashes of emerald golden and ruby fire. A girdle made of small plates of beaten gold studded with uncut jewels encircled his waist; bracelets, armlets, and anklets of the same precious metal similarly enriched and adorned his slender limbs; and from his shoulders there flowed nearly to the ground a mantle composed of the same delicate and beautiful materials as the tunic. A fillet of gold encircled his forehead and confined his long flowing hair; and in his right hand he bore a short staff or wand of office of solid silver.

The abrupt entrance of Richard of the Raven's Crest seemed to throw the Spaniards into no slight confusion. Ferdinand and Hernando Soto started to their feet, and grasped their swords with threatening gestures. Even Valverde's swarthy cheek turned a shade paler. Pizarro alone seemed unmoved, and regarded our hero with a keen, steady gaze.

"Keep your swords for your enemies, senors," said our hero, with a haughty glance at Ferdinand and Hernando Soto; "I am none, unless you choose to make me so."

Valverde had recovered his self-possession in an instant, and, bending over to the commander, he whispered—

"Be not hasty, noble Pizarro. Soothe the English cub with soft words. Our time will come anon."

Pizarro gave a slight nod, as if he fully understood the priest's motive, and then addressed himself to our hero

"Welcome, Senor Richard. Since thou art indisposed to rest, perchance thou wilt aid us with thy counsel, as we shortly hope that thou wilt do with thy strong arm."

"It would have been more courteous, noble Pizarro," returned our hero, shortly, "hadst thou

summoned me with the rest. Had it not been for my faithful follower, I had even now been ignorant of this assemblage."

Pizarro frowned heavily, and bit his thin under lip to restrain the angry words he would have uttered. Then he pointed with a quiet gesture to a stool, and again bade Richard seat himself.

"This is no time, senor," he went on, with a sterner ring in his voice, "for divisions amongst ourselves. Here, almost in the very hour of our landing, heaven has blessed our enterprise, and placed in our hands the sure means of conducting it to a successful issue."

"Truly," said Padre Valverde; "holy Church never deserts her children in the hour of need."

A murmur of devout assent followed the priest's words, and each one made the sign of the cross; for, strange to say, though the Spaniards were so rapacious and cruel, they were also extraordinarily devout, much resembling the Italian brigands of the present day, who will quit robbing and murdering the travellers they have attacked if they chance to hear the sound of the vesper bell; and, after telling their beads and muttering a prayer or two, return to their bloody work with an added relish.

"Yonder Indian, senors," continued Pizarro, pointing to the gorgeously-garbed Peruvian, "is the bearer of a message from Huoscar, who is at war with his brother Atahualpa for the sovereignty of Peru, asking us for our alliance, and offering, as a price, to fill our ships with gold. What say you, senors?"

The eyes of the Spaniards lit up greedily as they thought of the immense wealth contained in a country whose monarch was enabled to offer such a bribe.

"I say that we had better close with the bargain," said Ferdinand.

"My advice is, noble Pizarro," said Hernando Soto, "that you first hear what Huoscar's rival has to say. Doubtless when he hears of this offer he will be ready to give us twice as much."

"Why accept either," interposed Valverde, with a crafty smile. "Take my advice, noble Pizarro; dally with them both; let the rival Incas war against each other until they are so weakened that we can step in and seize—not the trifling bribe they offer us, but the whole wealth of the kingdom."

"By St. Jago!" exclaimed Pizarro, "a notable scheme, and one which will ensure success, without endangering our little band. What say you, senors, to the plan of the holy father?"

Ferdinand and Soto expressed an enthusiastic approval. Richard of the Raven's Crest alone remained silent.

"How now, Senor Richard?" said Pizarro; "what dost thou counsel. Hast thou a better plan to lay before us than that of Padre Valverde?"

"Ay, that have I. A better because a more honest one! What senors, think you it becomes Christian gentlemen to play such a shuffling game as yonder holy father, doubtless in jest, has proposed."

"And thinkest *thou*," retorted Pizarro, sternly, "that it becomes a stripling—a boy—to bestow such epithets upon the wise counsel of Padre Valverde. By St. Jago, thou triflest overmuch with my forbearance, Don Richard!"

"Heed him not, heed him not," said the Spanish priest, bending his crafty evil glance upon Richard of the Raven's Crest. "Time presses, senors; the messenger from the Inca waits his answer."

"Be it so," said Pizarro. "But remember, Don Richard, that he that is not with me is against me. Beware lest you force me to look upon you as an enemy."

"Look to yourself, then, Pizarro," replied our hero, haughtily. "See that your aims be just—your actions upright. I am English, and those of my race were ever enemies to craft and cruelty."

"Ha! Sangre de Dios. A threat!" ejaculated

Soto, rising from his seat and clapping his hand upon the hilt of his sword. "Give the word, noble Pizarro, and I will slay the English dog where he stands. Hath he not insulted holy Church in the person of Padre Valverde? He is a heretic, and accursed!"

"Dog, and accursed yourself, false Spaniard!" retorted Richard, his handsome face flushing redly to the very temples; while, even as he spoke, he snatched off his heavy gauntlet, and hurled it at Soto with such accuracy and force that it struck the Spaniard stunned and bleeding to the ground.

Then, springing backwards to the curtained entrance of the tent, his bright sword flashed like lightning from its sheath, and his clear, loud voice rang out its battle-cry—

"St. George for merrie England!"

With the quiet patience of a well-trained mastiff, Hubert had waited outside the tent till he heard the signal cry. Now he stepped forward, his heavy mace gripped in his strong right hand, while on his bronzed war-worn features there played a grim, ominous smile.

A fight, and a desperate one, too, seemed imminent. Ferdinand, his brow black as night with anger, had already seized the trumpet and sounded the first blast of an alarm, which would have brought a hundred swarthy and active Spaniards to avenge the insult to their commander, had not Pizarro strode forward and snatched the instrument away.

"Hold, Ferdinand!" he said, in a low stern tone; "and you, Don Richard, sheath your sword, and listen to me. Nay, not a word, Ferdinand, I *will* be obeyed."

There was something so irresistibly commanding in Pizarro's mien and gesture that his fiery brother shrank back, and let the half-drawn sword clash back into its sheath.

"Senor Richard of the Raven's Crest," Pizarro continued in a slow measured tone, "you seem to have forgotten that before we sailed upon this venture, and in consideration of the small number of our force, and the dangers that might threaten it, it was agreed that neither quarrel nor strife should be allowed between us, and that the first who dared to lift his hand against a comrade should be cast out from amongst us."

"And *you* forget, Pizarro," returned Richard, haughtily, "that to one of my race an insult is as hard to bear as a blow! The blood of Cœur de Lion runs in my veins, and I will shed it to the last drop ere I leave unresented a taunt from the haughtiest Spaniard in Castile or Aragon."

"Reflect!" said Pizarro, who knew well the value of Richard's strong arm and fiery courage. "Pause before the doom is pronounced which cannot be recalled: think of what your fate will be, cast off from us, alone in this vast country, swarming with enemies. I would fain look upon you as my own son, and you compel me to doom you to a lingering death."

"I defy thee, and thy doom too, Pizarro!" retorted our hero, sternly. "I shall be safer alone with my faithful follower, Hubert, than backed by thy crafty and treacherous Spaniards! Adios, Pizarro! A reverder la!"

And, thrusting his ponderous sword back into its sheath, Richard of the Raven's Crest drew his splendid form up to its full height and strode out of the tent, followed by Hubert.

All the evil of Pizarro's nature seemed to concentrate itself in his dark eyes, and flash out in the glance he shot after our hero's retreating figure.

For a moment it was in his thoughts to sound the alarm, and bid his soldiers hew to pieces the insolent English boy who had dared to defy him; but, in the midst of all his passion, he reflected that many a Spaniard would bite the dust ere Richard and Hubert could be brought low, and he dared not risk the life of a single man.

The crafty priest, watching narrowly the commander's features, read the dark thought that troubled him as easily as he could follow the lines of his breviary.

"Leave him to me, noble Pizarro," said Valverde, in his soft, persuasive voice; "I have that here which will tame the hot courage of these English perros* better and more easily than a score of thy best spearmen."

"What mean you, Padre?"

"See, here?" said the priest, taking from his bosom a small ebony box, curiously inlaid with silver, which, when opened, disclosed a phial of rock crystal, nearly filled with some clear fluid, sparkling in the light as if it had been distilled from a diamond.

"Well?" said Pizarro.

"One drop of that," said Valverde, in a low, soft whisper, "mingled with their food or wine, will send thy enemies as surely to their doom as though thy sword had pierced their hearts a dozen times. They cannot yet have left the camp; 'twill be easy to steal unseen into their tent—and then——"

"Well, be it so!" said Pizarro, after a few moments gloomy thought. "I would fain that they had died sword in hand, for this English lad is brave, and worthy of a brave man's death; but his example in abandoning me might spread the contagion amongst my men—no, he must die! And let it be done quickly, Valverde!"

CHAPTER III.

"A vision
Of calling shapes, and beckoning shadows dire;
And airy tongues that syllable men's names
On sands, and shores, and desert wildernesses."

RICHARD OF THE RAVEN'S CREST was young in years, and his anger cooled almost as quickly as it heated. Before his firm martial strides had covered the distance between Pizarro's tent and his own, he stopped suddenly and broke into a short clear laugh, and clapped Hubert lightly on the shoulder.

"Well, Hubert," he said in his fresh ringing voice, "what think you, man, of this brawl betwixt Don Pizarro and myself?"

"Why, I think, Lord Richard," replied the man-at-arms, gravely, "that we are well out of as likely a nest of hornets as ever I put this old head into. By 'r lady, I thought we should meet with but scant grace when you cracked yon black-visaged Spaniard over the skull with your gauntlet. I' faith, I had much ado to keep from giving you a cheer, as I saw him go down like an ox i' the shambles."

"'Twas a rash blow," said Richard; "yet I am not sorry that I struck it. I have none of the craft of those Spaniards, good Hubert, who can smile and dissemble their hatred, even while their busy brains are plotting how to poison their foeman or stab him in the dark."

"And that reminds me, Lord Richard," said the man-at-arms, in a lower voice, "that we are not safe an instant in this camp. The priest Valverde, did you note the evil look he bent on you while you were holding converse with Pizarro?"

"Not I," returned Richard, with a careless laugh. "As for departure, Hubert, the morrow will be time enough for that."

"The morrow!" exclaimed Hubert. "Say you, you mean to trust yourself within reach of a Spaniard's malice, and a Spaniard's dagger until the morrow?"

"Even so," returned our hero, "I was well within reach of both just now, Hubert, and they did not harm me."

"That was because—because you were awake, Lord Richard, with your good sword bared in your hand, and, perhaps, a faithful friend by your side, who would have given good account of half-a-dozen

---
* Dogs.

ere harm should have come to you; but, Lord Richard, when you are lying asleep, the veriest cur that ever called himself a Spaniard might plant six inches of steel between your ribs."

"What; and *you* by?" said our hero, with a laugh. "So ho, Hubert, I shall begin to think that you are turned craven. I say I have need of rest and thought, my trusty squire, and to-night I mean to sleep in yonder tent, were there twenty Pizarros and twenty thousand spearmen around me!"

"Pray heaven, it be not the long sleep that knows no waking!" muttered Hubert; but, knowing how useless it was to oppose his fiery young master, he followed him to the tent without further expostulation.

The night was beautifully clear and calm, and although there was no moon, the brilliant constellation of the southern sky gave quite as much light as ever Luna in her most obliging moments affords to the inhabitants of our cold northern clime.

It was when they were within a dozen yards of the tent that Hubert, looking towards it, fancied he saw a human form, dressed in a long robe, flit round its farther side, and disappear like a breath.

In an instant he had cleared the distance between him and the tent, and was on the very spot where he saw the figure vanish.

His keen eyes seemed to glance in every direction at once; and there was light enough for him to have descried a mouse, yet there was nothing.

At any other time Hubert would have passed the matter over without a further thought, but his suspicions were aroused, and he felt certain it was no phantasm that he had seen.

"Why, what ails thee, man?" said Richard, coming up with his henchman and clapping him on the shoulder.

"I' faith, Lord Richard, I scarce know!" replied Hubert, passing his hand slowly over his forehead. "Methought I saw——"

"What, man? Not thy wife?" laughed our hero. "Certes! Thou hast oft told me how Dame Margery threatened to follow thee to the ends of the earth, if thou dared'st to leave her to follow my broken fortunes; but sure she has not ventured herself here? How was she disguised, Hubert? As one of Pizarro's musketeers or crossbow men, mayhap?"

"Ay, jest on, Lord Richard," replied Hubert, in a sad, grave tone, most unusual with him. "Pray heaven we be not both lying on our backs by the morn, looking at the sky with blind eyes, and with a foot of Spanish steel in our medriffs by way of breakfast!"

"Peace man with thy croaking," said Richard of the Raven's Crest, impatiently. "Thou hast been passing the flagon too freely. What thou sawest was but a vision of one of those Spanish wine-skins which thou hast pierced so unmercifully."

"A murrain light on me if I have moistened my lips since sundown," replied Hubert.

"Then take a cup to cheer thee, man," said Richard. "By St. George, an' I lay me not down now; thy old woman's fancies will keep me awake till cock-crow. Trouble not to fire the torch, Hubert; there is light enough to see the flagon; and thou canst smell the wine-skin. Hand me a stoup, man, and then moisten thine own throttle."

Richard cast himself lightly down upon his couch, and, leaning on his elbow, watched with a dreamy look the stalwart figure of the man-at-arms, as he moved about the tent.

The flagon filled, Hubert approached the couch, and Richard of the Raven's Crest reached forward to grasp the measure; but yet, though his fingers had closed around it, there suddenly flashed into light, hovering in the air above the flagon, the apparition of a hand, its forefinger raised, as if in menace or in warning.

The ghastly hand was luminous, yet shed no light around it, and seemed to glow with an intense transparent heat, as if it had been newly drawn from some infernal furnace.

There was something so terrible in the appearance of the mysterious hand, hovering there alone in the darkness of the tent, that Richard of the Raven's Crest was held spell-bound by supernatural awe, gazing at it with dilated eyes, while Hubert, dropping the flagon with a crash, sunk upon his knees, and covered his face.

Whilst yet he gazed, Richard saw the luminous hand slowly rise itself, and write with its forefinger the following lines, each character of which stood out like living fire upon the murky blackness of the air.

"Stranger from a foreign shore,
Fly ere yet this hour be o'er;
Fly from false Pizarro's pow'r—
Follow where I lead.
Honour and wealth lie t'wards the west;
Be thine the task to choose the best.
Beware the Demon Tempter's test—
God help thee at thy need!"

It seemed to Richard as if each fiery word traced by the mysterious hand imprinted itself indelibly upon his memory. They vanished as quickly almost as they were written, but the hand still remained, and, pointing towards the entrance of the tent, floated slowly thither.

"Be it a message from fiend or angel, I'll obey it," exclaimed Richard, leaping from his couch. "Here, Hubert, rouse thee man. I'll to the horses. Up and away."

No mortal peril had ever yet made the veteran Englishman tremble, or blanched the bronzed hue of his cheeks. But in the presence of the supernatural he was a very child.

"Stay, Master Richard, what would you do," he said in a hoarse whisper, as he caught our hero by the arm. "It's the foul fiend, who would lead you to perdition."

"Fiend or not, I follow it. With thee, or without thee, so make thy choice, and quickly, Hubert. It can be the work of no fiend of evil, I tell thee man, else it had never dared to trace the holy name of God."

Catching the still reluctant Hubert in his powerful grasp, Richard of the Raven's Crest forced him towards the entrance; keeping his eyes steadily fixed upon the mysterious hand, which floated on, preserving always the same relative distance between itself and our hero.

The horses were tethered but a few yards away, and with a slow unwilling step Hubert of Chertsey sought them, and brought them to where Richard stood impatiently waiting; while he murmured to himself the last few lines traced by the mysterious Hand—

"Honour and wealth lie t'wards the west;
Be thine the task to choose the best.
Beware the Demon Tempter's test—
God help thee in thy need!"

"Ay," he continued, "I have lost so much for honour's sake already that I am little likely to be turned from its path now. Honour and wealth I will gain if I can; but wealth without honour—never. But what means the Demon Tempter's test? Yon mysterious hand still points steadily onwards—let it guide me where it will. Ha, here is Hubert with the horses!"

He vaulted lightly into the saddle, never once taking his eyes though from the mysterious hand, which glared there with its lambent, lurid light, contrasted with the deep blue sky like some meteor suddenly arrested in its fall.

"Lord Richard," began Hubert, venturing once again to supplicate his master not to go; but our hero's only reply was to put spurs to his steed, and gallop after the mystic Hand, which now, with pointed finger, moved swiftly onwards.

It was t.me, for the crafty Valverde had at that moment stolen to the tent to see if his subtle poison had done its work. The vacant couch, the overturned flagon, and the red stain of the spilt wine upon the sand, told him he had failed, and, rushing out, he raised a loud alarm.

"To arms, Spaniards, to arms! A thousand pesos to the man who brings back Richard of the Raven's Crest!"

CHAPTER IV.

A WILD RIDE—THE ABYSS—THE CATASTROPHE.

AS the alarm-cry rang out through the still night air, Richard involuntarily tightened his grasp upon his bridle-rein, and a flush of anger rose redly to his cheeks.

For a moment it was in his thoughts to turn, and bid defiance to the enemies who cried after him like a pack of hounds upon the scent. At any other time he would have done so, had it been to run the gauntlet of ten times the number of Pizarro's followers; but there was the mystery of the mysterious hand to discover, and with an irresistible power it drew him on.

Again and again, but more faintly at each repetition, sounded the hoarse cries of the Spanish spearmen, mingled with the clash of arms and armour, and the shrill neighing of horses. Hubert turned in his saddle, and saw the clear starlight gleaming on the morions of a score of Pizarro's veterans, galloping in pursuit.

"See, Lord Richard," whispered the free-lance, as he guided his horse close to his master's side; "there are but a score of them. 'Twill be a stain on your escutcheon to fly from such a handful, and will, certes, be spoken to your shame hereafter. Let us turn and engage them; you and I will make short work of them, I warrant me."

"Nay, Hubert," replied Richard, "no worldly power shall turn me back till I have followed yonder fiery hand to the end. Be it sent by the powers of good or evil, there is a mystery in it, which some irresistible impulse tells me I must fathom."

"But the shame," urged Hubert—"the taint upon your name?"

"Fear not for that," returned Richard, proudly. "Pizarro and I will meet again, and if he dares then taunt me with cowardice, I will thrust the lie down his throat with the hilt of my good sword."

Hubert was silenced, but not convinced. His dread of the phantom hand—which, floating in the air before them, seemed to be guiding them to some unknown mysterious destination—was so great, that he would joyfully have encountered the whole of Pizarro's band, single-handed, rather than follow it.

The very horses, too, Hubert thought, were under the influence of some supernatural power. They seemed to him to be galloping with a speed far beyond that of which any mortal steed was capable. Yet their hoofs made no sound, while their eyes flamed, and the breath of their nostrils was luminous with a sulphurous light.

On and on, with unabated speed, their chargers bore them, following the fiery hand, unguided by the bridle, unurged by the spurs of their riders. Three hours had passed away, and still they showed no signs of flagging, when the increasing ruggedness of the ground and the mass of rock scattered about showed that they were approaching the mountains.

Yet another half-hour, and they were galloping up a rocky defile with huge boulders of granite on either hand, and the towering mountain itself raising its majestic point upwards until its summit was hidden in the gloom.

The pass was so tortuous in its windings, the path so bestrewn with masses of rock, that even in broad day a traveller would have chosen to pick his way cautiously. It seemed sheer madness to dash along it at a gallop in the darkness of the

night, yet Richard of the Raven's Crest let his bridle hang loosely on his charger's neck, and, with his eyes still fixed upon the mysterious hand, sped onwards.

Never stumbling, never faltering, the horses relaxed not one iota of their speed, following the sinuous path and leaping the boulders and crevasses as safely as the chamois traverse the mountain passes of their native Alps.

Already the first faint flush of dawn was lighting up the eastern sky, and the stars were beginning to "pale their ineffectual fires," when Hubert suddenly uttered a cry of alarm, and, pulling up his horse with all the strength of his stalwart arms, forced it to rear almost upright upon its haunches.

There, at his very feet, yawned a vast abyss, deep, dark, and unfathomable, apparently, as the bottomless pit itself. So suddenly had it opened up before them that Hubert's warning cry came too late to save his master. Like a flash of light the white charger dashed by, and, with a bound, Richard of the Raven's Crest was gone, his eyes still fixed upon the mysterious hand!

A cry of horror and despair broke from Hubert's lips, but, before he had even time to realise to its full extent the fate of his young master, a loud reverberating roar seemed to rend the very air, and a mighty mass of rock rolled down the mountain side, and, with a crash that shook the solid earth to its foundation, wedged itself into the yawning mouth of the abyss and closed it up for ever!

CHAPTER V.

SHOWING WHAT BEFEL HUBERT OF CHERTSEY AFTER THE MYSTERIOUS DISAPPEARANCE OF RICHARD OF THE RAVEN'S CREST—THE SEARCH—HUBERT'S DESPAIR—HE DEPARTS ON A MISSION OF VENGEANCE.

THE concussion of that mighty mass of rock, as it fell into the abyss, sealing up, as it were, the yawning sepulchre of Richard of the Raven's Crest, hurled the free-lance many yards down the defile, stunned and insensible.

Some fragments of the granite had struck them both. The horse was killed upon the spot, its skull smashed in as if by a cannon-ball. A smaller piece had grazed Hubert's temple, and when he recovered consciousness he found the blood still trickling down his face.

It was morning now, and the slanting rays of the rising sun were darting like golden arrows amongst the crags and boulders of the pass, and, for a moment or two the free-lance lay on his back, staring up at the bright blue sky above him, dreamily wondering what had happened.

Then, like a flash of light piercing the gloom of night, there came to him the recollection of that awful abyss, the terrible gulf which had swallowed up his young master in its pitchy depths, and, with a shudder, Hubert leapt to his feet, and passed his hand across his eyes to clear away the blood, and perhaps the tears, that obscured them.

"And this is to be our parting!" muttered the veteran, mournfully. "He was but a lad in years, but a truer, braver one never drew the breath of life. He was a prince among his fellows, and made the noblest Spaniards of them all look like mongrel curs, when he held up his head amongst them. He was a bit hasty—true, and his blows came quicker than his words when angry, like the great Richard Cœur de Lion, whose blood ran in his veins. A murrain seize me for a craven fool! had I not reined in my horse, I should be with him now—dead perhaps, but better that than to be here alive, and without him."

And, with a bitter execration, Herbert smote the rock with his clenched hand, as if it had been some mortal foe. The steel-clad gauntlet struck out a shower of fiery sparks, and the echos ringing from the cragged sides of the ravine seemed to mock him.

Then the wild thought came to him that the abyss was perhaps not entirely closed. If it was not, thought Hubert, he would certainly descend and share his young master's fate, let that be what it might.

But a very slight examination showed him that even this desperate resolve was impossible of execution. The mass of rock, which was quite as large as an ordinary cottage, had not only closed the abyss, but had so blocked up the ravine that to pass it was impossible, while its further side rested against the side of the mountain itself. Nothing but an earthquake could have moved it from its position.

"No hope! no hope!" murmured the free-lance, bitterly. "And here am I now, left to wander these strange lands like a falcon that hath lost its mother. What strange fate was it that led young Lord Richard so early to his doom? What power of evil sent that mystic hand to lure him to his death? Methinks I can see it now, as it hovered above the black gulf, and beckoned him onward, while he——"

Hubert paused, and covered his face with his hands, while a strong convulsive shudder shook his powerful frame.

"Could I but think," he continued, "that it was some juggling of that false priest, Valverde? I have heard that many of them are skilled in the black art. But no. It was no trick, else my young master had seen through it. 'Fore heaven, were it not for the sin of the deed, I would sheath my dagger in my breast, and make an end of it."

Hubert's grief at the loss of his master was of no common order. His rugged nature—battle-worn, inured to almost every danger and hardship that ever befel a man on land or sea—was moved with difficulty; but when, as now, a great grief touched his heart to its inmost core—its very rarity gave it more power.

"I fought side by side with his father," so the mournful recollections of the faithful veteran ran on: "I carried him from the field, where he fell fighting like a hero, and knelt by his side when he was stricken unto death by a shaft from an arbolest—a murrain on the hand that sped it him! With his last breath he charged me to keep watch and ward over his little Richard, and until now I had never quitted him. Many a time and oft have I dandled him in these arms, for he was little even then, and when he grew older, who but I taught him to run, leap, wrestle, play quarter-staff, and sword and buckler—and now he is gone!"

And then the grizzled veteran, whom certainly nothing else on earth could have so moved, seated himself on a boulder, and again covered his face with his hands, while from between the gauntletted fingers there trickled and fell heavily upon the rocky ground some tears, mute witnesses of his great sorrow.

"Beshew me for an old woman!" he exclaimed, rising suddenly to his feet. "I have lost my manhood, certes, to let my eyes fill like those of some green-sick maiden. By St. George, I will find a manlier way to prove my grief for Lord Richard's fate!—for I can, at least, avenge it. I may not grapple with the foul fiend who lured him hither, but Pizarro and that crafty priest Valverde are as much to blame, and may this right arm wither if they feel not the weight of it."

Full of this new idea, which gave him an opportunity for action—a phase much more suited to his nature than inactive grief—Hubert thought for the first time of his horse, and, looking round, there he beheld it lying dead but a few yards away.

"Poor beast!" he muttered. "It was scarce worth the while to bring thee so far to lose thee so soon; that's no matter, 'tis but a few hours' longer journey, and my appetite for revenge will but be whetted by the delay."

He stooped down, and unfastened from the saddle-bow the petronel and mace which was slung there, and also the goat-skin haversack and water skin, out of which latter articles he helped himself to a mouthful of food, and a long drink of the refreshing fluid.

"Certes," he muttered, grimly, "it was fortunate that Pizarro's orders kept our horses ready saddled and equipped for a fray, else should I have had to march both hungry and thirsty. Lord Lord Richard was right—he is a good soldier, but none the less shall he feel the heaviest end of my mace, ere the sun sets."

Once again Hubert turned, and, doffing his helmet, bent his knee before the place where he had seen his young master entombed, and with that last silent farewell, strode quickly down the ravine, his heart now hardened to all tender feelings, the one thought in his brain—Revenge!

CHAPTER VI.

RICHARD OF THE RAVEN'S CREST IN STRANGE QUARTERS—THE FULFILMENT OF THE PROPHESY—THE HIGH PRIEST OF THE TEMPLE OF THE SUN TELLS OUR HERO A STRANGE STORY—THE LEGEND OF THE DEVIL'S DIAMOND.

NOW, leaving for a while Hubert stealing silently away on his mission of vengeance, let me return to our hero, Richard of the Raven's Crest, who we left a chapter ago in such dire peril.

His eyes had been fixed upon the phantom hand until the very moment when he was plunged into the abyss; and it was only when he felt the solid earth no longer resounding beneath his charger's hoofs, and the deep darkness of the chasm closed around him, that he knew what had happened.

For the next few moments everything seemed to happen as 'twere in a dream. He heard the awful crash of the falling rock above—he felt that his horse alighted safely, not with such a shock as he might have expected, a shock that would have hurled him straight from his saddle, but so gently and easily, that had he not been too bewildered to think, he might well have wondered.

All around him was perfect darkness—darkness so heavy and oppressive that, in the awful and expressive phrase describing the Egyptian plague, it might be felt.

Silent, too! So still, that the laboured breathing of his horse, and the beating of his own heart, were almost painfully audible to Richard. It was such a sudden change from the fierce excitement of that hurried gallop to this sepulchral stillness, that even his hot blood was chilled, and ran cold now within his veins.

The phantom hand, too, that had guided him into the abyss, where was that? Richard would even have welcomed its dread presence; but it was gone, its fiery fingers no longer glowed with lurid light in the murky blackness of that living tomb.

For a few moments he sat motionless in the saddle—it was only a brief period, that might have been counted in seconds—and then, as if by magic art, the whole scene was changed!

Gone in an instant! The awful darkness—the dread silence—the chilling fever which accompanied the horrible thought that he was immured alive! and in their place Richard's eyes were dazzled by the soft, mellow light beaming from myriads of lamps, sweet, low strains of such music as he had never heard before greeted his ears, and some exotic, delicate perfume was wafted towards him, instead of the earthy odour of a tomb.

"Merciful heaven!" thought our hero. "I am dreaming. This is some spell of sorcery cast over me!"

As his sight, confused at first, became accustomed to the light, Richard of the Raven's Crest saw that he was in a vast and lofty chamber, the magnificent proportions of which reminded him of the aisle of some great cathedral.

Suspended from the roof by golden chains were numberless lamps, while the walls and the high row of columns supporting the vault above reflected the light with a bright yellow radiance there was no mistaking. They were plated with sheets of gold. The wealth of a dozen empires seemed to be around him.

The ground was carpeted with a thick heavy matting screen, of some material strange to our hero, but it was so soft and elastic, that, though his horse sank fetlock-deep in it, there was no trace of his iron-shod hoofs upon it.

Richard glanced at the roof immediately above him, but there no sheen of lamp or glitter of gold met his gaze—all was gloomy and impenetrable darkness. Above him there lay the gulf into which his horse had leaped, but——

Before our hero could carry his speculations further, the music, which had almost died away, broke out into a fuller and louder stream, and he beheld approaching him, with a slow and stately step, the solitary figure of a tall old man, habited in a long flowing garment, white as the snow in colour.

His features were those of a race quite strange to our hero, but there was something in their expression so full of simple dignity, that Richard of the Raven's Crest involuntarily bowed his proud head as the white-robed priest advanced.

He halted as he reached the centre of the aisle, and, with a slow solemn gesture, raised both his arms. Instantaneously the music ceased, with an inexpressibly soft and plaintive wail.

Then there slowly filed in, in obedience to some signal unseen by Richard, some score of closely draped and veiled figures, bearing amongst them a curiously carved table and stool of some rare fragrant smelling wood, strange fruits, the like of which Richard had never seen before, piled up on dishes of massive gold, and a flagon and cup of the same precious metal, inlaid with enormous uncut jewels.

"It is a dream," thought Richard again; "I shall wake presently and find myself back in my tent. It must needs be a vision, and yet it seems too real."

"Welcome, stranger!" said the priest. "Sit and eat. A hundred years have passed over my head since I first heard thy coming prophesied. Each day since that time thy advent has been waited for, and I knew that I should not be gathered to my fathers till the prophesy was fulfilled. Welcome to the Temple of the Sun God!"

There was something so solemn in the strange being's words, and in the way in which he spoke of a hundred years, as if they had only been so many hours or minutes, that Richard of the Raven's Crest felt awed as in the presence of a supernatural being.

Silently, almost reverently, he dismounted, doffed his casque, and seated himself at the table. He then saw that there were, besides the fruit, several dishes of some viands, the appearance and odour of which were equally strange to him; but as he had in some degree recovered his self-possession, so his appetite returned, and he both ate and drank heartily.

"It is well," said the old man gravely, when Richard had concluded; "the prophesy is half fulfilled, the stranger hath come, he hath eaten and drank in the Temple of the Sun God—the rest lies yet hidden in the mystery of the future."

"What is this prophecy, reverend father," said Richard, breaking for the first time the silence he had observed. "Methinks I am in a dream, or is that vision of the fiery hand, my plunge into the dark abyss, and my presence here, all true?"

"As true as that thou livest and drawest the breath of life," replied the priest; "as true as the prophesy which foretold thy coming, ere yet thy grandsire came into the world, as true as that thou art the distant saviour of the empire of Peru."

"I?" repeated Richard.

"Even thou. The fiery hand which guided thee hither traced upon yonder wall, beneath the sacred image of the Sun God, full a hundred years ago, the prophecy telling of the misfortunes which should distract the empire of the Incas, and showed how, by thee alone, could they be averted."

"This is marvellous, reverend father!" said Richard, amazed—as well he might have been—at the old priest's revelations.

"Thy name and call are alike unknown to me," the old priest continued. "This only I know, that thou art not of that detested nation who first landed on the shores of a neighbouring nation, now many moons ago, and armed with strange weapons which belched forth fire and smoke with a dreadful noise."

"You mean the Spaniard, Cortes, reverend father," said Richard.

"May his name and race be accursed!" the old priest said. "May his bones be unburied, and the dogs of the plains devour him. I was one of the hapless Mexicans when he, under pretence of friendship and of peaceful trading, marched into their country. They were an innocent and guileless people, and they believed him, looking upon Cortes and his men as superior beings, understanding not the strange animals on which they rode, neither the weapons which had the power of dealing death with a flash of fire. They loaded him with wealth, for the Spaniard courted the gold which they valued not. But his avarice grew as the riches of the country were revealed to him. He tortured, maimed, burnt alive, racked with the most cruel torments all those whom he thought had treasures hidden from him. Neither youth, age, nor sex, conscience nor belief, could restrain the monster, Cortes, from his purpose."

"All this I know," said Richard; and a blush came to his cheek as he reflected that it was one professing the religion of Christ, the Prince of Peace, who had done these deeds.

"The prophesy which the Fiery Hand, the messenger of Manco Copae,* traced, told that the same calamity would come upon us. That a band of strangers, coming from far over the great water, mounted on strange beasts, armed with the lightning, clothed in invulnerable garments, and strong and merciless as death, should fall like a pestilence upon our people."

"The prophesy is fulfilled, then!" exclaimed Richard; "for even now, reverend father, Pizarro, with more than a hundred of his hardiest veterans, is but a day's march from where we stand."

"I know it," replied the old priest, gravely. "The poison and the antidote have arrived together. But time is short—there yet remains much to be done."

"First, reverend father," said our hero, "let me tell my name and lineage, and the purpose which brought me to these shores; then, if you think fit, let me hear what is your purpose with me."

The old Priest of the Sun inclined his head gravely, and our hero continued—

"My name is Richard of the Raven's Crest, my lineage—though it befits me not to speak of it—is derived from the princes of the mighty kingdom of England, a country lying far beyond the great water that washes these shores. I sailed hither with the Spaniard, Pizarro, believing that his cause was just and honourable. Not many hours ago it was revealed to me that he intended to emulate the infamous Cortes in his treachery, and——"

"You quarrelled with Pizarro, and left him," in-

---

* This is the name given by the Peruvians to the founder of their religion—a being half mortal, half divine—who first taught them the arts of civilization and established the dynasty of the Incas, which the Spaniards were destined to overthrow.

terrupted the priest. "All that I knew, for hath not the prophecy foretold it? Again I say to thee, thou art the destined saviour of the empire of the true Incas, and it is thy hand which will destroy the might of the Spaniard, and turn Pizarro, baffled and beaten, back upon his course."

Richard thrilled with a strange wild impulse, as he listened to the old priest's words. Now that Pizarro had shown himself in his true colours, our hero felt no scruple in opposing him—now that he knew the Spaniard's object to be plunder and extermination, instead of the noble aim of converting to the new faith, and instructing in the arts and civilization of Europe the inhabitants of the country he had come so far to visit.

"I am ready, reverend father," he said firmly. "Tell me what you require of me, and if it be aught that a Christian knight may attempt, I will essay it."

"Mount thy horse, then," said the priest, "and follow me."

Richard's trained charger stood quietly where he had left it, showing no signs of impatience, but only testifying his delight at his master's return by a low whining and a toss of its small delicate head into the air.

Wondering into what strange scene he should next be introduced, and still scarcely able to divest himself of the idea that he was in a dream, Richard seated himself on the saddle, and moved on after the High Priest of the Sun.

As he approached the extremity of the aisle, Richard saw that a vast curtain, embroidered with gold and the feathers of humming birds, formed the boundary to that end of the vaulted chamber. Before it, the high priest halted, and then, raising his hand, smote them together thrice.

At the signal, the curtain was drawn aside by some invisible means, the sweet streams of music broke forth again, the high priest fell upon his knees and bent his face to the ground, and Richard was in the presence of Atahualpa, the monarch of Peru.

The Inca (who was not only obeyed as a monarch, but worshipped as a divinity by the Peruvians) was seated upon a throne of solid gold, continued with the same rich feather-cloth which adorned the curtain, and studded with enormous jewels. On either side of the throne, and leading from it to the threshold of the audience chamber, were two rows of the chief caciques of the empire, all kneeling, and with their faces bowed to the earth, as if they thought themselves unworthy of even looking upon their emperor.

And indeed, as Richard gazed upon the Inca, he thought that the simple Peruvians were hardly to be blamed for the devotion they paid to him, for never had he seen a face of such mild angelic beauty as that of Atahualpa. His form was slight, but exquisitely moulded; his features of marvellous softness and regularity, and the calm, gracious, yet almost sorrowful expression they wore, was akin to that which the inspired painters of old transferred to the features of the Saviour.

While the sensation of religious awe was gradually stealing over his senses, the high priest had arisen, and, advancing a few steps nearer to the throne, spake in his own language to the Inca.

The monarch bent his large dark eyes upon our hero, and then replied to the high priest in the same soft, musical language.

Richard, who still sate motionless upon his horse, was struck with the solemn splendour which surrounded him. He seemed fascinated. His will, usually so strong and impatient under restraint, was subdued by the supernatural mystery which had enveloped the last few hours, and he waited for the high priest to address him.

"Noble stranger," said the priest, "the monarch of Peru—the mighty Inca, Atahualpa—greets thee. He accepts thee as the champion, selected by the will of his divine ancestor, to save the empire from the power of the Spaniard. Dismount, Richard of the Raven's Crest, and receive the greeting of the Inca!"

Our hero dismounted, and at the same time Atahualpa arose from his throne, and advanced to meet the gallant Richard, extending a hand soft and delicate as a woman's. Our hero took it in his mailed gauntlet, and raised it almost reverently to his lips.

The Inca then unclasped from his slender wrist a bracelet so thickly studded with jewels that the metal was barely visible, and handed it to Richard, signing to him to clasp it on his own arm.

Our hero could hardly repress a smile, for the jewelled ornament was a world too small for his sinewy wrist; but, with a bow to the emperor, he placed the bracelet in his pouch, and, stepping back a pace or two, folded his arms over his broad chest, and waited for what was next to come.

Up to this time the caciques (the nobles of the Peruvian empire) had remained in the same reverential posture—kneeling, with their faces turned towards the floor; but, at a few words from the high priest, they arose, and advancing towards Richard of the Raven's Crest, prostrated themselves in turn before him, and touched his right foot with their lips.

"It hath pleased the Inca," said the high priest, as soon as the ceremony was over, "to signify his imperial pleasure that from this day forth thou art his equal in this empire, being, as the phantom hand hath decreed, the chosen champion and saviour of the empire. Henceforth all must obey thee and do thee reverence, even as obedience and reverence is paid to the divinely-descended Atahualpa."

Still wondering, still doubting whether all this was not a dream, Richard heard the priest's words, but barely understood them.

"This day," the high priest went on, "the edict of the mighty Inca will go forth throughout the length and breadth of the land, and the issue of the fulfilment of the prophecy will make the usurper, Huoscar, tremble."

Richard's thoughts at once reverted to the scene in Pizarro's tent, and the Peruvian messenger he had seen there, and in a few words he told this to the priest.

"It is indeed the time to act. There yet remains one ordeal to go through, noble Richard, and that no eyes, save mine and thine, may witness."

"Lead on then," replied our hero. "I will not flinch from aught now that my foot has once trodden the path."

The high priest once again waved his arm high in the air, again the solemn stream of music burst forth, and two richly-dressed slaves entered, the one bearing a curiously-shaped flask of crystal, stoppered with a single emerald, while the other bore upon a golden salver a goblet of the same precious metal.

"Then act now, noble Richard," said the high priest; "submit to undergo the first test which will fit thee for thy task, and complete the fulfilment of the prophecy. I may not reveal to thee what that ordeal is; this only can I say: Thou goest now in search of the lost jewel of the imperial crown—a diamond which hath not its equal in the whole world, neither for beauty nor for the mystic qualities it possesses. Five centuries ago two brothers quarrelled for its possession, and to gain it the one basely slew the other. From that time it was accursed—the evil spirit who had prompted the murder haunted it, and haunted its possessor to the death, till Manco Copac caused it to be buried deep in the bowels of the earth, where none should find it till the time appointed in his prophecy. That time has come, and thou, stranger, art the one destined to deliver the Devil's Diamond from the curse that haunts it."

"I am ready, reverend father," said Richard, firmly. "Why should I fear to face the foul fiend, when my cause is just and my heart is firm?"

"Drink, then," said the high priest, pouring out of the crystal flask into the goblet some fluid that sparkled like liquid topaz. "It is the sacred wine of the Incas, which none but those permitted by the Sun God may touch and live."

The high priest handed the goblet first to the Inca, who raised it to his lips and drank some of the contents, then with a grave, sweet smile, he passed it to Richard, who, without the slightest hesitation, drained it to the dregs.

Then, almost before the goblet left his lips, all around him seemed to grow dark, his senses reeled, his strong limbs tottered and gave way under him, and he sank to the ground, insensible!

CHAPTER VII.

THE FREE-LANCE ALONE—THE COMBAT.

WHEN Hubert of Chertsey at length reached the bottom of the defile, and stood once more upon the open plain beyond, he halted, not because he had changed his purpose, but because he was uncertain which direction to take.

The horse's hoofs had left no imprint in the rocky ground that Hubert's eye was capable of discerning, and there was no fiery hand to serve him as a beacon.

"Chance must decide," muttered Hubert, gloomily. "Pray heaven that it may guide me straight to Pizarro. Perchance the men he hath sent out are still searching for us. Ha, what is that moving yonder?"

His keen eye had detected the outline of a human form far away to the east, and, using his hand as a shade, he gazed towards it long and earnestly.

"It is no Spaniard," muttered Hubert, "else could I note the glitter of morion and breast-plate. Ha, there is another, and yet another. 'Fore George, they are coming out of the very earth by dozens!"

Without losing a moment, Hubert hastened on towards the figures. They were not Spaniards, therefore they could not be his foes: and if they were some of the natives of the country, he might be able to glean some information from them.

They were fully a mile away; but Hubert's sturdy limbs could have covered the distance in ten minutes; but to his astonishment, before he had gone half way, the figures disappeared as silently and mysteriously as they had come into view.

"By St. George!" muttered Hubert, "this is an accursed land—a land peopled with demons and unholy things."

Putting forth now his utmost speed, Hubert soon reached the spot where he had seen the figures.

It was like the rest of that part of the plain that stretched from the mountains to the sea-shore —barren and rocky, with large boulders and frag- ments of granite scattered here and there; but he could see no trace of a living creature.

"My eyes must have played me false," thought the free-lance. "'Twas without doubt the sunlight playing on those crags, that deceived me into the belief that they were moving human beings; but still——"

He paused and turned suddenly as he thought he heard a low mocking laugh behind him. On that instant he was seized by a dozen rude and powerful hands, and the priest Valverde, stepping out from the shelter of a huge boulder, confronted him.

"So," said Valverde, regarding Hubert with a cruel, crafty smile, "you have fallen neatly into the the snare, amigo mio. But where is that head- strong cub, your master, Richard of the Raven's Crest?"

Valverde spoke in Spanish, a language of which Hubert knew but very little. He comprehended the drift of the question though, recognising his young master's name, and he smiled grimly at

"Where is my master?" he repeated. "Gone, you sallow-skinned hypocrite, where you will be little likely to see him again: though, if these black-muzzled spearmen would but free my arms, I would quickly give you your passports to the other world."

"What says he?" demanded Valverde, im- patiently. "Dios mio, the language of these English is as rough and rude as their manners. Bind him securely, men; and then some of you make further search for his master, while I return to Don Pizarro with the prisoner."

Hubert had remained so quietly up to this time, offering no resistance to his captors, that three of them instantly let go their hold to procure the necessary cords. Instantly the stalwart free-lance seized his opportunity, wrested his arms free from the two who held him, and, with a couple of tremendous blows from his huge fists, levelled them with the ground.

His mace was still slung to his wrist, his strong right hand was swung above his head, and, before the astonished Spaniards could unsheath their swords, he had stricken three of them to the earth with as many mighty blows.

Valverde's sullen face was overspread with a sickly green hue, as he saw that the prowess of the Englishman was defeating his well-laid plan of ambush.

The three Spaniards whom Hubert's heavy mace had stricken down were all bleeding and senseless on the ground, but there yet remained three others, and the priest Valverde.

These soldiers, like all those who accompanied Pizarro in his expedition, were men of tried and desperate courage, and, unsheathing their long, straight swords, they advanced with silent ferocity upon Hubert.

The free-lance had taken up his station with his back against one of the huge boulders, so that he could not be attacked from the rear, and swinging his heavy mace in his right hand, he waited the attack.

"Three to one," muttered Hubert; "and they are armed with their long toasting-irons, which will never suffer me to get near enough to their thick skulls to crack one or two with my mace. I care not, though my time be come, if I may but deliver one good blow upon the bald pate of Valverde."

The Spaniards advanced steadily, but cautiously, for they were not unacquainted with the strength and skill of the English veteran. They halted when they were within striking distance, and then, with a loud shout, attacked him simultaneously.

Two of the blows Hubert avoided by leaping to one side, and, clutching the sword of the third soldier with his gauntlet hand, the free-lance dashed in under the guard, and dealt his opponent s terrible blow with his heavy mace, crushing the steel morion as if it had been pasteboard.

Then, with the rapidity of thought, Hubert snatched the sword from his foeman's nerveless grasp, and brandished it triumphantly in the air.

"We are at evens now!" he said, as he made the heavy sword whistle through the air. "Come on, ye caitiffs, and taste the quality of your own steel while an English hand is wielding it!"

The two remaining Spaniards were startled for a moment by the fall of their comrade, but set- ting their teeth firmly, and with their dark eyes flashing fire at the stalwart veteran, they advanced shoulder to shoulder upon him.

Hubert was so much engrossed with the combat that he had not noted how the priest, Valverde, with an evil, crafty look upon his face, was slowly creeping towards him in the shadow of the rock.

Slowly, step by step, he advanced, until he was within a few paces of Hubert, his right hand ex- tended and grasping a small phial; then, before the free-lance was aware of his presence, he raised the phial, and, with a sudden motion, threw some of contents in Hubert's face.

THERE, BY THE LIGHT OF THE DIAMOND, THE DEMON STOOD REVEALED.

No. 2.

The Englishman reeled backwards, gave a strange vacant stare, and then, dropping his weapon, fell heavily to the ground. He had been proof against the steel of the Spanish soldiers, but not against the subtle drugs of the Spanish priest.

"See," said Valverde, with a half-concealed sneer; "one little drop of the fluid, colourless as water, has effected more than half-a-dozen of ye, covered in steel, and armed with sword and spear, could do. Take him up, ye need not trouble to bind him; he will not recover his senses for six hours to come."

"He is not dead, then, reverend father," said one of the soldiers.

"No; the subtle liquid which I cast upon him will only deprive him of his senses for a certain time. He must not die yet. Pizarro, our commander, hath need of him and of his master too."

"A malediction light on him," growled one of the Spaniards. "By San Juan, I shall care little to face our captain and tell him how we have let one thick-pated Englishman knock over four of us as if we had been so many starveling curs. How is it with them, Pedro—all dead?"

"Ay, as St. Catherine," replied Pedro, after a brief examination of his fallen comrades. "José there still breathes a little; but his skull is cracked past mending, and there is no leech at St. Michael."

"Ay de mi!"* returned the other; "'tis a pity, for José was as good a Spaniard as ever passed wine-skin or twanged a guitar. Would that we had those cursed English in Seville or Madrid; Padre Valverde yonder would soon give them a taste of the holy office."†

"Had we brought out our muskets," grumbled Pedro, "four of the best companions that ever set foot on a galleon might yet be alive and merry, as one bullet from my petronel would have silenced the Englishman quite as quickly, and more effectually, than the reverend padre's elixir."

"Why have taken the trouble to come after them at all?" said the second soldier. "Once gone, we were well rid of them. Senor Richard was a spirited gallant, and liberal enough with his pesos,‡ but too proud and haughty for me."

Valverde was standing by the prostrate, insensible form of Hubert, regarding it with a moody air, for he was sorely perplexed. It was necessary to his and Pizarro's plans that Richard of the Raven's Crest should be arrested, and how to effect this purpose he knew not.

"Beyond doubt," thought Valverde, "we should find him in the mountains, whence this fellow came and fell into the trap I had prepared; but I have only two men left wherewith to attack him, and Richard of the Raven's Crest hath all the fiery courage and strength of his ancestor, Cœur de Lion. If I could steal upon him unawares, and drug him as I did his squire, even now! But no, that would not be safe. Malediction! I know not what to do!"

It was, in truth, an awkward position in which the wily Valverde found himself. True, he had secured Hubert, but not before the strong arm of the free-lance had slain four out of the six Spaniards. Then at any moment Richard of the Raven's Crest, alarmed at the absence of his squire, might, so the priest feared, come in search of him, and Valverde knew that he might expect scant mercy.

He was, of course, unaware of the strange adventure which had befallen our hero, and his only hope now lay in his being reinforced by the band which Pizarro, in person, was leading.

He ordered the two surviving soldiers to drag the dead bodies of their companions behind the rocks, and then stationed them so as to command a view of the plain, from any quarter of which

Pizarro might be coming, while he employed his own keen eye in watching the mountain pass whence he dreaded the arrival of Richard.

Two hours passed away in this slow and tedious manner, and then José hurriedly returned from his station to report that a small body of horse was rapidly coming up from the eastward.

"It is Pizarro," said Valverde. "Go you, José, to meet him, and signal him to come on here at once. We shall yet have the English cub safely in our clutches. Go, man—and haste."

The Spaniard set off at a run, and Valverde, scarcely able to restrain his own impatience, watched the rapidly approaching horsemen with an anxiety contrasting strangely with his usual cold, impassive demeanour.

In a quarter of an hour the Spanish leader and his band of twelve chosen horsemen reined up their steeds by the boulders, and Valverde, with a troubled, almost anxious countenance, advanced to meet Pizarro.

"How now, reverend padre?" he said, as he quickly dismounted. "Has fortune favoured you? But I need scarcely ask, for the expression of your face bodes evil."

"Evil and good too, noble Pizarro," replied Valverde. "We have one of the traitors safe enough; but ——"

"But what, padre?"

"The foul fiend must have aided him," the priest continued. "He—'tis of Hubert I speak—fought like a demon, and slew four of the men you sent with me in less than as many minutes. It would have gone hard with the rest had I not tried upon him the power of this drug."

"Sangre de Dios!" burst out Pizarro, while his face grew dark and threatening as a thunder cloud. "And has that English hound sent four of my best men to their account?"

"Even so, noble Pizarro," replied the priest. "They fought well, and did their devoir manfully; but they were no match for one armed by the powers of evil. They lie yonder—the dead and living in company."

"Lives he yet?" demanded Pizarro, with a cruel smile hovering about his thin lips.

"He does, but lulled into insensibility by the power of the subtle drug I cast in his face. He will not waken yet for hours to come."

"It is well," said Pizarro. "When he does revive, it shall be to taste such tortures as never yet racked mortal frame with anguish. And what of the other?"

"He is yonder, in the mountains," said Valverde, "no doubt awaiting the return of his squire, whom he sent out to spy upon us. I waited but your coming, noble Pizarro, to track him to his hiding-place."

"Time presses," said Pizarro, thoughtfully. "Even now another message from Huoscar awaits me, bringing fresh presents, and entreating my alliance against his rival Atahualpa. This is a glorious opportunity, and must not be neglected, Valverde, and yet——"

Pizarro paused, and the cloud of thought grew heavier on his brow.

"Can it be," he resumed after a few moments, "that Richard of the Raven's Crest has constituted himself my rival, and joined Atahualpa. His is but a single arm, but it is a strong one. We might be drawn into an ambush yonder, and the sending out of his squire is but a subtle device."

"If Richard of the Raven's Crest hath really joined the rival monarch of Peru," said Valverde, "the more necessity, noble Pizarro, of thwarting him at once. He must be in lurking yonder in the mountains close at hand. Hubert would never leave him for long."

"We will make the essay," said Pizarro. "He must not escape my vengeance; and, once again in my power, he shall never live to carry back the

---

* A Spanish exclamation of sorrow or pity.
† The Inquisition.
‡ A Spanish coin of the sixteenth century; value about four shillings and sixpence.

story of how he thwarted Pizarro! To your horses, men; forward, to the mountain! Ride cautiously, and keep your eyes and ears open for the faintest sign of danger. You, Padre Valverde, had better stay and guard yonder senseless carrion. The potency of your drug may be less than you imagine!"

And, placing himself at the head of his little squadron, Pizarro moved away at a slow pace towards the rocky defile, unconscious that a thousand eyes, unseen by him, were watching his every movement as he hastened towards the trap he was baiting for another.

CHAPTER VIII.

THE DEMON—THE GIFT AND THE PROPHECY.

WHEN our hero awoke, as from a calm refreshing sleep, it was to find himself once again in almost impenetrable darkness.

The faint light, if light it could be called, which revealed nothing, was more like the unwholesome exhalations which flitter over marshy ground and deserted graveyards, than the reflection even of the fair light of day, and only served to render the surrounding gloom more heavy and oppressive.

As he raised himself slowly on one arm, a strange chill convulsed his frame, and, passing his hand over his body and limbs, he found that he was naked, save for a waist-cloth of some soft, silk-like material.

"What is this!" muttered Richard, vainly endeavouring to pierce the gloom that surrounded him, as it were, with an impenetrable yet impalpable wall. "I am dreaming, surely."

He rose to his feet, shook himself, rubbed his eyes, and stamped upon the floor; but just then a sharp point of rock wounded his right foot, and convinced him that he was indeed awake.

"What can it be," muttered Richard again. "What fresh mystery is this? Was that wild ride in chase of the fiery hand—that leap into the dark chasm—that interview with the strange old priest who boasted twice a century of existence—that splendid hall dazzling with gold and jewels—are all these visions? No; the memory of them is too real, and yet how came I here?"

To fear, as our readers know, Richard of the Raven's Crest was a stranger. Yet the deep gloom—the awful silence—the mystery which now seemed to pervade every hour of his existence—chilled him, and he could not repress an involuntary shudder.

The darkness was so great that he could not at first discern any object, but as by degrees his vision adapted itself to the gloom, Richard made out that he was in a cavern of apparently vast dimensions, the floor of which was strewn with huge masses of rock.

"Fool that I was," muttered our hero, bitterly. "I see now that I have been sacrificed to some superstition of these Indians. I have heard of their human sacrifices, and I have been selected as the victim of some legend or tradition. But that fiery hand and its prophecy—what did that mean?"

The thought had scarcely passed through Richard's mind, than he thought he saw, in the remote corner of the cavern, the dim outline of a shadowy form.

There was a quivering halo of light around it—pale-phosphorescent—indistinct at first, but gradually growing clearer and brighter, radiating from one central point, till at length Richard of the Raven's Crest discerned a tall, semi-human figure, standing with something that glittered and sparkled like a living light, between the outstretched fingers of its right hand.

The face was such as no human being ever wore. The features were there—human in outline—but endowed with an expression of Mephistophelian mockery, absolutely demoniac.

Richard of the Raven's Crest leaned forward,

spell-bound, his limbs rigid, his eyes fixed upon the weird apparition—as if, like Medusa, it had the power of turning into stone all those who gazed upon it.

Suddenly there broke from its lips a low mocking laugh, and, slowly raising its hand, it let the light of the diamond fall full upon its face.

That laugh broke the spell that had held our hero motionless, and, lifting his handsome head proudly, as if ashamed of the momentary chill of awe which had crept over him, he said—

"Who, and what art thou?"

The Demon laughed again, but again without any visible alteration of the demoniac smile which wreathed its features.

"I say again—who and what are you?" said Richard, with a stern, angry ring in his voice. "Man or fiend, I command you to answer me!"

"Command!" repeated the figure, in the same clear, unearthly tones. "Ho! ho! ho!"

Its mocking laugh, though perfectly distinct to Richard's ears, yet seemed to arouse no echoes in the cavern. It was the very ghost of a sound.

A belief in the supernatural was much more general then than it is now, when so-called science has reduced even the dread mystery of creation to the level of the manufacture of the commonest goods that Birmingham or Manchester produces.

Our hero fully believed that what he saw before him was no creature of earth, but he had no dread of it, and the mocking tones of the Demon made the hot blood flush into his cheek as though it had been an insult from some mortal foe.

"Speak!" he said. "Answer me—whether you be of earth or hell—whence come you? What would you with me?"

"Behold!" replied the Demon, waving the diamond in its hand until it seemed to scatter a shower of brilliant sparks around it; "here is my answer. You are destined to relieve me of the charge of this jewel, over which I have kept watch and ward for many a weary century. Take it—but take my warning with it."

"The Devil's Diamond!" thought Richard, as he gazed at the jewel sparkling with an unearthly radiance; and then the warning traced by the fiery hand flashed into his mind—

"Beware the Devil Tempter's test—
God help thee in thy need."

"What fresh ordeal is this?" thought Richard. "Be it what it may, I will go through with it; steadfast and strong in truth and right I cannot err."

"Take the diamond, Richard of the Raven's Crest," said the Demon again; "but take my warning with it. So long as you hold it let your thoughts be pure, your actions just, and no man shall prevail against you, for so it is written in the prophecy. All that mortal can desire—wealth, honours, power—all will be yours. Your enemies shall be powerless as the straws which the whirlwind sweeps before its breath."

"And Pizarro?" said Hubert, as the memory of the vindictive Spaniard crossed his mind.

"He has his destiny to fulfil," replied the Demon, "and you have yours. But beware of this—when you and Pizarro meet in deadly conflict, face to face, and sword to sword, be sure that you have the diamond with you; one sparkle of that will avail you more than if you possessed the strength and skill of a hundred trained warriors."

"Strange and mysterious being," said Richard; "one question more, and I have done. What is this mystery of the diamond? Why am I selected to fulfil the prophecy."

"That," replied the Demon, solemnly, "is the will and purpose of a higher power than mine; the diamond, with all its properties, to curse and to bless, now passes into your hands. Take it, and remember my warning! Before many hours have passed you will learn its power!"

Richard of the Raven's Crest involuntarily extended his hand; the Demon placed the sparkling jewel within it. There was a sudden flash of light that dazzled our hero's eyes, and when he looked again the Demon had vanished!

CHAPTER IX.

RICHARD OF THE RAVEN'S CREST FINDS HIMSELF IN POSSESSION OF THE DIAMOND—THE DUMB SLAVE—TREACHERY—THE POWER OF THE DEMON—THE FATE OF THE SLAVE—FREE ONCE MORE.

FOR a long time after the Demon disappeared Richard still stood in the same entranced attitude, gazing at the gloomy corner of the cavern which his mysterious presence had just lit up.

The whole affair seemed so weird and unreal, that our hero could with difficulty believe it until he glanced at the jewel in the palm of his hand.

It was indeed as the old priest had described it—a gem fit for the diadem of the greatest monarch the world ever saw.

Perfect in shape, pale as a dew-drop in colour, and sparkling with a light that seemed not to be reflected, but to emanate from the diamond itself, it might have excited the sin of covetousness in the most determined despiser of wealth that ever existed.

"A marvel of beauty," thought Richard, as he turned the jewel over. "I hold here in the hollow of my hand enough wealth to gratify the avarice of a dozen Pizarros. All the gold of the earth could not purchase the equal of this."

Had Richard of the Raven's Crest but turned his head at that moment, he would have seen peering from behind a mass of rock something that sparkled with scarce less lustre than the diamond—two eyes which followed his every movement even as the shadow follows the substance.

"And what now," murmured Richard. "What fresh ordeal am I to undergo? What is the wealth of all the Indies to me, shut up here in this gloomy cavern, separated from my faithful Hubert, and with my enemy Pizarro free to work his will? Give me the free air of heaven once again, and let the baubles, wealth and power, bestow themselves where they will."

Just then, as if it had been some genii singing a powerful incantation, there rose up from behind the boulder the tall, gaunt, dark-skinned figure of a man, naked, save only for a waist-cloth such as Richard wore, and a plain fillet encircling his head.

In the gloom of the cavern his stature seemed to be gigantic; he seemed like a vast shadow, but for his eyes, which glowed like incandescent embers.

Slight as was the noise he made in rising, Richard heard it, and turned and faced him.

"What is thy purpose?" said our hero. "Say on, if thou hast aught to tell me. I have supped full of wonders to-night, but I can hear thee."

The figure slowly shook its head, and pointed to its mouth, to signify that he was dumb. Then, kneeling on the ground, he took Richard's right foot gently up, and placed it on his head, in token of submission.

"A slave," thought our hero, "sent to conduct me from the cavern, now that the diamond is mine, and my mission here ended. Certes, I shall be glad indeed to see the light of day once more. My eyes were never made to glower like a bat's i' the dark. Methinks it would be but decent to light a torch, for the way is rough, and my feet are bare."

The dumb slave seemed to understand him, for he paused suddenly, and, turning round, pointed to the hand in which Richard still held the diamond.

Richard involuntarily opened it, and then, with a gesture swift as light, the slave snatched it from his hand, and, with a hoarse, inarticulate gutteral sound, held it aloft.

With a bound like that of a panther Richard of the Raven's Crest sprang upon him, but the slave seemed gifted with preternatural strength, and, keeping our hero off with his left hand, he waved the fatal diamond once more aloft, and then, thrusting it into his mouth, swallowed it.

For one single instant he stood erect, his arms extended. Then, as if struck by a flash of lightning, he fell prostrate to the ground, while, horrified, Richard saw a lambent flame leap from his lips, while his whole body seemed lit up with an infernal fire.

The whole scene seemed to pass as quickly as a thought—the fire flared up brightly for one brief moment—a dreadful sickening stench filled the whole cavern—and there was no other sign of what had happened but a heap of grey ashes on the rocky floor, in the midst of which shone out the Devil's Diamond.

Sick and giddy at the terrible sight. Richard staggered back and leaned against the rugged wall of the cavern for support.

"Heaven shield me!" murmured Richard. "But this is an awful sight. What mysterious power dwells in yonder sparkling jewel which, in one brief moment of time, could reduce a living human being to a heap of smouldering ashes?"

Just then the soft delicious strains of music, which Richard had before heard, sounded plaintively through the cavern, a flood of light dispelled the gloom, and, when Richard's dazzled eyes had recovered, he saw slowly advancing towards him the old Priest of the Temple of the Sun.

"Welcome, thrice welcome!" said Richard, hurrying eagerly towards him. "In good truth, reverend father, I would sooner face Pizarro and his whole band of spearmen than pass another hour in this cavern!"

"It was thy fate," replied the old priest, gravely. "Thou wast stout of heart and free of mind, else thou had not been selected for this deed. But the diamond? thou hast it?"

Richard pointed to where the jewel lay embedded in the heap of ashes, and in a few words told of the fate of the slave.

"His doom was just," said the priest, solemnly. "It was his task to guard the entrance to this cavern, and he knew that his fate would be death, by the most cruel torture, should he attempt to penetrate its sacred mysteries; but the Demon of the Diamond hath saved him from our vengeance."

"To doom him to a worse," said Richard, with an involuntary shudder. "His agony lasted only one brief moment, but there was a whole eternity of torment in his look."

"Such or worse will be the fate of all who design to injure thee," said the Priest of the Sun. "Such also will be thy own if thou usest the power it giveth thee for aught but the cause of right and truth."

"I have no fear," said Richard, proudly, as he stooped and took the precious gem once more within his hand. "Lead on, reverend father. I am ready."

The priest carried the golden lamp he bore in his right hand, and threw its light into a narrow fissure in the rocky wall of the cavern, and, motioning Richard to follow him, passed through it.

"This," said the priest, "is the secret passage leading from the sacred council chamber of the Temple of the Sun; and, save myself, none but thou and that slave who has paid the penalty of death for his curiosity, have ever trodden it since the diamond was placed here by Manco Copac."

It sloped gently upwards, and was only high and broad enough to admit of the passage of a single person. Richard, indeed, was forced to stoop his stately head, while his broad shoulders were bruised and torn against the rocky sides.

The passage seemed to have been purposely designed to baffle any curious intruder. It wound about in such a tortuous manner—seeming to cross and recross its own track; but in half an hour the end was reached, and, the priest clearing aside a heavy curtain, ushered Richard into a small but exquisitely appointed chamber.

Its walls were hung with the beautiful feathers of which Richard had already seen so lavish a display. In the centre of the floor, carpeted with a rich, velvet-like material, was a large golden bath, from which some aromatic water sent forth a delicious perfume, and on a soft, luxurious couch of sandal-wood there lay carefully arranged Richard's clothes, his weapons, and his armour.

"Bathe, and refresh thyself," said the priest. "Food and wine will be brought to thee when thou art ready, and then——"

"And then?" repeated Richard.

"The Inca will be ready to receive thee," answered the priest; "and thou, at the head of twice a hundred thousand of the choicest warriors of Peru, shalt go forth to conquer Atahualpa's enemies and thine own!"

And with a stately, solemn gesture the old priest left the chamber.

"What said he?" mused Richard. "Twice a hundred thousand men. By my faith, a goodly force! But perchance the usurper Huoscar has as large an army to lead against us. Well, be it so; whatever the odds, Richard of the Raven's Crest turns not his back upon Pizarro."

Then, his heart beating high with pride and hope, our hero cooled his limbs in the refreshing aromatic waters of the golden bath, and, donning the bright armour that became so well his stately figure, waited.

It was not long before the priest returned, and a faint smile of satisfied admiration played over his aged features as he gazed upon the noble form of Richard.

Then, extending his hand, with a grave and kindly gesture he led Richard across the chamber towards a doorway screened by a heavy curtain, which the old priest signed to Richard to draw aside.

He did so, and, stepping forward, found himself standing upon a terrace of polished granite, and gazing down upon a scene of such sublimity and grandeur, that his brain seemed to reel, and his senses were intoxicated with the sight!

The terrace upon which stood Richard of the Ravens' Crest overlooked a vast square, in the centre of a great city, the buildings of which were of a shape and material strange to him.

It was built in a valley, surrounded on every side by majestic mountains, whose snow-topped crests told of their towering height. But Richard's glance wandered only for a moment, and then his rapt attention was fixed upon the scene below him.

There assembled were the flower of the Peruvian warriors, thousands upon thousands, packed so closely that each man had scarce space to raise his arms. Only just beneath the terrace on which our hero stood was a space cleared, where, radiant in their richest robes and ornaments, the caciques who had remained faithful to Atahualpa were clustered.

Every face was upturned, every eye directed towards Richard as his stately figure came in sight, and then, as with a simultaneous impulse, each warrior waved his weapon in the air, and such a shout went up from that mighty multitude as seemed to make the massive foundations of the city tremble.

"Hearest thou that, noble Richard?" said the high priest, who now stood by our hero's side. "Such is the welcome which the warriors of Atahualpa give to their chosen commander."

"It is a right royal one," said Richard; "but tell me, reverend priest, how comes it that the Inca himself hath not marched against Pizarro. It needs not my aid to sweep the Spaniards into the

sea with such a vast number of warriors at his command."

"I will tell thee anon," said the high priest. "Now there is not time. Draw thy sword, noble Richard, wave it thrice in the air, and pronounce the word—'Metzalacapal.'"

Richard did so; and, as his bright sword flashed in the sunshine, and his clear, powerful voice uttered the word, the vast body of warriors prostrated themselves, their foreheads touching the ground.

"It is done," said the priest, solemnly, as he took our hero by the arm and led him into the inner chamber. "Henceforth thou art the equal of the Inca—the sovereign master of Peru—and not a warrior or cacique amongst them all but would plunge his spear into his own breast if thou bade him."

CHAPTER X.

PIZARRO BAFFLED — THE RETURN TO THE ENCAMPMENT — PIZARRO QUESTIONS THE INCA'S MESSENGER — ON THE ROAD TO THE GOLDEN GATES OF CAXAMALCA.

IT is almost unnecessary to tell our readers that Pizarro's search for Richard of the Raven's Crest was without result.

They advanced up the defile as far as the huge mass of rock that had closed the entrance to the subterranean temple. They had seen the dead body of the horse, which Pizarro at once recognized as Hubert's charger, but that was all; of Richard of the Raven's Crest there was no trace.

Pizarro's brow was clouded, and the expression of his face so stern and angry, that his men drew back when he turned his horse's head and gave the order to return.

"El capitano is in a black mood to-day," said one of the band. "By St. Jago, I would not give much for the life of the man who crosses his will within the next hour!"

Dark and angry indeed were the thoughts that overspread Pizarro's brain, and if such a man as he was could have been susceptible of fear, the mysterious disappearance of our hero would have caused him to feel it.

"A malediction light upon him!" he muttered, as he gnawed his heavy moustache. "Whither has he gone? What is he doing? Something hath happened, else why that slaughtered horse. Hubert must know, and if fire can burn, and sharp knives wound, I will wring the truth from him."

He urged his charger into a trot, and a few minutes sufficed to bring them to the spot where Padre Valverde had been left in charge of the insensible form of Hubert.

"And hast thou found him, noble Pizarro?" said Valverde, eagerly.

"I have not," replied Pizarro, gloomily; "nor care I to search further. But let him once cross my path, should he be living, and he will learn what it is to thwart the schemes of Francisco Pizarro!"

"Should he be living?" echoed Valverde. "Think you that he is dead, Don Pizarro?"

"I know not," replied the commander, in the same gloomy tone. "Yonder Englishman can tell, and when the potency of thy drug, Valverde, hath passed away, his fortitude shall be tested. Thou hast had some practice in the Inquisition, padre; and thou shouldst know how to wring the truth from a rebellious throat."

"Ay," replied Valverde, "that do I, Don Pizarro. The holy office hath had servants far less zealous in her cause, than Vincent de Valverde. Trust me, noble commander, I will wring an answer from his lips."

"But," said Pizarro, with a meaning look, "it must be a *true* one, padre. Well wot I that racks and thumbscrews can wrest an answer from unwilling lips, but as oft as not the last breath is laden with a lie. But enough of this; we must away before night falls. I join Huoscar, and march with him against his brothers. Once Atahualpa is disposed of, and the Peruvians terrified by a display of my power, I can make what terms I please, and the vast wealth of this empire will be ours."

"And the empire too," said the ambitious Valverde. "Charles of Castile will know how to reward thy faithful service, noble Pizarro; and, as viceroy of the countries thy strong arm hath conquered, thou wilt possess a dignity which thou hast rightly earned."

Pizarro smiled. The crafty priest had well measured the height of his leader's ambition. Power, as well as wealth, was coveted by him, and it is impossible to withhold some measure of admiration from the strong will and daring courage that with so small a force could not only attempt but achieve the conquest of a mighty empire.*

The desertion of Richard of the Raven's Crest from his standard was the first check Pizarro had experienced. To that he traced the subsequent misfortunes and the loss of four of his best and bravest soldiers, who had fallen beneath the strong right arm of Hubert.

Of such importance did he deem the departure of our hero that he had not hesitated to halt his forces and detach three separate parties to scour the country in search of him. With what success we have seen. Hubert was a captive, but at the price of four precious lives.

Pizarro and the mounted men rode hastily back to the camp, one of the troopers carrying the insensible form of Hubert in the saddle before him. Already he had lost a day in the useless search, and the prosecution of his ambitious schemes admitted of no further delay.

Hernando del Soto, who had headed the third party sent in search of Richard, was already at the camp, waiting the account of Pizarro. It needed only one glance at his face to see that he too had failed.

"Strike the tents!" said Pizarro. "Where is the messenger from Huoscar, who is to guide us to Caxamalca?"

"In yon tent, capitano," replied del Soto. "Need you his presence?"

"Mount him on one of the best horses," said Pizarro; "but first send hither with Philippillo, the interpreter."

The two Peruvians soon came, and as they neared the Spanish commander, prostrated themselves to the ground. The simple Indians regarded these strangers as something more than mortal, and paid them the reverence due only to a divinity.

Pizarro's questioning was brief and stern—

"How far is it," he demanded, "from here to Caxamalca, where your Inca waits our coming?"

"Two days' march, mighty Pizarro," said the interpreter, after putting the question to the messenger. "Caxamalca lies beyond the mountains which rear their lofty crests before us, but the only pass by which they can be crossed lies far to the east."

"Ask him if there is a shorter road," said Pizarro, impatiently; "no matter how difficult or dangerous."

"There is one, mighty stranger, says the messenger of the Inca," was the interpreter's reply; "but it is a secret path known only to the High Priest of the Temple of the Sun. It may not be defiled by any feet less sacred than his."

"Would that I had that same priest here!" said

Pizarro. "Sacred or not I would wring the truth from him; but since better may not be, bid him mount and lead the way with all haste!"

The Peruvian glanced tremblingly at the snorting charger, which at Pizarro's command was led up. He regarded it with amazement and awe, but he dared not disobey.*

The Spanish leader saw his terror; and, smiling scornfully, bade two of the soldiers lift the Peruvian on to the horse, and bind him there securely.

"Should the rest of his race prove as faint-hearted as yonder fellow," said Pizarro to the priest, "we shall scarce need to draw our swords. Padre, the very sight of us will terrify them."

"May it prove to be so," said the priest; "for if what Philippillo says be true, Huoscar can bring a hundred thousand men into the field; and were they the veriest cowards that ever drew the breath of life, their numbers would be sufficient to stay our progress."

"Ay," said Pizarro, "and for that reason, reverend padre, I mean to follow thy advice. We must league with Huoscar, and march against his rival Atahualpa; then, when they have cut a few thousands of each others throats, and so done half our work for us, we can turn upon them both, Valverde, and——"

"Then," said the padre, with his crafty, evil smile, "hail, Francisco Pizarro, Vice-king of the Golden Americas!"

The next moment the trumpet sounded the advance; and, placing himself at the side of the guide, Pizarro moved forward towards the doomed city of Caxamalca.

CHAPTER XI.

RICHARD OF THE RAVEN'S CREST SEEKS TIDINGS OF THE FREE-LANCE, HUBERT—THE VISION IN THE GRANITE CHAMBER.

IT must not be supposed that Richard of the Raven's Crest was so careless or ungrateful as to have wilfully dismissed from his mind all thought of his faithful squire, Hubert of Chertsey.

The strange events that had succeeded each other with such startling rapidity had kept his senses in a whirl, and even now, at times, he doubted the reality of what was passing around him.

But now that he and the high priest were alone in the inner chamber, and his freedom of thought had in some measure returned, the fate of Hubert flashed into his mind, and it was with a feeling of bitter self-reproach that he reflected that for so many hours he had not devoted one single thought to the free-lance.

"My follower, Hubert," he said, abruptly; "what of him, reverend priest. Know you aught of his fate? Came he not hither with me?"

"Thou wert alone," replied the high priest, calmly; "none but thou wert to descend into the abyss, and fulfil the prophecy of the fiery hand."

"Alas, poor Hubert!" exclaimed Richard, sorrowfully. "I warrant that he has not so easily forgotten me as I him. I must seek him at once. I would not for the wealth of a hundred Incas that aught of evil hath happened to him."

And then in a few hurried, impassioned words Richard told the old priest of the relations that existed between himself and the veteran Englishman—told him of the strong affection the free-lance bore towards him, and how until that moment they had never been separated since Richard was a child.

"It speaks well, noble stranger," said the high priest, "for the goodness of thy heart to regard

---

* The force with which Pizarro marched into Peru consisted of only one hundred and two foot soldiers and sixty-two horsemen. Of these, but a very small proportion was armed with muskets and cross-bows. Two cannon completed the equipment, but these were of such trifling dimensions that in our days they would be considered as toys fit only for playthings.

* Until the advent of the Spaniards in the sixteenth century, the inhabitants of America were totally unacquainted with the horse. The strange appearance of these (to them) unknown animals, their strength and swiftness, filled the Peruvians and Mexicans with a supernatural dread.

with an equal affection one who hath been true and faithful to thee; but time alone can reunite thee to him."

"I tell you, sir priest," said Richard, with a touch of his old haughty impatience at having his will opposed—"I tell you that I must seek him at once. Show me the way, or stand aside, and let me find it for myself."

"It may not be," returned the priest, calmly.

"And why not?" demanded Richard.

"There is but one entrance to the Temple of the Sun and the city of the plain of Cuzco, and that closed up for ever when thou entered it."

An exclamation of despair and disappointment broke from Richard's lips. The fate of his faithful Hubert was no trifling matter to him; indeed, as he had said, the wealth of a hundred Incas was as naught in the balance weighed against the life of the free-lance.

"Is there no way," demanded Richard, "no matter how difficult or dangerous, reverend priest?"

"None, noble Richard. These mountains which enclose the sacred city of Cuzco, present an impenetrable barrier to the east. My people believe that on the side from which thou comest dwell a race of beings, surpassing the children of men in strength and beauty, and gifted with immortality. Hence the reverence they pay to you, and the fear with which they regard the coming of Pizarro and his followers."

Richard stamped impatiently on the ground with his foot, and a cloud of sorrow seemed to settle upon his handsome features.

"'Fore George!" he muttered. "I would give all I have, and all I hope to have, to be once more by thy side, my trusty Hubert! Should Pizarro have tracked him, I know well that they will show him little mercy."

The high priest watched Richard's features with a quiet, grave attention, and then, laying his hand lightly on our hero's arm, he said—

"Would'st thou know, noble Richard, the fate of thy follower?"

"Ay, that would I," replied our hero, eagerly "It would be the next best thing to having him here safe and sound by my side."

"Thou shalt have thy wish, then," said the high priest. "Follow me, Richard."

And with a slow and solemn step he passed out of the inner chamber into a smaller one, which, unlike all those Richard had yet seen, was utterly destitute of ornament—floor, walls, and ceiling were of solid granite.

There was a dim, misty light in it, proceeding from no particular point, yet pervading the whole room; and Richard noticed that as the priest entered, the luminous vapour seemed to be agitated, and concentrate itself in a halo around him.

"Be silent," said the high priest, in a low tone, "and stir not till I bid thee, or the charm is broken."

Then, stepping forward a few paces, he began a low, monotonous chant, moving his hands with a slow, regular motion towards the wall opposite.

Then the room grew suddenly darker and darker, and the luminous vapour that had filled it floated towards the wall, and spread itself into a circular patch, which grew brighter and brighter with every moment.

Upon this Richard riveted his gaze, while the low chant or incantation of the priest grew louder and clearer, till suddenly he stopped, and, laying one hand upon Richard's arm, pointed with the other towards the centre of the luminous circle.

There, shadowy and indistinct as the mirage—wavering and uncertain at first, but gradually growing clearer and sharper—were the outlines of some human figures. Richard of the Raven's Crest held his breath, and he could count the quick, hard beating of his own heart, as they grew plain to his sight, and he recognized the

form of Pizarro, the priest Valverde, Ferdinand, and del Soto grouped round some figure lying on the carpeted floor of Pizarro's tent.

Richard could not see the features of the recumbent figure, but he knew involuntarily that it must be the free-lance.

"He is dead!" he thought, "or dying; and I, recreant that I am, have left him to his fate."

Richard turned to the priest with a passionate manner, and would have spoken, but a warning gesture stayed him.

"Speak not, if thou wouldst see more," he said. "Take heed of what thou seest, for the time is brief."

Richard looked again, and, as he did so, the figure of Pizarro and his companions separated, and then he recognised in the recumbent figure on the ground the features of his faithful Hubert.

His arms and legs were bound, and he seemed to be awaking from a deep sleep, for, as he looked, Richard saw the free-lance struggle into a sitting posture, and gaze wonderingly around him.

"My poor Hubert!" thought our hero. "It is even as I feared, and he is in Pizarro's power—but see. Pizarro seems to be questioning him—and now—Hubert is laughing. Ha! coward that he is, the Spaniard has struck him—an unarmed and helpless man! Now Valverde makes a sign, and three soldiers enter, and clear a space around Hubert. Ha! what is that they pile about him? By heaven, 'tis a heap of brushwood, and now one of them has fetched a torch and fired it. Villain, stay your murderous hands!"

Richard of the Raven's Crest had drawn his sword, and dashed at the wall, as if the vision he beheld was a reality; but in that instant it faded, the wall was blank, and he and the priest were alone once more.

CHAPTER XII.

OUR HERO'S RESOLVE—THE ASSEMBLY OF THE PERUVIAN WARRIORS—THE RETURN OF THE SPIES FROM CAXAMALCA—THE WARNING—THE DESTRUCTION OF THE CITY OF THE PLAIN.

BEFORE Richard of the Raven's Crest had recovered from the bewilderment which the strange scene had caused him, and while yet the flush of anger was on his brow, the high priest had taken him by the arm and led him forth into the inner chamber.

"Thou wert mad, noble Richard," he said in an agitated voice; "to disregard my warning. Hadst thou not been under the protection of the fiery hand and the chosen champion of the Incas, thy life had paid the penalty."

"Pardon, reverend priest," replied Richard. "But what I saw seemed so real, so horrible, that I could not have stayed my hand had I a thousand lives, and each one depending on my silence. But tell me, is the vision that I saw but now the representation of a reality, or only a shadowy vision sent to mock me?"

"It was, or will be true," replied the priest; "that only can I tell thee, noble Richard. Whether shadows of the past or visions of the future, thou mayst be sure of that."

"Tell me, then," said Richard, eagerly, "how to avert that awful doom? If it is yet in the bosom of the future, there is time—surely, your skill can give me that hope?"

"Who can avert the inevitable?" replied the priest, gravely. "What is written—is written; what will be—will be."

"I am no fatalist," said Richard; "no believer in that pernicious creed which would deprive life of the only thing that renders it tolerable — hope. Set me free, I say, and I will cut my way to Hubert's side and save him!"

"Impossible," said the priest, in a grave, solemn voice, that sounded to Richard as though it had come from a tomb. "I tell thee again, noble stranger, that unless thou could'st borrow the wings of the eagle, and soar over the tops of yonder mountains, thou canst not hope to see thy follower till the Great Spirit wills that you shall meet."

"If what you say be true," replied our hero, sorrowfully, "I needs must put my trust in Heaven; but if the vision that I saw were true, then let Pizarro and that subtle Valverde look to themselves; for every pang inflicted on my faithful Hubert they shall feel a thousand. No fiend has e'er imagined such tortures as I will rack their bodies with. Up and away, reverend priest, if it will please you. I have need of action, or I shall vent the anger that burns within me upon these senseless walls."

"All is in readiness," said the High Priest of the Sun. "We await but the return of the spies sent to watch Huoscar's movements, and then, noble Richard, you can lead our warriors against the foe."

"Be it as soon as you will," replied Richard, his brow contracting in a stern, dark frown, that boded little good to his foe. "It cannot be too soon for me. Alone, or with your myriad warriors at my back, I swear to avenge the fate of Hubert."

But passionate and impetuous as he was, Richard of the Raven's Crest did not lose sight of the fact that, in encountering the usurping Inca, allied with Pizarro, he would have need of caution as well as courage to insure success.

There was an army of two hundred thousand men ready to follow him blindly, implicitly to the death; but such an army, Richard well knew, could not be handled as easily as he managed his sword or guided his trained charger.

Their usual method of fighting, as he learned from the high priest, was to charge with a wild tumultuous rush upon the enemy, and trust to superior numbers or individual courage for success.

Richard's martial instinct and education told him what would be the inevitable fate of such a vast body of men opposed to the trained and warlike veterans of Pizarro, and eager as he was to revenge the fate of Hubert (for he never doubted but that the vision he had seen was true), he had yet prudence enough to take the best means of securing it.

"How long will it be think you, reverend priest, ere the spies return from Caxamalca?"

"But two days, at the farthest," replied the high priest; "and till then, don Richard, thou must restrain thy impatience."

"I will make good use of the time," said our hero. "It will all aid to further my revenge."

These two days were well employed by Richard in instituting some sort of discipline. He divided the army into two equal parts, the one to act as a reserve in case of the defeat of the other.

Each of these divisions Richard further divided into troops of five thousand men, placing them under the command of the caciques, whose duty it was to bear a standard of a particular shape or colour, and only lead his men against the enemy when, by hoisting a similar flag, Richard should himself give the signal.

These manœuvres were so simple that even the caciques, unused to the art of warfare, except in its most primitive form, readily comprehended them. At the end of the two days they had learned their lesson, and our hero knew that he would be implicitly obeyed.

At the end of that time the spies returned, bringing information that Huoscar was encamped outside Caxamalca with the whole of his army, numbering nearly two hundred and fifty thousand men, and that Pizarro was on his way to join him.

"They must never meet," said Richard. "In how short a time, reverend priest, could our forces march upon Huoscar?"

"In three days," replied the high priest. "The roads are good, noble Richard, and Huoscar will suspect nothing. He knows not that the royal Atahualpa is preparing to punish his treachery."

"Then must we delay no longer. Huoscar must be attacked, defeated, and the city of Caxamalca taken before Pizarro suspects aught. Then, when he does arrive, instead of an ally, he will find Richard of the Raven's Crest burning to retaliate upon him the wrongs he hath inflicted on my faithful Hubert. Let the caciques assemble their troops, I pray you reverend priest, and let my charger be brought forth. I here vow not to doff mine armour or sheathe my sword till my trusty Hubert be restored to me—or avenged?"

The signal was given, the long silver trumpets, or horns, of the Peruvians sounded their low, melancholy notes, and, as if by enchantment, the vast square in front of the temple was filled with the warriors, each man ranging himself, with some appearance of order, under the standard of his particular chief.

A slight satisfied smile passed over Richard's face as he noted the improvement he had already effected. He doubted not now that the undisciplined troops of Huoscar would be scattered like sheep before the warriors of Atahualpa, animated as they were by the belief that he who led them was more than mortal.

The Diamond, which had come so strangely into our hero's possession, he now wore gleaming in the front of his helmet, where the hands of the high priest himself had set it in a circlet of solid gold.

There, flashing and glittering like a living light, it was indeed a jewel fit for the diadem of the mightiest monarch that ever wore a crown. But Richard thought not of its value—he longed only to test its power on his enemies.

With a burning, feverish impatience Richard watched the passing of the troops; and, as each cacique led his men out of the great gate of the city, he uttered an exclamation of anger at their tardy movements.

"Bid them haste," he said. "By St. George, it will be sundown ere one-half of them have defiled upon the plain beyond the city gates! Each moment that we waste here delays the execution of my vengeance."

"Patience, noble Richard," said the priest, gravely. "When thou hast lived until thy brow be wrinkled and thy hair grey, thou wilt have learned its value. To him who knows how to wait nothing is impossible."

But patience was a quality of which our hero possessed very little. His youthful blood coursed far too hotly in his veins, and not until the snows of age had silvered his clustering locks, and chilled the fire of his nature, would he learn the truth of the old priest's lesson.

Hour after hour passed on, and still the throng of warriors pressing forward to the gates seemed endless. Richard, unable to control his impatience, passed to and fro with the restless tread of a caged panther, his hand ever upon the hilt of his sword, his eyes fixed upon the moving masses that slowly and steadily passed onwards to the gates.

He was alone now, for the priest had left him, to perform some duty in the temple—an invocation to the Sun God to favour the enterprise, the issue of which should restore the rightful Inca to his throne and scatter his enemies like chaff before the wind.

Richard could hear the low solemn chant of the priest, mingled with the sweet melody of the music which had accompanied his first entrance to the Temple of the Sun.

As he listened, a strange calm seemed to steal over him, and soothe the fiery passions which were stirred within his breast. He associated it in a curious manner with the soft lullaby which had hushed him to rest when he was a child. He stopped in his restless walk, and, throwing himself upon a couch, gave way to the dreamy influence of the music, and gradually fell into a slumber.

His dreams were as sweet and pleasant as the music which had caused it, for he thought that he was once again at home in Merrie England, a happy child, listening with eager ears and wondering eyes to Hubert's tale of battle and adventure; then, anon, he would be contending with the old veteran at quarter-staff or sword and buckler, or bending the bow which Hubert's own hands had fashioned from a yew bough for him, till suddenly his arm was roughly shaken, and he awoke to find the old priest standing by his side, with such an expression of awe and terror upon his aged features as Richard had never seen before.

"Awake!" he cried. "Up and away, Richard—the city of the plain is doomed! 'Tis the earthquake!"

Even as the priest spoke, our hero felt the ground vibrate with a curious shuddering motion, the walls rocked to and fro, while a thunderous roar, like that of some mighty cataract, filled the air!

CHAPTER XIII.

THE EARTHQUAKE—RICHARD TO THE RESCUE.

EVEN our hero's magnificent physical powers were shaken by this awful convulsion of nature. In the sublime record of the creation, man is created to dominate over every other living thing, but in this instance nature herself seemed to be bent upon the destruction of her children, and every thing that lived and moved and had being bowed before her.

The sky—but a brief while since radiant with the golden glory of the sunshine—was black as midnight now, save when at frequent intervals the vivid lightning lit up its murky horrors. The birds flew low, uttering shrill, discordant cries; the fierce jaguar and the timid llama crouched side by side, trembling with a common terror, on the mountain sides; but the chief horror had accumulated in the plain, and the full power of the earthquake had concentrated on the city of Cuzco.

It was the first shock that Richard of the Raven's Crest had felt, and it lasted but a minute. In that brief space of time he was fully awake and alive to the danger. Catching the old priest in his arms, he bore him towards the curtain which screened the entrance to the balcony, but with an effort of almost supernatural strength, the old man wrested himself free.

"No, noble Richard," he said, with a simple dignity, which even at that awful moment impressed our hero. "I may not desert the temple of the deity I serve. Let the dread earthquake wreak its will upon these sacred walls, and rend these stones asunder, Rimac still remains faithful to his trust."

Richard saw that it was useless to oppose the determination of the high priest. He felt, indeed, that it would be little less than sacrilege to attempt to force him to desert his guardianship; so, with a hastily spoken "farewell," our hero vaulted lightly over the parapet, and dropped into the square beneath.

The scene was indeed terrible. In that one brief moment the work of centuries had been undone.

The splendid edifices which the hands of man had slowly and laboriously built up piece by piece were scattered like a house of cards which the breath of a child has touched. Ruin, devastation, and destruction were all around, but the worst was not yet come.

The great square was yet filled with warriors, who, at the first shock of the earthquake, had cast themselves upon the ground, there to await their fate. According to their superstition, they believed that the deity was offended, and they deemed it useless to attempt to avert the effects of his wrath.

Huge masses of granite had been hurled by the first shock into the square, crushing them by dozens at a time; but the rest made no effort to escape, but lay there, passive as slaves led to the sacrifice.

But it was not to these that Richard's attention was directed. He heard arising from the ruined city the wails and lamentations of women and children. To hear these cries was enough for our hero. To give aid to a woman in distress was with him a religious duty.

The square was literally paved with the Peruvians, and Richard had no time to pick his way amongst the cowards, as with a bitter contempt he called them, so over their prostrate bodies he strode, and many a warrior gave vent to a shriek or groan as our hero's heavy foot trode mercilessly on his unprotected body.

He had not yet traversed half the breadth of the square, when again that low, muttering growl—unlike any other sound that he had ever heard—heralded the second coming of the earthquake. Again the wails and lamentations broke forth, and Richard redoubled his speed; but, ere he could reach the gate, that terrible trembling shudder shook the earth again to its foundations, and our hero was thrown forward with such violence that the shock almost deprived him of breath.

He was on his feet again in an instant, and, holding to the sides of an immense block of granite, looked bewildered at the terrible scene of ruin. Even as he gazed a wide chasm opened in the ground before him, and with its hideous jaws vomiting a thick, black smoke, swallowed up all that lay within their reach. Twice a hundred living men were there but a moment since—then, like a breath, they were gone, and the chasm closed once more with a crash, leaving no trace behind it.

Richard muttered a brief prayer for the hapless wretches who had gone to such an awful doom, and then steadying himself, dashed onwards. His path was clear of human forms now. The hideous jaws of the chasm had closed on them for ever, and passing through the tottering remnants of the granite gate, our hero was in the main street of the city.

Immediately opposite him was what had once been the stately palace of the Incas of Peru. It was so solidly built, though, of massive granite blocks, dovetailed into each other, that it had apparently suffered less than any other portion of the city.

The entrance, though partly blocked by the ruins of the pillars which had once decked its front, was still open, and Richard paused, as he heard, proceeding from within, the sounds of some solemn chant, such as he had heard in the Temple of the Sun.

A ponderous block of granite, which had been the key-stone of the arched entrance, overhung the passage, retained only from falling by its having caught upon a slender ledge, from which it almost seemed that a child's weight might bring it down.

Crouched just beneath it there lay a woman with a child pressed closely to her breast, and just beyond, the body of a man was huddled up, crushed by a huge heap of masonry.

It needed but one glance at the woman, who from terror seemed to have frozen into rigidity, to realize to Richard the awful fate that threatened her.

It seemed as if the lightest touch of a finger would send that massive block of granite crashing down, and even as Richard hurried towards her the low muttering sound, presaging the third shock, shivered in the air.

With one tremendous leap our hero reached the spot, and striding over the helpless form of the woman, he with a mighty effort, worthy of his ancestor, Cœur de Lion, kept the falling masonry in its place.

Only just in time ; for the next instant came the third shock of the earthquake—a more terrible and violent one than either of the others. The granite block was wrenched away from the ledge, and only the vast power of young Richard's arms sustained it.

"Fly !" said our hero, forgetting that the Peruvian mother understood not a word of his language. "Fly, and save yourself !"

But she neither heeded nor heard him. In the first dread shock, she had seen her husband and her brother crushed into a shapeless pulp by a falling pillar, and little cared she now if the same fate was shared by her.

Richard still struggled with the tremendous weight that was bearing down upon him. The muscles of his sinewy arms stood out like knotted ropes, his sinews strained until they creaked, the veins in his forehead swelled almost to bursting, and he felt that he could not hold out much longer.

To have relinquished his hold, though, would have been to doom not only the woman, but himself, to certain death ; if he gave way but an inch, that ponderous mass would come crashing down, bringing their fate with it.

There was only one chance, and that was to topple the block forwards so that it would fall harmlessly into the palace ; and Richard, setting his teeth hard together, braced up every nerve and muscle for the effort.

Just then, the solemn chant that he had heard before, arose again, mingling with the wails of agony, and the cries of the wounded ; and, looking beyond into the courtyard, Richard saw advancing from the ruins of the palace, the Inca himself, accompanied by the few caciques whom the earthquake had spared.

In another moment, they too would be within reach of that crushing mass of granite. The Inca had already seen and recognised him ; and, with that sweet gracious smile that had already so impressed our hero, raised his hands in a gesture of welcome.

Richard of the Raven's Crest felt his strength going, the strain was too great for mortal muscles to bear much longer. He made a last despairing effort to cast the huge block from him—he felt the stubborn rock slowly yield—another effort, and it toppled over and fell crashing inwards within a yard of the advancing Inca.

CHAPTER XIV.

HUBERT OF CHERTSEY IN THE POWER OF PIZARRO—THE QUESTIONS, AND HOW THE FREE-LANCE ANSWERED THEM—THE ORDEAL BY FIRE.

THE vision which the High Priest of the Sun had shown to Richard in the granite chamber was a true one, and represented as faithfully as a mirror a prophetic picture of the fate which Pizarro had destined for Hubert.

The Spanish commander's heart was full of bitterness and hatred towards our hero and his faithful squire. He hated Richard because of the contempt and abhorrence which the daring English youth had openly expressed for his craft and cruelty, but above even this feeling was the sense of uneasiness—almost of fear—at his strange disappearance and its motives.

Pizarro had settled in his own mind that Hubert of Chertsey could disclose the truth, and he resolved to wrest the solution of the mystery from his lips.

It was near sunset before the effects of the powerful drug Valverde had administered wore off, and that Hubert showed signs of returning consciousness.

He had been narrowly watched, by Pizarro's orders, and the instant that this intelligence was conveyed to him he commanded a halt and had Hubert borne to his own tent, and laid upon the ground.

Then, as in the vision which Richard had seen, the Spanish leaders gathered round him, and awaited for his waking.

"Dios mio," growled Pizarro. "How much longer must one dance attendance on this English hound ? Hast thou no drug, padre, which will quicken his sluggish senses into life without more delay ?"

"None, noble Pizarro," replied Valverde ; "but I have plenty which will for ever still his pulse, and pass him from life into death without a struggle."

"Nay, reverend padre," said Pizarro, grimly, "that would be too merciful a death for one who hath not only defied and resisted my authority, but shed the blood of my best and bravest men. Besides, thou knowest I have that to demand of him which he must answer."

"Trust me, noble Pizarro," replied Valverde, with his old evil crafty smile. "We of the holy office know how to administer the question* to the refractory. True, we lack both rack and thumbscrews, but fire can burn and knives flay, as well in Peru as in Castile or Aragon."

Pizarro smiled grimly again, and bent his dark eyes down upon the recumbent form of Hubert, which now began to move uneasily, as one awaking from a deep sleep.

Then the veteran Englishman unclosed his eyes, and gazed wonderingly around him, but recognising the familiar features of the Spaniards, he made an effort to rise, but his bonds prevented him.

"Why," he muttered, "how now ? A prisoner, am I ? St. George ! how came this about ?"

As our readers already know Hubert comprehended but very imperfectly the Spanish language, and the same ignorance of English prevailed amongst the Spaniards, with the exception of Ferdinand, who had spent some time at the court of Elizabeth, then Queen of England.

At a sign from Pizarro he now advanced, to act as interpreter.

"Ask the English dog," said Pizarro, roughly, "what has become of the traitor, Richard of the Raven's Crest ?"

"Tell Pizarro," retorted Hubert, his bronzed cheek flushing an angry red, as Ferdinand put the question to him, "that he shall sooner tear the tongue from my mouth than force me to answer one who dares to call my noble master traitor."

"Be politic, Don Pizarro," said Valverde. "These English are obstinate, as you well know. Soothe him with softer words, until you have gained from him the knowledge you require ; then treat him as you list."

"Be thine, then, the task," said Pizarro. "I cannot look upon him, padre, without the desire to spurn him with my foot, like the dog he is."

Valverde questioned Hubert in his turn, but with no better success. The veteran had resolved that the enemies of his young master should never know, at least from him, the fate that had befallen him.

"Let them do their worst," thought the free-lance. "At worst they can but send me to follow Lord Richard, and I have risked my life too many times with him to care much about losing it now that he is gone."

"By St. Jago," muttered Pizarro, "the dog laughs at us, padre. Let us see if he will be so hardy when his skin is cracking and turning brown before the heat of the fire which Spanish hands can kindle."

The glance that he shot at Hubert as he said this might well have quelled the courage of many a man ; but Hubert only laughed—a short, contemptuous laugh too—that sent the hot blood mantling into Pizarro's face.

---

* The "question" was the term usually employed by the familiars of the Inquisition to denote the tortures to which heretics or infidels—reluctant to reply—were submitted.

"Laugh now, rebellious hound!" hissed the fiery Spaniard, as with his sheathed sword he struck Hubert a sharp blow in the face. "Take that as an earnest of what is in store for thee."

"Coward," returned Hubert, scornfully, using about the very words which had escaped our hero's lips when he saw the vision. "Coward, to strike a bound and unarmed man. Set my limbs free, if you dare, and then strike."

Pizarro's only reply was a scowl of intense malignity, and then turning to Del Soto, he whispered a few words, and, shortly after, three soldiers entered the tent, two bearing an armful of dry grass and twigs, and the third a lighted torch.

These, following Valverde's instructions, were heaped around the prostrate form of Hubert, closing him in on all sides at a distance of some two feet.

"Ah!" muttered Hubert. "The caitiff Spaniards think to wring an answer from me by torture; but 'fore George, they shall find that we of the mastiff breed can keep our mouths fast when we like, for never a Spaniard of them all shall make Hubert of Chertsey yelp."

"Ask him once again, Ferdinand," said Pizarro "Bid him disclose the hiding place of his traitorous master, and he shall not only go free, but I myself will reward him with a thousand pesos."

"And again I answer, no!" returned Hubert. "Not for all the gold told ten times over, that Pizarro's avarice deems within his reach, will I answer. Bid him in his turn do his worst, Hubert of Chertsey defies him!"

"Fire the pile!" exclaimed Pizarro, in accents choking with wrath; "and let the flames wring an answer from this boasting Englishman. Stand by there, two of you, with water, and if he complies with my demand, and tells us where the traitor lies hidden, extinguish the fire. I have no wish to kill him body and soul."

The soldier who held the lighted torch advanced, and stooped to fire the dry grass; but before the flare had caught, a vivid flash of lightning seemed to illuminate the tent for one brief moment with an unearthly light, then followed a crash of thunder, so loud, so deafening, that those who heard it recoiled as if stricken by a heavy blow.

"Santa Maria shield us!" exclaimed the soldier, dropping the torch and starting back; while the rest, excepting Pizarro and Valverde, devoutly crossed themselves.

It had grown so suddenly and intensely dark, that, but for the fitful glaring of the torch, as it lay flaring on the ground, all in the tent would have been invisible.

Pizarro gave utterance to an angry exclamation, and struck at the soldier with his gauntleted hand.

"Muerte de Cristo!" he said. "What, have I been gulled into bringing weak children from Spain, instead of men! A pestilence on ye, to start at a flash of lightning and a peal of thunder!"

As he spoke, Pizarro himself strode forward and picked up the fallen torch to apply it to the pile; but ere he could accomplish his purpose, a second flash of lightning shot from the heavens and seemed to pass through the very centre of the tent. It was followed, or rather, accompanied by a peal of thunder so terrifically startling, that Pizarro paused.

It was doubtful, though, whether his iron nerves and his strong will would not have accomplished the task he had set them, but for an event which made even Pizarro think that heaven had set itself in opposition to his cruelty.

CHAPTER XV.

HUBERT SAVED—THE FLOOD—THE VETERAN FREE-LANCE IN PERIL—THE CAMP OF HUOSCAR, THE RIVAL INCA—HUBERT'S WARNING.

IT was the earthquake which the storm had heralded, and which, so many miles away, was desolating the grand city of the plain, where Richard of the Raven's Crest was battling with its might.

At the very moment when our hero had heard its low, muttering, threatening voice, and felt the first shuddering motion of the earth, as if Nature herself were in the throes of dissolution, it swept down upon the tent where Pizarro stood, eager to vent vengeance upon Hubert.

He held the blazing torch yet in his hand. The lighting had no power to weaken his strong nerves, and another moment would have seen it thrust into the dry grass and brushwood, when suddenly the ground shook and quaked with a violent motion, and a hideous chasm opened with a terrible rending noise, vomiting from its mouth blue sulphureous flames, and nauseous sickening smoke, that seemed the very breath of hell itself.

This chasm had opened out across the very centre of the tent, presenting a barrier between Hubert and the Spanish leader, which even his hardihood would not attempt to bridge.

Ferdinand, Del Soto, and the soldiers had hurried out of the entrance, awed and terrified, for the dreadful phenomena of an earthquake were new to them. Valverde alone remained by the side of Pizarro, and, reckless and unscrupulous man though he was, he was cowed.

"Come, noble Pizarro," said Valverde, hastily. "Yonder chasm is widening, and if we stay here we shall be engulfed."

Even as he spoke the second shock of the earthquake convulsed the ground—the hideous chasm widened—the sulphureous flames leaped up fiercer and higher—and the stench of the smoke became quite insupportable.

"Your enemy will never trouble you more, noble Pizarro," said Valverde, grimly; "bound and helpless as he is, his fate is sealed."

"He is a dog," said Pizarro, fiercely; "let him die the death of one. Would only that his master had shared it with him."

Even the awful aspect of convulsed nature had no power to turn Pizarro's mind from the object of his hatred. The scene around him might have caused even a non-superstitious man to believe that the last day had come; yet the thought uppermost in the mind of the Spaniard was that of his enemy, young Richard of the Raven's Crest.

Many of the soldiery were on their knees praying devoutly—others, as soon as Valverde emerged from the tent, ran to him and clasped his dress, as if the mere touch of his robe had power to save them. A little apart stood the Peruvian, looking with wonder, not unmixed with contempt, at the fear displayed by the Spaniards at a phenomenon which to him was common.

"Get ye to your horses, ye cowards," shouted the Spanish commander, angrily. "Sangre de Dios! Am I leading a pack of old women—to be terrified by a dark sky and a flash or two of lightning. To horse, I say. The last man in the saddle I will fling into yonder chasm with my own hands."

Pizarro turned, and pointed, with a stern gesture that there was no mistaking, towards the chasm. It seemed as if that gesture and those words had been the invocation of a demon; for on the instant the third shock of the earthquake came, the hideous chasm closed for a moment, then opened again, and belched forth, not a torrent of fire and smoke, but a volume of black pitchy water, which spread with inconceivable rapidity.

Before they had time to realise the fact, the water was upon them, knee deep almost, and

THE SLAVE FELL, AS IF STRICKEN BY LIGHTNING, AND A BRIGHT FLAME FLASHED FROM HIS LIPS.

No. 3.

spreading in every direction. It was as if one of the rivers of the infernal regions had escaped, and forced its way into the upper air.

"To horse! to horse!" shouted Pizarro. "The higher ground towards the mountains! Quick, for your lives! Dios mio, padre; but I could well believe that Satan himself is in league with these English hounds!"

The Spaniards, so accustomed to obey when their commander spoke, seemed to have broken the spell of fear which had enchained them. They rushed towards their horses, untethered them, and mounted; while such as were on foot, headed by Ferdinand, ran at the top of their speed towards the mountains.

But fast as they ran, the pitchy water went faster. With the force and rapidity of a mountain torrent it gushed up from the mouth of that hideous chasm, gathering strength and volume with every minute.

Snorting and curvetting, the horses needed no urging from their riders, but plunged on, knee deep, splashing the foul water high on every side, and bearing their riders nearer and nearer to the high ground where alone safety lay.

Leaving Pizarro and his men to struggle as best they may with the enemy their leader's own evil passion seemed to have conjured up, let us return to Hubert of Chertsey, our hero's faithful squire, and ascertain how he has fared in the plight in which we left him.

*   *   *   *

The nature of the old free-lance was not one given to despair or despondency; but when he lay there helpless on the ground, saw the flaming torch in the Spaniard's grasp, and noted the cruel glitter in his dark eyes, he thought for a surety that his last hour had come.

The awful advent of the earthquake, the opening up of that fearful chasm that saved him from his enemies, seemed to Hubert to be the effect of magic, in which he was a firm believer.

"It's that fiery hand," muttered the veteran, "of a surety. I have said more evil of it than it deserved. It hath saved me; why not, then, Lord Richard, who so much more deserved it?"

The clouds of smoke which the chasm belched forth, hid Pizarro and the Spaniards from his sight; but he heard the cries of the affrighted soldiers, and, though half choked and blinded himself, he could not repress a grim laugh at their discomfiture.

"'Fore George," he thought, "'tis an old saying that the devil takes care of his own! but in this instance he has turned traitor to his friends, and baulked yonder black-a-vized Spaniard of his prey."

Just as these thoughts passed across the mind of the old veteran, the second shock of the earthquake made the earth tremble to its foundations, and hurled the free-lance against the further side of the tent with such force, that he was driven bodily through, and shot out upon the open ground beyond so violently, that every joint in his body seemed to suffer dislocation.

It was of service to him, though, in two important matters. First, he was removed some distance from the dangerous vicinity of the chasm; and, secondly, his bonds were so far loosened, that, with a little effort, he succeeded in freeing his legs from the cords which yet bound them.

Then came the third shock; the tent was levelled with the ground, and the chasm poured forth its volume of pitchy water.

From where he lay. Hubert could hear the stern voice of Pizarro issuing his orders; but he could see nothing, for the sky was black as midnight, and only the pale sulphureous glow that seemed to overspread everything was visible.

"They think," muttered the veteran to himself, "that the chasm hath swallowed me up, or that the fire it belched forth hath consumed me, body and bones. 'Fore George, when Pizarro and I meet again, as we *shall* do, I will prove to him that I am yet a living man, with all the will and power to avenge mine injuries upon him. Ha!" he added, half aloud, "what is that? The sound of rushing water."

The next moment it was upon Hubert, sweeping over him, filling his mouth and nostrils and stifling him with its pungent, pitchy odour.

He strove to struggle to his feet, but his arms were still bound, and he was helpless.

The flood was not deep, but the current was tremendously strong, and, in spite of his physical power, Hubert was borne along, rolled over and over, and bruised against the rocky ground, in his vain efforts to stay his course.

Fortunately for himself, he was an excellent swimmer, and, finding, in a very brief time, that he could not check his course, the free-lance turned upon his back, and, paddling gently with his legs, drifted with the current.

The water was hot, sulphureous, pitchy—nauseous alike to taste and smell and feeling. The thirstiest traveller in the desert of Sahara would have turned with disgust from such a draught; but Hubert had no choice—he was at its mercy; and, firmly shutting his mouth and breathing only through his nostrils, he drifted with the current.

Whither he knew not. It was still dark, and only the mountains, looming heavily like gigantic shadows in the gloom, could be dimly discerned.

Far to his right Hubert could still hear the shouts of the Spaniards, growing fainter and fainter, as they pressed madly on towards the rising ground, but the free-lance had no idea of whither the current was bearing him. In truth, he cared but little, and but for the hope—dim and shadowy enough—that had again began to spring within his heart that his young master was still alive, he might have abandoned all effort to preserve his life.

"'Fore George," he thought, as he was thus borne onwards much as a cork is swept along in a mill-race, "this is no land for Christian folk to dwell in—a country where the very earth gapes wide and swallows men, vomiting out fire, and smoke, and water in exchange. Let me but once be safe on dry land again, and sure of the fate of my young master, and Hubert of Chertsey will carry his old bones back to Merrie England. Such doings as these were never heard of there, and never will be i' faith."

For the first part of his journey Hubert was painfully conscious that the water was shallow, as he was being constantly reminded by the bruises he received from the rocks and boulders; but suddenly he was drifted sharply to one side, and knew, with the instinct of a swimmer, that he was in deep water.

The sky, too, at the same time cleared with magical celerity. The veil of darkness which had overspread the face of nature, was drawn aside, and the sun once more illumined the wild magnificence of the landscape.

It revealed at once to the free-lance the nature of his position. He could see but little, for he could not raise his head, but he saw enough to tell him that he was drifting with great rapidity down a ravine, the steep sides of which rose full fifty feet above the level of the water.

The nauseous smell and taste, too, of the water had, in a great measure, disappeared, from which Hubert judged that he had floated into the channel of some mountain watercourse, but whither would it lead him?

He was drifting, too, towards the range of mountains, not from it, as would have been natural, but the free-lance had already become so habituated to the strange and wonderful that this circumstance troubled him but little.

He tried more than once to stay his course

but that was impossible, owing partly to the strength and swiftness of the current, but chiefly to the fact that he had not the use of those strong arms and hands which had so often saved him in peril.

Nearer and nearer towards the mountains, lifting their eternal heads high into the vault of the sky; and farther and farther too; now whirled about in an eddy; now carried to this side of the stream, now to that; till at length, Hubert felt something touch his feet, as if a bird had alighted on them; then his progress was stayed, with a sudden quick jerk; and as he felt himself drawn towards the bank, he heard a loud sound as of human voices raised in a cry of joy or exultation.

The old veteran had but just time to note that the voices he heard were shouting in some language strange to him, when, by the rapidity with which he was dragged along, his head was forced under water, and he was compelled to hold his breath for a few moments until he reached the shore, when a dozen hands were laid upon him, and he was lifted to his feet.

Shaking himself, much as a big Newfoundland dog scatters the water from him after a swim, the sturdy veteran, with no intention of behaving so roughly, threw four or five of those who held him to the ground.

His eyes, being cleared of the moisture that had obscured his vision, Hubert saw that he was standing in the midst of a crowd of Indians, whose slight, effeminate build accounted for the ease with which he had cast them off when he shook himself.

There were many hundreds of them, all armed with lances, bows and arrows, and clubs, so curiously and delicately carved, that they seemed more fit for toys than warlike weapons.

Some of them had bent their bows and poised their lances with unmistakeable demonstrations of hostility when Hubert with so little ceremony, threw the Peruvians to the earth; but they still kept at some distance, and showed no desire to come to closer quarters.

The veteran quite comprehended that he was in danger, and made a desperate effort to free his arms, but his bonds were wetted, and had shrunk, until the cords cut deep into the muscles of his arms.

"What the plague mean they?" muttered Hubert. "Here I stand—one man, bound and helpless, against five hundred, armed—and yet they dare not loose a shaft from the bowstring. 'Fore George, if these are the foes Pizarro has to encounter, he will make short work of them!"

Still, helpless as he was, the veteran faced them —as he ever faced his foes—with a smile and a form that never shook or trembled.

Suddenly this crowd of warriors divided, and, opening out, gave place to a man who, with slow measured strides, advanced towards Hubert.

He was dressed—or undressed, as the reader pleases—in the slight garb which the Peruvian warriors wore when on the war-path, but in manner, features, costume, and physical proportions he was altogether different.

Instead of the slim, smooth limbs of the Peruvians, his form was muscular and heavy, while his lips and chin were ornamented with a heavy beard and moustache.

"'Fore George," growled Hubert, "an' that be not an Englishman I will be content to eat him and myself too, should the saints deem it possible."

If he had any doubt, the new comer soon dispelled them. He seemed at first almost as much startled at the appearance of Hubert as the veteran had been at his, but after a long steady look, said—

"Art thou English?"

"That am I," replied Hubert. "And ——"

He never got any farther with his speech, for the strange warrior dropped his weapons, and, rushing forward, caught him in his muscular arms.

Strong as the free lance was, the grip of those powerful arms compressed him so tightly that he was fain to cry out for aid.

If his own limbs had been free Hubert would have returned the embrace in the same hearty manner that it was given, but he was powerless to resist, and could only growl forth his displeasure.

"A murrain on ye!" he roared, at the top of his stentorian voice, the while he bestowed a couple of sound kicks upon the other's shins; "thinkest thou I am a wench at a country fair, or a maypole, that thou claspest me so tightly?"

"What, Hubert, old friend?" said the strange warrior. "'Tis but ten years since we were like brothers, and at our first meeting since, you bestow a curse upon me!"

Hubert's eyes opened to their widest and fullest extent, and he stared wonderingly at the strange warrior.

"What," he said, at length, and in a voice of bewilderment, "is't thou—William of Wyckham?"

"Ay, the same, brave Hubert. Once a man-at-arms, when thou knewest me; then a follower of the daring Genoese, Columbus; and now, a chief among these Indians."

"Half-a-dozen of whom I laid sprawling on their backs when I but shook myself," said Hubert. "But pardie, man, I am glad to see and shake thee by the hand, that is, if thou wouldst but cut the cords that bind my arms."

Almost before the words had left his lips William of Wyckham had drawn an arrow from the quiver he carried on his back, and severed the rope with its sharpened point.

Up to this time the Peruvians had remained motionless, waiting for the orders of their leader; but now, upon a signal from him, they opened out into a double line, and William of Wyckham, taking his old comrade by the arm, led him onwards.

This sudden discovery of an old friend had utterly bewildered Hubert, accustomed as he had been of late to strange events.

"'Fore George, William," he said, "methinks I have been in a dream since I landed on the coast of this strange country. I have lost my master, and I have found an old friend, and both events have happened in so mysterious a manner that I can but think that either the foul fiend hath bewitched me or that I am dreaming, and shall awake presently, and find myself in Merrie England."

"And I too, Hubert," said William of Wyckham, "would fain believe even as you do. The touch of your hand and the sight of your face seems to annihilate the events of the past few years. But there—enough of the past, old friend; let us talk of the present, and of the strange chance which has brought you and I together again."

A few brief words sufficed for Hubert of Chertsey to tell his story, and by the time it was concluded they had reached what was evidently the encampment of a large army.

Everywhere they passed Hubert noted, even in his bewilderment, that William of Wyckham was received with the utmost tokens of respect.

The caciques bent their plumed heads almost to the ground, while the warriors prostrated themselves in the dust, a tribute that was only usually paid to the Inca.

Before one of the largest and most handsomely decorated of the tents, William of Wyckham halted. A guard, composed entirely of the chiefs, surrounded it, and these, as William and his new-found friend approached, lowered their lances, and opened out a passage for them.

The interior of the tent was the first glimpse that Hubert had, as yet, had of the luxury and magnificence of the Peruvian empire.

It was lined all through with a rich feather cloth, composed of the skins of humming birds.

A single table stood in the midst, of carved sandal wood, ornamented with silver.

Two couches of the same rare materials reclined against the sides of the tent.

The ground was richly carpeted with furs, upon which were scattered numerous drinking vessels and dishes of solid gold.

Hubert gazed around him for a moment in silent wonderment.

But William of Wyckham, as if the sight of such rich ornaments were a matter of every-day occurrence, kicked aside those that stood in his way, and bade Hubert be seated.

"'Fore George, William," said the free-lance, "you are lodged like a prince, man."

"And such am I," returned William, with a laugh. "To tell truth, comrade, I would rather be at the head of a hundred of our English bowmen; but needs must when the devil drives, as the old proverb hath it."

"'Tis a good devil," replied Hubert, echoing William's laugh, "that has driven you into such quarters as these. By all the saints in the calendar, there is enough in this tent of yours to send Pizarro and his men wealth-laden back to Spain."

"Pizarro!" said, William. "What of him?"

"What of him?" echoed Hubert. "Let me tell you this, old friend, that you had better have the devil himself at your heels than this same Pizarro. Have you heard naught of his approach?"

"I have," replied William, gravely. "But, Hubert, let me tell you this: he comes, not in the character of an enemy, but of a friend."

"A friend!" laughed Hubert, bitterly. "A friend to whom, old comrade? To himself, and to none other."

William of Wyckham rose from the seat, and his countenance assumed a grave expression.

"Speak out, Hubert," he said. "What know you of Pizarro and his purpose? Even now we await the return of the messengers who were sent with friendly words and rich presents to buy his alliance."

"If you knew Pizarro," returned Hubert, "you would know, too, that all the wealth the country possesses would not satisfy his greed. Heaven must have sent me hither to warn you of his purpose, old comrade. The very earthquake that snatched me from his vengeance will be the means of saving you from his rapacity."

It was William of Wyckham's turn now to be bewildered.

He had dwelt so long amongst the simple-minded Peruvians, that deceit and treachery had become ideas quite unfamiliar to him.

But when, in his rough, rugged diction, Hubert of Chertsey told the story of Pizarro's treachery, the eyes of the white chief were opened, and an angry flush rose to his bronzed cheeks.

"I cannot doubt your word, Hubert," he said; "you were ever in the old days too short of speech to frame words enough for a lie. The earthquake, of which you spoke of but now, has been indeed of service, when at one time it gives me an old friend and rids me of a foe."

"As to giving you a friend, good William," returned Hubert, "that is true enough—I may call myself that without fear of contradiction. But as to ridding you of a foe—why, time must tell. Pizarro and his men have the lives of cats, and, till the time comes when the foul fiend shall claim them for his own, they will live. Be sure of it."

"Stay a moment, Hubert," said the white chief, slowly. "Let me think this out. My thoughts are as unused to wile and deceit as my tongue to utter the words of our dear native language."

So great was the disturbance wrought in William of Wyckham's mind by Hubert's revelation that he neglected the hospitality which he intended to extend towards his friend.

But the free-lance was made of tougher material.

He was sore, bruised, hungry and thirsty, and the wants of nature pressed their claims upon him.

He reminded William of Wyckham of his want of hospitality by rising and searching for himself among the dishes and goblets that lay scattered about for the means of satisfying his hunger and quenching his thirst.

But they were all empty, and Hubert, with a growl of dissatisfaction, sent a dozen of them, with a couple of vigorous kicks, spinning across the tent.

The clatter aroused William of Wyckham from his reverie, and, stopping suddenly in his hurried walk, he said—

"What ails thee, Hubert?"

"What ails me?" repeated the free-lance, surlily. "An empty belly, a dry throat, and a friend who has naught to give me but words."

That gentle reminder was enough for William of Wyckham.

His heart was English still, although his outward garb was so changed that naught but the keen eye of friendship could have pierced the disguise.

He made the best apology for his neglect that was possible.

He clapped his hands, and a dozen slaves appeared.

He uttered a few words in the mellifluous language of the Peruvians, and with magical celerity the empty vessels and dishes were cleared away, and replaced by a repast fit for a king, and sufficient for a score such as Hubert—hungry as he was.

They brought a bath, too, filled with perfumed and spiced water, and a change of clothes, such as the Peruvian nobles wore.

These latter, though, Hubert regarded with a grunt of contempt.

"'Fore George," he said, as he settled down to his meal, "this old buckram suit and I have been comrades far too many years to be parted, for the sake of a wetting; I would as lieve part with my skin. And as for you, old friend, if you have not changed your nature, like your coat, don an honest suit of mail, and let me see William of Wyckham standing before me as he used to do when we were young in Merrie England."

"Your coming, Hubert," said William of Wyckham, "has changed me far more than my strange garb has altered me in your seeming. Until my my face looked in yours, and your hand touched mine, the past seemed like a dream—bygone, almost forgotten. An hour ago I was even as the simple people surrounding me, and regarded the coming of Pizarro with almost as much curiosity and wonder. You have awakened in me, Hubert, all that I thought dead, and I am once again an Englishman!"

"You never were anything else," said Hubert, bluntly. "The sun might tan your hide, and the strange garb you wear may disguise you, but not at heart, William—not at heart."

"It needs not for me to say," returned the white chief, "that your words are true good Hubert, for I feel them to be so; but I am sore perplexed, old friend, and, i' faith, I know not what to do."

"That is soon told," said Hubert, with a grim laugh. "You have men enough here, William, even were they weak as women, to scatter Pizarro and his men like thistles down upon the autumn breeze."

"Ay," returned William of Wyckham, sadly, "I know that, Hubert; but that is not all. The Inca——"

"The Inca! What's that?" cried Hubert.

"The emperor, or king, as you will, of this country," replied William of Wyckham. "He is all powerful, Hubert, and I am but his subject—trusted, it is true; powerful—but only in his name. The whole army, to a man, has received orders to do all honour and reverence to Pizarro and his followers. My commands would be as naught, if I attempted to lead them against the Spaniards."

"Then," said Hubert, "there is but one thing to do, William. Your course is clear; you cannot doubt but that what I have told you is true. Tell the Inca—or the emperor—of the treachery that Pizarro intends towards him, and, let his decision be what it may, *you* will have done your duty."

"You have solved the riddle, Hubert," said the white chief, as he grasped the free-lance's hand firmly in his own. "The Inca is but a day's march from here. You and I, old friend, will go to him, and from our lips he shall learn what woe and desolation Pizarro brings in his train."

CHAPTER XVI.

THE TWO FRIENDS START ON THEIR MISSION—RICHARD OF THE RAVEN'S CREST PUNISHES THE TRAITORS—AFTER THE BATTLE—DANGER.

BEFORE an hour had passed, the two old friends, so strangely united, were on the road to Cuzco, the imperial city of the Incas of Peru.

In that country, and at that time, beasts of burden were utterly unknown; the Incas and the great nobles of the empire were borne by slaves in palanquins, such as are now in use in India.

It was in this way that the white chief wished himself and Hubert to be carried to their destination. But the veteran free-lance disdained such a childish method of progression.

"What!" he said to William of Wyckham, when the elaborately embroidered palanquins were brought out, "do you think, old comrade, that so many years of toil and hardship have softened me into the likelihood of a child, or of a woman? No, while these old legs can bear the burden of my body, Hubert of Chertsey will never consent to be carried, like a child in a go-cart."

William of Wyckham had long been unused to such a method of progression, for he—an elected noble amongst the Peruvians—had almost, of necessity, adopted their manners.

But from the moment of contact with the veteran, he had felt the English blood stir again within his veins, and he stepped out once more with the same free swinging steps with which he had formerly trod the green swards of his native land.

The distance from the camp to the city was but some fifteen miles.

William of Wyckham had called it a day's march—and such indeed it was for the indolent Peruvians; but when Hubert settled into his long military stride, the day's march became an easy walk of four hours.

It was late in the afternoon when they had started, and the deep darkness of the tropical night had settled down upon the scene ere Hubert and the white chief came within sight of the granite walls of the city of Cuzco.

At the great westward gate the torches of the sentinels lit up, with a glittering radiance, the massive golden gate.

At a word from the white chief, the gates swung back on their huge hinges.

*　　　*　　　*　　　*

Now let us return for a brief period, and follow the fortunes of our hero, Richard of the Raven's Crest. We left him when, by a gigantic effort, he had hurled the block of granite harmless to the earth.

The surrounding nobles, who had regarded the person of their sovereign as sacred, and incapable of receiving injury by any mortal means, looked on with a calm wonder as they saw our hero, flushed, triumphant, arise from amidst the ruins, and approach the Inca.

The earthquake was over now. The ruin was complete—the devastation entire.

Of that palatial city, scarce one block remained above another to tell the tale of what it had been.

The silence was as the silence of death—solemn and awful.

But a moment ago, as it seemed to Richard, the air had been filled with the crash of masonry, and the cries and groans of the wounded and the dying.

Now, all was hushed, as Richard stepped from out the gloomy passage, and, by the Inca's side, moved into the midst of the ruined city.

As he did so, the solemn chant again broke out, and Richard of the Raven's Crest beheld the high priest coming with a slow and stately step towards him, followed by the assistant priests bearing the symbols of their worship.

Glad, indeed, was our hero to see that the old priest's devotion had not sacrificed him upon the altar of his faith, and with a cry of welcome he advanced to meet him.

"Great is the power of the Sun God!" said the old priest, gravely. "He hath spared those destined to serve him, even while he scattered those who were unworthy."

"What mean you, reverend father?" said Richard.

"This, my son," replied the priest. "Treachery was at work even within the walls of this sacred city. But this hour I have learnt it from the lips of a dying wretch, whom a falling block had crushed."

"Treachery!" repeated Richard.

"Ay, my son, treachery of the deepest and blackest dye," replied the high priest, gravely. "The earthquake which hath laid the city waste, was also the means of punishing those who had it in their hearts to attempt to violate the sacred person of the Inca; and even now, if there be aught left of them without the gates, our days are numbered."

"Not so," said Richard. "Not while my sword is sharp, and my arm strong. Give me my horse, reverend father, and we will soon see if these same traitors can stand against me, armed with truth and right."

"You will have your wish, and sooner than you thought," replied the priest, as he pointed onward with a gesture of his right hand.

Richard turned, and saw, crowding on over the ruins of the western gate, a body of warriors approaching, with a grim, determined aspect that there was no mistaking.

They were foes—their look told that, and the priest had told him that they were foes to the Inca.

"My horse!" he said, while his hand involuntarily sought the hilt of his sword.

"It is here, noble Richard," said the high priest, and, uttering a few words in his own language, four of his attendants disappeared, and a moment after came back, leading by the bridle Richard's noble white charger.

Our hero could hardly have welcomed his dearest friend—not even Hubert—with more warmth, and the noble animal seemed to respond with almost human feeling.

"Now," said our hero, as he vaulted on the back of his horse, "let those come, who dare. Richard of the Raven's Crest defies them!"

"Thou art but one against a host," said the priest; "but thou art strong in truth and right. See—even now the traitors send their arrows into our midst."

It was even as the priest had said. Some three score arrows shot up into the air, and fell a few yards off the Inca.

"They have been tampered with by Huoscar," said the priest, hurriedly. "He has led them to believe that our monarch, Atahualpa, is an usurper, and this earthquake has but confirmed them in their belief. They think it a judgment sent by the deity to punish him."

"They shall suffer for their treachery!" exclaimed Richard, fiercely, as a second flight of arrows, better aimed, flew through the air, wounding four of the caciques surrounding Atahualpa. "S'death! Stand clear there! God and the right St. George for Merrie England!"

And, with the far-famed battle-cry upon his lips, Richard was in their midst, scattering them like chaff !

The noble horse seemed to enjoy the fight as much as did his master. A dozen were swept away at the first leap he made—another bound, and his hoofs were gory with the blood of the slain.

Our hero might have contented himself with riding his enemies down, so thoroughly did the horse seem to know the will of its rider.

But Richard of the Raven's Crest was not idle. His long bright sword had left its scabbard and played around his head like a flash of forked lightning, and each time it descended the life blood of a traitor gushed out.

There were enough there to have crushed him by sheer force of numbers, but he seemed to them like an avenging god.

Some few shot their arrows or darted their lances, but the weapons recoiled from his armour, even as the dew falls from a rose leaf.

"Die, traitors !" cried Richard, as his sword swept through the air. "Oh, that my trusty Hubert were here ! We would then give such an account of your falsity as should make the whole land ring !"

In a quarter of an hour the rout was complete. There yet remained some who were faithful to Atahualpa, and these warriors, arming themselves, completed the work that Richard had so well began.

Our hero seemed endowed with superhuman vigour; the diamond in his helmet blazed with a more than mortal light, and wherever its magical rays alighted there fell a foe.

Some few of the caciques, who had been bribed or persuaded into making the attempt upon the sacred person of the Inca, strove to rally the warriors, but they failed utterly.

That white horse, bestrode by the mailed figure of Richard, seemed everywhere. Like the sword of the avenging angel, his weapon descended heavily, remorselessly ; and, bright as the awful glare of the lightning, flashed the Devil's Diamond in his casque.

The faithful warriors following completed the work which Richard left undone, and many of the foe turned round upon their friends and plied lance and club with a desperate desire to save themselves.

Within half an hour, Richard of the Raven's Crest had achieved a victory as complete as if an army had followed at his back.

Disordered — disorganised — deprived of their leaders—the Peruvians became panic-stricken, and fled in their thousands before the strong right arm of Richard of the Raven's Crest.

Once his triumph secured, our hero drew in his reins, and stayed his hand. It was no longer fighting, but indiscriminate slaughter, to ride down the wretched fugitives, and such a deed as that was contrary to Richard's nature.

He wheeled his noble charger round, and, wiping the blood-stained sword upon its mane, sheathed the weapon, and rode slowly back.

The victory was gained, but at what a fearful cost !

The whole of the square was strewn with the bodies of the wounded, the dying, and the dead, over which Richard of the Raven's Crest was forced to guide his charger.

He was a terrible enemy in battle, and when that fiery light shone in his eyes it boded ill for anyone who crossed his path, but once his sword was sheathed, Richard was as quiet and tender as a woman, and more than once on his return he dismounted to remove some wounded warrior from the path.

The High Priest of the Temple of the Sun had watched the progress of the fight with no little satisfaction. The city was laid desolate, it was true, but the chosen champion of the Inca had well performed his duty, and the empire was saved.

"Well and nobly hast thou redeemed thy trust, noble Richard," said Rimac, the priest. "The traitors were but as grass before thee."

"Let the praise be given to the righteous cause for which I struck," replied Richard. "I am but the instrument of an avenging Providence."

"In honouring the instrument we honour the deity who chose it," replied the priest, gravely. "It is the will of our master, the Inca, that you take a place beside him in the Imperial palanquin. Henceforth, noble Richard, and until the traitors who have striven to deprive him of his birthright are subdued, you are the monarch of Peru."

The kingly blood that coursed in Richard's veins thrilled with a quicker pulse at the high priest's words. He was born to rule, and now the destinies of a mighty empire were in his hands.

Almost the only building that had withstood the triple shocks of the earthquake was the Temple of the Sun, and that, sculptured in the very bosom of the mountain itself, had sustained but very little damage.

Thither Richard and the Inca, seated side by side, were borne, and there a repast worthy of the Imperial host was prepared.

But matters more important had not been neglected. The high priest, at Richard's earnest request, had sent some messengers to stay the slaughter of the conquered rebels, while such of the artificers as the shock of the earthquake had spared, were with busy hands removing the ruins which cumbered the streets and squares of the city of the plains.

Then ensued a long and ardent discussion between Richard and the high priest, regarding their future actions.

"Our army," said Rimac, "is scattered, for the spirit of rebellion hath gone forth in its midst ; but it needs but the voice of its leader to make it once more faithful to the true cause."

"And that voice ?" said Richard.

"Is thine, noble Richard," returned the priest. "Those whom thy strong arm hath conquered look upon thee as a deity. There is no longer rebellion in their hearts, for fear hath driven it out."

"But, Huoscar," said Richard, "what of him. Ere now, reverend priest, we should have been well on the way to Cuzco—burning to punish his treachery."

"That is so, my son," replied the priest. "but it is not yet too late. Pizarro cannot have joined his forces to those of Huoscar, and to-morrow will be time enough for us to start."

"We have an old proverb in my country, reverend priest," said Richard, "which tells that delay is dangerous. Heaven grant that it prove not so in this enterprise."

"Have no fear, my son," replied the priest. "This very night our spies will go forth again, and bring us tidings of Huoscar's movements. Take thy rest, then, and sleep in peace."

Richard of the Raven's crest did so, for he was weary ; but little slumber would he have had, had he only known that at that very moment the enemy were slowly, but surely, environing the walls of the doomed city !

CHAPTER XVII.

THE NIGHT MARCH—RICHARD IN CAPTIVITY.

THE information which the high priest had obtained was as true as it was startling. Some of the principal caciques had been indeed corrupted by the spies of the rival Inca—Huoscar—and those in their turn had influenced more than half the army, who, on being led to battle, were to march over to the camp of Huoscar, and, joining him, turn their weapons against their rightful monarch.

The plot had been well laid, and would, without doubt, have succeeded; but the earthquake had precipitated the course of events, and when the rebellious troops, hoping to take the Inca and his champion at a disadvantage by attacking them in the midst of the confusion and dismay, the strength and courage of Richard of the Raven's Rest in that terrible charge had, as our readers have seen, completely routed them.

But the dying conspirator, whose latest breath had told the high priest this, had expired ere yet he was able to give the most important portion of the secret, and that was that Huoscar, impatient at Pizarro's delay, was marching himself with all the picked troops of his army upon the city of Cuzco, and that they were almost within sight of its walls when the earthquake took place.

So little did the army of Atahualpa apprehend danger from such a source, that no sentinels were posted at the ruined walls of the city, all the available men in fact being employed in burying the dead, attending the wounded, and repairing as much of the damage as the limited time allowed.

The merciful darkness of the night soon fell, and wrapped the scene of desolation in its mantle, shutting out from view the grief-stricken mothers, who, frantically beating their breasts and tearing their hair, sought for their children amidst the ruins of their homes, or bent over the dead bodies of brothers or husbands, bitterly bewailing their loss, while here and there flared the ruddy light of torches, by which men were working silently and sadly to extricate the bodies of some friends or kinsmen from the heap of ruins.

But at midnight the scene was changed. As if by enchantment, the tens of thousands of Huoscar's warriors appeared in the midst of the ruined city, and completed the work of desolation and destruction which the earthquake had so well begun.

Soon the air was hideous again with the shouts of the combatants, the shrieks of the women, and the groans of the dying; and, while the fell work was being accomplished, Huoscar himself, with a large body of his most tried and bravest warriors, surrounded the Temple of the Sun, while some twenty of the stoutest and strongest entered in search of the Inca and his champion, Richard of the Raven's Crest.

The spies who acted as guides were perfectly acquainted with the intricacies of the temple, and before it was possible for the few guards on duty to give the alarm, the Inca, the high priest, and Richard of the Raven's Crest were bound, and with such dexterity and swiftness, that they were hardly awake when the thing was done.

Richard's brow was black as night with anger, and he turned his head half angrily in search of the priest. For an instant—but an instant only—he suspected him of the treachery.

But Rimac was in as bad a plight as Richard. Disregarding the reverence which was usually paid by the Peruvians to their priests, he too had been bound, and by no gentle hands, only his lower limbs being left free; and now he stood regarding Huoscar with a steady, reproachful glance.

"Beware, Huoscar," he said. "Thinkest thou that the deity whom even thou must fear will leave this outrage upon his sacred temple and his servants unpunished.

"It is thyself, Rimac," retorted Huoscar, "who art the victims of his just wrath, thou and my unworthy brother here, the usurping Atahualpa."

"Blaspheme not," returned the high priest, sternly, "lest a heavier judgment than that which will surely follow overwhelm thee."

"Silence," said Huoscar. "Thou hast abused thy sacred office, in advising Atahualpa to usurp the throne. Another will replace thee, and thou shalt suffer thy just doom. My brother, Atahualpa, too, must die, for by our laws death is the meed of him who rebels against the true Inca; and as

for the stranger, the keenest tortures which my executioners can devise shall be his. Remove the prisoners; see that they hold no converse with each other, and if they attempt to speak, gag them."

Richard's helmet was on a seat by the side of his couch, and as the usurper Huoscar turned to leave the apartment, the glitter of the splendid jewel set in its front attracted him.

"Ha!" he exclaimed. "What is this? I swear by the sun 'tis the lost jewel of the Incas, the diamond of Manco Copac."

"Thou sayest right, Huoscar," said the high priest, with a peculiar smile. "Thou art fortunate, for at one and the same time thou hast made thine enemies captive, and recovered the richest treasure the world possesses."

He just had time, taking advantage of the excitement caused by the discovery, to whisper to our hero—

"We are saved, noble Richard! If Huoscar takes the diamond his doom is sealed—the demon guardian will avenge thee and me."

The next moment two of the guards roughly dragged the venerable priest from Richard's side. Others would have treated Richard in the same unceremonious fashion, but there was a dangerous glitter in our hero's eyes that warned them back, bound and unarmed as he was.

But the words of the priest made a deep impression on him. He had seen the awful power of the diamond exercised upon the unfortunate slave, and he half expected, half dreaded to see the same terrible fate befal the Inca.

But no such change came over him, as he tore the jewel from the golden fillet, and, tossing the helmet contemptuously away, carefully placed the fatal diamond in an embroidered pouch that hung at his belt.

The high priest glanced at Richard with a calm, satisfied smile, that seemed to say—"Be of good cheer; his doom is certain—'tis but averted for a brief period."

Up to this time the captive Inca had not spoken, only regarding his traitorous brother with a calm reproachful look, but as Huoscar gave the order to move onwards, he said in that sweet, musical voice, which had so thrilled Richard—

"And art thou then, Huoscar, determined to carry to the bitter end this unnatural strife? Remember, the same blood courses in our veins, the same father gave us life, and from the same divine ancestor we trace our descent. Beware ere you provoke their wrath, and call them from their high throne in the sun to wreak their vengeance on you!"

To this appeal of his brother Huoscar deigned no reply, save a bitter sarcastic smile. He held the power in his hands now, the fire of ambition had devoured every other better feeling, and, in his own heart, he had already doomed Atahualpa to the cruellest of deaths.

He still had some remnant of respect, though, for the imperial lineage of his unfortunate brother. Though watched as closely and strictly as the other prisoners, Huoscar ordered that he should be separately lodged and waited on during his captivity, in a way somewhat befitting his rank.

Our hero was treated with no ceremony at all. He was bound so tightly and skilfully, that the utmost exertions of his great strength could not suffice to loosen his bonds in the least; and so, helpless, but with the fury of a caged lion raging in his breast, he was borne away by half-a-dozen of the strongest warriors, who staggered beneath the weight of his stalwart limbs, and cast unceremoniously into the little granite chamber where the high priest had shown him the vision.

"Dolt that I am!" muttered our hero. "This is my fault. I might have prevented it if I had but attended to the commonest rule of warfare, and seen that outposts and sentinels kept watch and ward, like good men and true. But what is done, is done. Let me sleep now, if I can, and gather strength should I need it. I have hope yet that the mysterious Demon of the Diamond may do me good service in the time to come."

And so, composing his limbs into as convenient an attitude as his bonds permitted, Richard of the Raven's Crest sought in sleep a present panacea for his troubles. His eyes closed, and he was soon in dreamland, free and happy once again.

CHAPTER XVIII.

THE MARCH TO THE EMPIRE CITY—RICHARD AND WHITE THUNDERBOLT MEET AGAIN — THE TRIUMPHAL ENTRY.

IT seemed to Richard that he had been asleep but for a few moments, when a strong guard of Huoscar's warriors entered the granite chamber and aroused him, and bade him, by signs as unmistakeable as spoken speech, arise—they having first cut the cords which confined his legs, in order to enable him to get upon his feet.

Refreshed by his slumber—short as he thought it, though it had in reality extended over some six hours—Richard sprang up, and his first impulse was to use the recovered freedom of his limbs, and endeavour to make his escape.

But a second thought convinced him that he could have but little hope of effecting the object while his arms were bound, and with a hostile army in his path; so, with his graceful, powerful form towering full a head above the slight, effeminate figures of the Peruvians, he strode from the chamber, the guard surrounding him with lances levelled, and their eyes watching keenly for the slightest motion indicating an attempt to evade them.

So, with the same care and precaution, our hero was conducted through the stone corridors of the temple, and into the great square of the city, where he found assembled not only the victorious army of Huoscar, but such of the legions of Atahualpa as, through fear or bribery, had deserted their master's cause.

But the massacre of the previous night had spared few indeed. The corpses of the unburied slain lay in gory heaps about the square, and choked the narrow by-ways of the city, while over head, flocks of the huge condors of the Andes waited the departure of the living, to make their hideous meal upon the bodies of the dead.

There, too, already were the captive Inca, Atahualpa, and the high priest, both of whom—the former, in consideration of his rank, the latter, by reason of his advanced years—were mounted in palanquins borne by slaves.

But no such conveyance was prepared for our hero. Still bound, and bare-headed, he was conducted to a place just in front of Huoscar's palanquin, and with a doubled guard of armed warriors, waited for what was next to come.

In a little while the arrival of the usurper was heralded by the long-drawn, melancholy notes of the Peruvian war trumpets, and Huoscar, entering his palanquin, without even deigning a glance at his captives, gave the signal to march.

Richard had looked at him, though, and noted that he now wore the diamond, set in the diadem of gold and feathers that encircled his forehead. He fancied, too, that the features of Huoscar were paler, and that his expression was worn and anxious, as that of one who had passed a troubled and sleepless night.

"The demon has paid him a visit," thought Richard. "The spell begins to work, else why that troubled mien. Pray heaven that I may be freed, and suffered to wreak vengeance on Huoscar with my own right hand."

The appearance of the Inca was the signal for the army to march, if such a scrambling, irregular method of progression could be dignified by such a name.

On they went—leaping the fallen masses of granite, climbing over the ruined walls at the first available points, singing the wild, rude chants of triumph in honour of their victory and in praise of their own valour.

Richard thought to himself how easily a few disciplined horsemen could charge and rout such a confused, disorderly rabble.

"Pizarro and his spearman," he muttered, "will make no more account of them than if he laid lance in rest, or drew his sword against an ants' nest. 'Fore heaven! it makes me mad to think that I have suffered myself to be captured by such an insignificant enemy; but I will have vengeance yet for this, if I have to charge Huoscar and his army single-handed. Would that Hubert were with me; but he is doubtless slain, or in as hard a plight as I."

But his attention was soon absorbed by the difficulty of keeping his footing on the ruin-strewed ground. The cords had been replaced so that he could just walk, and no more, and still the guard of warriors gathered round him with their levelled spears.

It was just as they gained the open plain beyond the city walls, that Richard caught sight of his favourite charger, which a number of warriors were guarding as strictly as Richard himself. It was still saddled and bridled, and on its back were fastened Richard's armour, his sword and dagger.

Four of the Peruvians were leading it by cords attached to the bridle and the saddle girths, and each time that the restless charger curvetted or played and champed the bit between its teeth, the warriors retreated as far as the length of their cords would allow them.

A slight contemptuous smile curved Richard's lips, and the next moment he gave a shrill, sharp whistle, thrice repeated.

The noble animal stopped short, laid back its short delicate ears, reared up, and darted towards Richard with a loud whinny of delight, upsetting in an instant the warriors who had it in charge.

In a few bounds it was by Richard's side, rubbing its soft muzzle against our hero's shoulder, in token of its delight at having recovered its master.

Bitterly then Richard regretted his powerlessness, and the multitude of his enemies. Had his arms been but free, how he would have leaped upon the back of White Thunderbolt, and with his good sword cut his way to freedom!

The desperate thought crossed his mind that he would seize the stirrup between his teeth, and, giving the signal to his horse, suffer himself to be dragged along; but a moment's reflection convinced him of the madness of such an attempt, and he returned the caresses of White Thunderbolt with a few encouraging words.

There was so much disorder and confusion already amongst the myriad warriors of Huoscar's army, that this incident passed almost unnoticed save by those immediately concerned. It is fortunate that this was so, for the horse was regarded by them as a strange and terrible animal, more to be feared than the white men, whose weapons dealt death with a lightning flash and spoke with the voice of the thunder.

They did not attempt to meddle with the noble charger again. The warriors closed in with weapons ready, but at a very respectful distance; and, seeing that Richard made no effort to escape, those who had fitted arrows to their bows restored the weapons to the quivers, and the march was resumed.

A long and tedious march it was. Mounted on his noble horse, Richard could easily have covered the distance from Cuzco to Caxamalca in half-a-day, but the sun had risen and set full four times ere the foremost warriors of Huoscar's army came within sight of the capital of the usurping Inca.

A few swift runners had been sent on before, to announce the victory and the capture of Atahualpa, so the golden gates were widely opened, and the whole town blazed with the light of innumerable lamps and torches, while shouts of welcome from tens of thousands of voices vibrated in the air.

"A plague upon the curs who open their throats to yelp so loudly!" muttered Richard. "Would that my arms were free—I would give them better cause to shout! So-ho! steady lass!" he added, as his charger showed some signs of alarm at the noise of the shouting and glare of the torches; "our time will come anon—a time when thou shalt ride fetlock deep in the gore of these heathen churls!"

The sight of the illuminated city, and of the thousands of richly habited Peruvians who had assembled to give a welcome to the conquering usurper, was a magnificent one, but Richard saw little of it, for he and White Thunderbolt were hurried into the courtyard of the palace of Huoscar, which, surrounded as it was by high walls, permitted no view of what was passing in the city.

A quantity of dried grass was spread in a corner for the accommodation of Richard and his horse, the latter being evidently regarded by the Peruvians as being endowed with human intellect, and more than mortal powers.

It was on this account doubtless that they brought precisely the same description of food for the horse as was supplied to our hero, and their wonder was great when they saw White Thunderbolt turn from the viands in disgust, and satisfy his appetite with the dried grass intended for his couch.

If our readers will picture to themselves a caged lion endowed with human reason and feelings, they may have a tolerably accurate idea of what Richard of the Raven's Crest experienced in his captivity.

It was the first time that he had been aught else than free, and his fiery spirit chafed in bondage till he was nearly maddened by the degradation to which he was subjected.

To be a prisoner was enough, even had his fetters been of solid gold, and his place of confinement a palace, but to be housed and treated like a dog, with a thousand curious eyes watching him as he ate, drank, and slept, was torture to his kingly spirit. The angry glitter in his steel-blue eyes boded ill for his enemies when he should be once more free to confront them sword in hand!

But how long would it be ere that time came?

CHAPTER XIX.

THE TRIUMPH OF THE INCA—HUBERT FINDS HIS HOPES DEFEATED—RICHARD OF THE RAVEN'S CREST IN THE ARENA—THE CONTEST WITH THE GIANT PATAGONIAN.

HUOSCAR had wished to celebrate his triumph in a manner that should be worthy of its importance.

He was diplomatist enough to know how much the pomp and glitter of Imperial state influence the minds of the people, and he had issued orders for such pageants and processions as Peru had never yet seen even in her palmiest days.

All business was suspended by the Inca's decree, no handicraftsman was permitted to pursue his calling upon pain of death, in case of disobedience. The prisoners were set free, excepting those who had offended against the sovereignty of the Inca, which last were ordered to be sacrificed solemnly as a tribute to the Sun God.

Meanwhile, William of Wyckham, or the white chief—as we prefer to call him for the present—and our old friend Hubert had been anxiously waiting the return of the Inca from his expidition, for the purpose, as our readers already know, of warning him of the treachery intended by Pizarro.

So, at the earliest available moment, the white chief presented himself before the conquering Inca, leaving Hubert in the centre court of the palace, anxiously awaiting the result.

He was not long absent; but Hubert could see, by the expression of his friend's face, that he had failed.

"'Tis useless, old comrade," said the white chief. "These Spaniards must have charmed him with some magic spell, so bent does he seem upon his own destruction."

"There is hope yet, William, since thou and I are here," said Hubert. "Without a leader, I own that they would be as chaff before Pizarro and his spearman; but thou knowest what a skilful and courageous leader may effect, even with such men, if men they be, which I somewhat doubt, as thou hast here."

"They are well enough," returned William of Wyckham; "and they will fight like wild cats when pitted against each other. But Pizarro's horses, his cannon, and muskets will effect, by the terror they excite, more mischief than ten thousand spearmen could do."

"Are they deer, then, or hares?" said Hubert, contemptuously, "to fly at the flash and the report of a firelock."

"You are too hard upon them, old comrade," replied the white chief. "A new and unknown danger strikes more fear to the heart than one which a man is accustomed to face day after day."

"Well—well," said Hubert, with a grim smile. "They are your own chickens, William; it is right that you should shelter them under your wing when my rough tongue assails them. But what of Pizarro? Can nothing be done to check his advance?"

"Nothing, old friend—unless I induced my warriors to desert the Inca's cause, and march them against Pizarro myself."

"I know not what course to take," said Hubert, reflectively. "Would that my young master, Lord Richard, were here; his clear wits would soon solve the riddle which puzzles my thick skull."

"We must wait, Hubert," said the white chief, as he striked his grizzled beard with a meditative action. "The Pizarro after all may not mean harm, and if his only purpose is to get gold, why he can have enough of that for the asking, to send his galleons deep laden back to Spain."

"You know not his insatiable avarice—his lust of power and conquest. I know but little of his lingo, but I can read his face plainly enough. William—his character is written there, as clearly as if framed in good Saxon English."

"We must be on our guard, then, you and I, old comrade; and be sure that at the first sign of treachery from Pizarro, I will drive my lance into his throat!"

"And I will do the same for that shaven-pate, Valverde!" growled Hubert of Chertsey, whose invincible dislike to the Spanish chaplain seemed to increase each day in strength, for he regarded him as the principal cause of the misfortune which had befallen his young master.

Had Hubert only known, though, that Richard of the Raven's Crest was at the moment a prisoner in the city, doomed to a lingering and cruel death, that knowledge would have conquered every other feeling—but that time was not yet come.

The sight of that splendid city — the myriad throngs of the inhabitants, mingling with the plumed and painted warriors—the busy preparations that were going forward in the great square—formed such a striking and picturesque whole that even Hubert, sorrowed and anxious as he was, could not avoid being interested and even amused.

"'Fore George," said Hubert at length, and after a long interval of silence, "the more I see, old comrade, of the riches of these people the more I dread the effect the sight will have upon Pizarro and his Spaniards. Be assured they will not rest content with less than all they see."

"Enough of him and his greed," replied the white chief. "Let us talk of something pleasanter, Hubert. You were wont to be foremost in the revel when we were young in Merrie England—ever first when a wine-cup had to be emptied, a good song sung, or a pretty lass kissed."

"Your memory is as long as your sword, William," returned Hubert; "and you were wont to boast that it was the longest, keenest, and readiest of any in the realm. But anent these sports ; will they be such as a christian man may look at and like."

Ay, that are they, Hubert—feats of skill and strength, darting the lance, shooting the bow and arrow, running, wrestling, and leaping, and other exercises with which you are as yet unfamiliar. In particular, I hear, that the Inca hath taken a captive in his expedition against Atahualpa ; a stranger, who will be exhibited in the arena."

"Who is he ?—of what land and nation ?"

"That I know not. He is jealously guarded by a large body of the Inca's best warriors, and even I cannot gain access to him."

"He is dangerous then, it seems."

"It would appear so, Hubert. They have, too, an animal of a strange and unknown shape, captured at the same time, which breathes fire and smoke from its nostrils."

"By my patron saint," laughed Hubert, "'tis the dragon of St. George that they have caught. Would that the saint were here too ; or, better still, my young master, Lord Richard—but that is past hoping for."

How little the free-lance suspected that the strange captives of whom William of Wyckham spoke were none other than our hero, Richard of the Raven's Crest, and his noble charger.

It was fortunate for the free-lance, perhaps, that he did not know, else had his devotion to the service of his master cost him his life.

* * * *

Seldom has the sun shone upon a spectacle so gorgeous as that presented in the great square of Caxamalca on the day appointed for the triumphal pageant in honour of the Inca.

Of itself the city and the people were always sufficiently rich and beautiful to strike with wonder the unaccustomed eyes of a visitor from the colder climes of the north. But on this occasion it seemed like a reflection of the sun itself, intermingled with a myriad rainbows, so gorgeously magnificent was the display of wealth and colour.

And the very centre, the focus of all that glitter and beauty, was in that portion of the arena where sat the Inca, looking indeed more like the divinity from which he claimed descent than an ordinary mortal, while grouped around him the great caciques of his empire seemed scarcely inferior in splendour.

Hubert and his old friend William of Wyckham were stationed just in the rear of the Inca's throne, in full view of the arena and the sports.

But the veteran free-lance soon manifested a great distaste for the exhibition, and expressed his opinion in such free language, that had he been understood by the Peruvians crowded round mischief might have come to him.

"They are woman, even as I told you, Will," he said, contemptuously. "There is not one amongst them whose skull I could not crack with a fillip of my finger."

"Stay a moment," said the white chief. "See, yonder comes one who would make no more of pitching thee over his shoulders than I would of swallowing a stoup of wine—and look there, Hubert, is the stranger of whom I spoke to thee two days since !"

As William of Wyckham spoke there strode into the arena a very giant—a huge Patagonian—whose enormous muscles stood out in his brawny limbs like a ship's cable, and whose long black hair fell upon his shoulders like a mane.

A tremendous shout of applause and admiration rent the air as the giant took his place in the centre ; but another, and a louder one made the very earth vibrate, as there advanced to meet the Patagonian the magnificent form of Richard of the Raven's Crest, his splendid figure looking white as marble, by contrast with the dusky skin of the Patagonian, while his bright golden air floated in the sun like the aureole of a divinity.

Hubert saw him—started, and staggered back as if an arrow had pierced him to the heart !

CHAPTER XX.

SCENES IN THE ARENA—THE DEFEAT OF THE GIANT—HUBERT'S WARNING.

HUBERT stood, like a man in a dream, gazing at the figure of his young master. The stately form he knew so well was no longer garbed in knightly armour ; those flowing golden curls were unconfined by the steel casque, but the faithful free-lance knew him, and tried to call his name, but his tongue and lips refused to do their office.

"What ails thee ?" said the white chief, looking wonderingly at his friend, and shaking him roughly by the arm. "Hath the sight of that giant Patagonian unmanned thee, or what ? Speak !"

"Let me go, Will," exclaimed Hubert, in a strange, constrained voice. "Yonder is my lost young master—Lord Richard !"

"Say'st thou !" replied the white chief, forcibly holding Hubert in his powerful grasp. "Then if thou lov'st him, hold thy hand, man—naught can be done now. Keep back, I tell thee ! Would'st thou destroy him and thyself too ?"

With a vice-like grip William of Wyckham drew Hubert back until his cooler senses returned, and told him of the danger that a rash attempt to rescue his young master then and there would cause.

"I am calm now," he said, "but the sight of Lord Richard was almost too much for me. I thought him lost to me for ever—swallowed up in the bowels of the earth—and in good sooth 'tis little better now ; for is he not a captive and a slave ?"

"But alive," said the white chief, "and if strong arms and stout hearts can achieve his deliverance, old friend, it shall be done."

Hubert thanked him with a close pressure of the hand, and then bent his eyes upon the scene in the arena.

The Patagonian and Richard of the Raven's Crest were now standing within a few paces of each other, the former's giant form towering high above our hero ; who, with his arms folded across his broad chest, regarded his opponent with a calm, defiant look.

"They are about to wrestle," said the white chief to Hubert. "Thy master is a lad of mettle, and with the thews and sinews of a Hercules ; but, by my patron saint, yonder huge fellow will be too much for him. Why, he looks as if he could crush an ox in his arms !"

"A hulking, ill-conditioned brute," said Hubert. "He is strong enough, I grant you, but that said, all is said. My master is as quick of eye and as active as the leopard which he quarters on his shield—so let yonder giant look to it !"

"Ha, the signal sounds ! they engage, Hubert ! 'Fore heaven, then, thou wert right. Yonder Patagonian is as slow and heavy as a lumbering Flemish cart-horse."

The silver trumpets had given out their long melancholy sounds, the signal for the wrestlers to close ; and the Patagonian, with his huge hands extended, reached forward to grasp the slight figure of his opponent

But Richard, without even unfolding his arms, stepped back a pace beyond the giant's reach, and still regarding him steadily in the eyes, laughed contemptuously.

The Patagonian uttered a hideous cry, half-yell, half-roar, and made a clumsy leap at Richard; but our hero, with a graceful easy movement, sprang aside, and then, with a motion so rapid that the eye could hardly follow it, leapt upon his antagonist, gripped him round the body with his powerful arms, and, with scarce an effort, hurled the giant headlong to the earth.

It was so quickly, so easily done, that it seemed more the effect of magic than of physical strength; but as the spectators realised the fact, and saw the splendid form of Richard proudly erect, while his gigantic foe lay stunned and prostrate on the earth, a mighty shout of admiration rent the air.

And, rising high above the shriller cries of the Peruvians, rose the hoarse strong voices of the two Englishman, blending in a hearty cheer, such as has so often struck terror to the foeman's heart upon the battle-field, or hailed a hard fought, and well-won victory.

"Hurrah!" roared Hubert, unable to contain his delight. "St. George for Merrie England!"

"Hush, Hubert, man; 'tis enough!" said William of Wyckham, in a warning tone. "Draw not his attention upon thee, or 'tis like enough that he will spoil all in his gladness at finding thee again."

It was only this consideration which could restrain the veteran free-lance within the bounds of prudence, and it was fortunate that the white chief had checked him in time, for our hero had heard the well-known voice of his esquire, and was glancing round the arena.

"'Twas fancy," muttered Richard; "yet methought I could have sworn 'twere Hubert's voice. But that could hardly be—were he here, and free, he would soon be by my side. I beg his—— But how now? what fresh task have these barbarians in store for me? Better this, than to lie bound in the cold inactivity of a prison."

Some dozen slaves now advanced into the arena, and, approaching the Patagonian—who had partially recovered his senses, and was staring stupidly about, as if wondering how he came there—offered him a large earthen pitcher full of wine.

The giant leaped to his feet, and scowled heavily at our hero, who, in the same calm easy attitude, confronted him.

"By St. George," he thought, gloomily, "if we try another fall I will have no mercy on the ungainly brute, and, unless his head prove as thick as my steel morion, I will find a way to crack it."

But now the second part of the programme had to be played out, and it was one utterly strange and novel to Richard of the Raven's Crest.

A slave came forward, bearing a long coil of rope, made of strips of tanned hide, flexible as gutta-percha, and strong as steel, to the ends of which were attached two balls of stone, each as large as a man's head, and weighing about thirty pounds.

Richard noticed with what a gleam of savage joy the Patagonian clutched the strange weapon—if such it was—as the slave handed it to him; but he only noted this for an instant—the next his own features were flushed with a glad smile, for a second slave approached him, leading his charger, White Thunderbolt, and bearing his unsheathed sword.

The noble animal was unsaddled, for Richard had taken the opportunity when his arms were unbound that morning to release his horse from the burden of the heavy demi-pique saddle, and to take the bit and bridle from his mouth.

To have replaced these was more than the Peruvians knew how to do, or cared to attempt; but our hero required them not. With a bound he was on the gallant horse's back, and, snatching the sword from

the slave, he tossed it high into the air, catching it deftly by the hilt as it fell.

Then putting his horse to the gallop, guiding it only by the pressure of his knees, Richard of the Raven's Crest rode it full speed around the arena, the while the fiery blood coursed more rapidly through his veins, with the joyous sense of having his horse once more bounding beneath him.

In the exuberance of his delight he had forgotten the Patagonian, till a stentorian voice from out the crowd near the Inca's throne shouted out in English the single word—

"Beware!"

As the cry was uttered, Richard stooped forward almost instinctively to check his horse. It was fortunate that he did so, for at that moment something whizzed just above his head, with a sound like that made by a cannon-ball in full career.

Wheeling Thunderbolt quickly round, Richard looked with a flushed and angry cheek for the cause. He had not far to seek, for there, some thirty yards distant, was the giant Patagonian, rapidly gathering in his long "lariat," or rope of skin, the heavy stone ball making a deep grove in the sand as it was dragged along.

Then Richard saw what a narrow escape he had had. It was the first time he had ever seen this peculiar weapon, in the use of which the Patagonians are so expert, but he was certain that had it not been for the timely cry the deadly missile would have stricken him dying and senseless from his horse.

"By St. George," muttered our hero, as he gripped his sword more tightly in his strong right hand, "'tis not again that Richard Plantagenet will be fooled with the same device."

And urging his horse onward, Richard shouted his battle-cry, and rode straight at the Patagonion giant, with the force and fury of a whirlwind.

But the savage had already gathered up the coils of his lariat; and, whirling one of the stone balls round his head with tremendous velocity, he launched it suddenly at our hero's head.

Swift as it flew, Richard's sword swept more quickly through the air, severing the lariat, while the ball whistled harmlessly by him, and the long rope coiling up, dropped harmless as a scotched snake to the earth.

The Patagonian turned to fly; but Richard was already upon him, his sword uplifted, gleaming like a lightning flash, ready to descend.

The giant cowered to the earth, one huge arm uplifted to ward off the blow; but Richard could not strike, his noble nature ever prompted him to spare a conquered foe, and he dashed past, leaving his foe untouched.

The Peruvians, little accustomed to see mercy shown to a fallen enemy, were nevertheless quick to appreciate Richard's generosity, and again and again their shouts of applause vibrated in the air.

"Beshrew me, but he is a gallant youth!" said the white chief, heartily. "It warms my old blood to see him there, looking more like a divinity than a man of mortal mould."

"You say sooth, Will," replied Hubert, his bronzed cheek flushed and his cheek lighting up with pride and pleasure. "'Fore George, I can scarce restrain myself from rushing out and clasping him in these old arms, which dandled him many a time before he was as high as my knee."

"Think not of it, Hubert," said the white chief, hastily; "the time for his rescue has not yet come. But let me assure ye, old friend, that I will spend my last drop of blood ere harm come to him. See, now, what fresh trial will they put him to?"

At a sign from a gorgeously habited cacique, who acted apparently as ludi magister, or master of the sports, there now advanced a single warrior, armed only with a bow and arrows.

A second sign, and a slave moved towards our

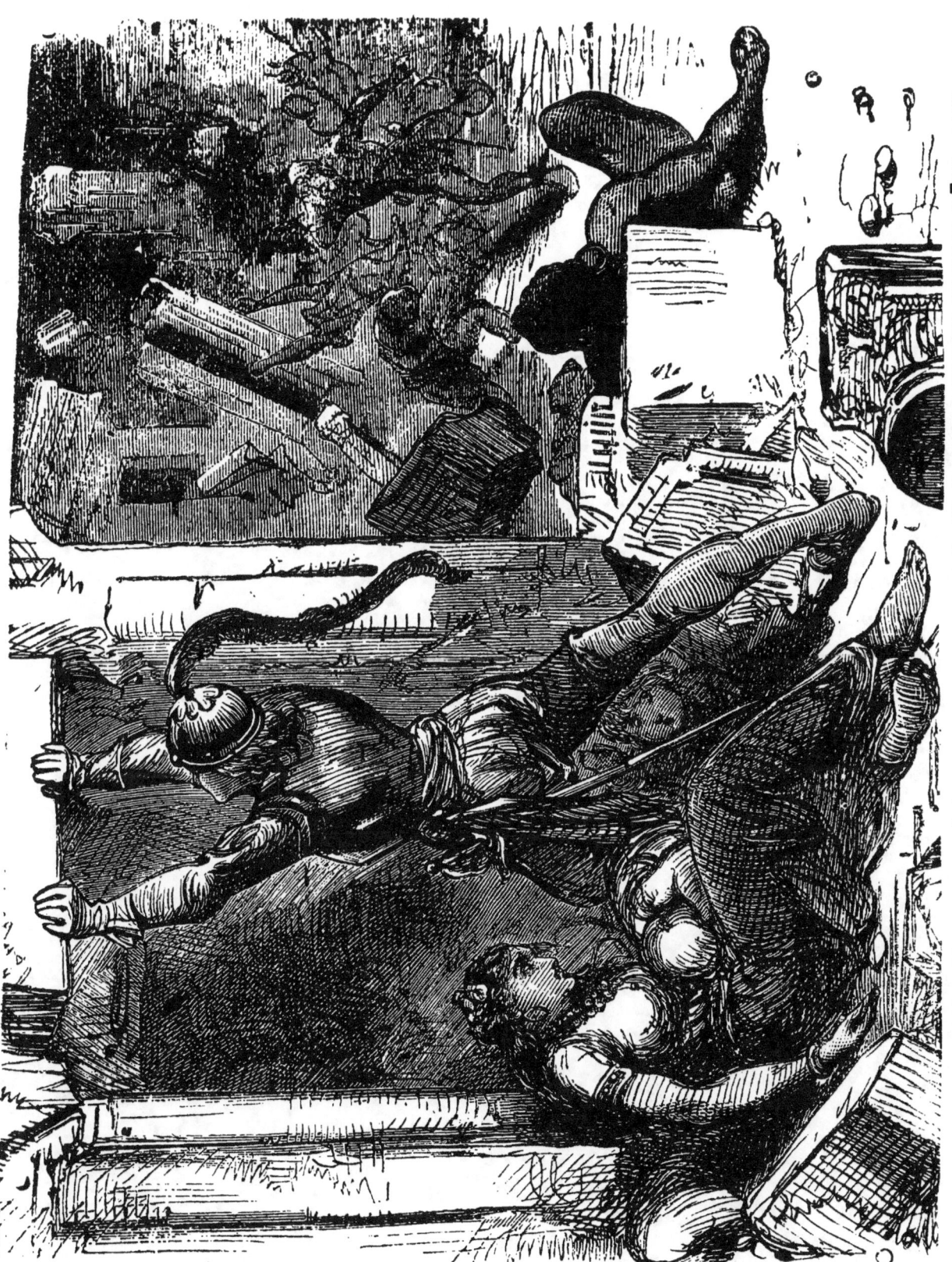

WITH A MIGHTY EFFORT, WORTHY OF HIS ANCESTOR, CŒUR DE LION, RICHARD KEPT THE FALLING MASONRY IN ITS PLACE.

No. 4.

hero, and signing to him with a respectful gesture to dismount, offered him weapons similar to those borne by the warrior.

Richard complied with a proud contemptuous smile, and, giving up his sword to the slave, took the toys, for such they seemed to be in comparison with the six-foot bows and clothyard shafts which English bowmen knew so well how to use.

Hubert's opinion seemed to be similar, for he shook his grizzled head disdainfully.

"'Tis a plaything," he said aside to the white chief. "Give Lord Richard but a good yew bow, 'stead of yonder jimcrack, and I will wager my life that he wets the goose-feathers of his shaft in the heart's blood of an enemy at twice a hundred yards."

"Despise them not, Hubert," replied the white chief. "Those warriors have not, I grant you, the thews and sinews of an Englishman, but they are unerring shots. Yonder fellow is one of Huoscar's bowmen, and can send an arrow through the head of a humming bird at fifty paces, and repeat the feat fifty times without missing."

"'Fore George then, Will," said Hubert, with some trace of anxiety in his tone, "if these arrows are sharp, he will prove a more dangerous enemy than yonder giant Patagonian, who stands scowling and sulking there in the corner."

"Fear not," replied the white chief. "'Tis not Huoscar's purpose that his captive should die so easy and painless a death. Thy master is doomed to the torture; such torture, old friend, as would make your blood run cold to hear."

"Never," said Hubert, grimly, "while thou and I are alive, Will."

"Keen wit and cunning will be of more avail to thy master, in this strait, than a dozen strong arms, and sharp swords, Hubert," replied the white chief. "I will tell thee of my plan anon; but hark, the signal sounds!"

As the trumpets rang out, the Peruvian fitted an arrow to his bow, and, holding a weapon in readiness, forced his keen, dark eyes upon Richard of the Raven's Crest; who, though standing motionless as a statue, was no less observant of the enemy.

Suddenly the Peruvian dropped upon one knee, and, drawing the arrow to its head, let fly the shaft with unerring aim at Richard's shoulder.

Quick as the warrior was, our hero was no less prompt. Almost at the same instant, the twang of his bowstring was heard, and, by an almost miraculous piece of skill, or fortunate chance, his shaft, sped with a stronger hand, met the other in mid-career, and shattered it to pieces.

Then, before the warrior had time to recover from his astonishment, Richard placed another shaft upon the silken string; straight and unerring it speed through the air, and pinned the Peruvian's left hand to his bow.

"Saw'st thou that?" exclaimed Hubert, excitedly. "By my patron saint, 'tis worth ten years of a man's life to see such a feat so deftly performed! Robin Hood himself could not have bettered that shot."

"'Tis a gallant sight, i'faith," said the white chief. "'Twill be many a long day ere yon gallant archer forgets or forgives the last shot of thy master. 'Twas a marvellous shot; but such, I fear me, Hubert, that the skill and strength Lord Richard hath shown will make our task of releasing him the more difficult."

"How so, Will?"

"Huoscar knows now, that it is no slight thing that could keep his prisoner within bounds, and, if necessary, he will guard him with half his army, —a number, good Hubert, which even Lord Richard, with thee and me to aid him, could not break through."

"We can try," said Hubert, grimly.

"Ay—and fail," retorted the white chief.

"Go to, man," the veteran said, with some touch of indignation. "What has changed thee since the old days, Will, when failure was a word to which thine ears were deaf?"

"Prudence, good Hubert," said the white chief, calmly. "When we're young and blood-hot we attempt impossibilities, but age has a wonderful knack of teaching men that running their head against stone walls is apt to result in no other advantage than a cracked crown."

"Call'st thou that prudence?" retorted Huber "Had any other man so spoken to me, I shoul have termed it cowardice."

"Trust all to me, old comrade," said the whit chief, quite unmoved by Hubert's half-angry words, "and if aught of harm befalls thy master, I give thee free permission to call me coward, and traitor to boot. But see there—'tis even as I said—the Inca has ordered the guards forth to conduct Lord Richard hence."

"A moment—a moment!" said Hubert, hurriedly. "Let us but give him a sign that friends are near, and 'twill comfort him until we bring him freedom."

"An' thou wilt, Hubert," said the white chief; "but be cautious. Those Indians are quick to suspect, and a single false step may betray and destroy us all. Come this way. I will so station thee that he can see us as he passes."

Making their way through the throng of caciques, who readily enough gave passage to the white chief, who had made himself feared and admired by all, Hubert and his friend mingled with the guards appointed to conduct Richard back to the palace, and placed themselves by the side of the barrier through which our hero would have to pass.

In a few moments they saw him coming—his stately form drawn proudly erect—his face paler than usual, and wearing on it an expression of mingled contempt and weariness, telling almost as plainly as if he had spoken the words, that he submitted because he despised them too much to lift his hand against them until his own time came.

With a feeling of nervous anxiety, which very seldom troubled him, Hubert waited until his young master was opposite, and so near that he could almost have touched him with an outstretched hand.

Then he uttered a peculiar low, long whistle, a sound that had served as a signal between them many a time before.

Richard started, and, looking round, saw Hubert with the forefinger on his lips, and a look of warning in his eyes.

Our hero understood him at once. He walked calmly on between his guards, but there was a brighter light in his eyes, and a flush upon his cheeks, that had not been there before. He knew that the faithful Hubert was planning his deliverance, and would never rest till he had compassed it.

CHAPTER XXI.

RICHARD OF THE RAVEN'S CREST STILL A PRISONER—HOPES OF FREEDOM—THE ARRIVAL OF PIZARRO—TREACHERY—THE ESCAPE.

"IT is done—it is enough," said the white chief, as his keen eyes noted the look and sign that passed between Richard of the Raven's Crest and Hubert. "Thy master is a lad of prudence as well as mettle, old comrade."

"He hath a keen and ready wit," said Hubert, "if that is what thou meanest by 'prudence;' and now, Will, for the plan. I am all impatience to be up and doing. I' faith, I am as restless as a war-horse that hears the clash and clang of steel in battle."

"Then curb thy restlessness, Hubert," replie the white chief; "for there is much to do, an scarce time in which to perform it."

"An' I had my way," grumbled the free-lance, "there would be little to do, and that little would be done quickly."

"How so, Hubert?"

"Faith, thou and I would go straight after yonder crew of painted women, cut our way through them, put a sword in Lord Richard's hand ——"

"And fall, pierced with a score arrows and lances ere we had got as many yards towards the gates," said the white chief, concluding the sentence. "Faith, Hubert, I think that Time must have stood still with thee, for thou art as rash and headstrong as a boy of fifteen."

"And thou as cold and pulseless as an old dotard of eighty," retorted Hubert, good humouredly. "Well, take thine own way, Will. I promise to be guided by thee."

"On thy word as a soldier?"

"I swear it on the cross of my sword, or I would do so, had I the good fortune to have it with me."

"'Tis well. Then stay thou here till I return. I will leave thee in charge of a cacique whom I can trust. He will not understand English, nor wilt thou comprehend a word of his language. But 'tis all the safer perhaps, for then that tongue of thine cannot lead thee into harm."

"A plague upon thee, Will," growled Hubert. "Thinkest thou that I am old woman, to let my tongue run away with my discretion?"

But the white chief had moved away in search of the friendly cacique, with whom he returned in a few moments, and, whispering something to him in the Peruvian language, pressed Hubert's hand, and hurried away.

"William of Wyckham treats his old friends with but scant ceremony, methinks," grumbled Hubert. "Here am I left with this be-feathered and painted heathen, who would call himself a soldier. I dare swear, if he knew how, while Will has gone—the saints alone know where. He hath a good heart, and I can trust him, though he might have taken me with him, knowing that I rest on thorns till Lord Richard is free."

The cacique was one of those in attendance upon the person of the Inca; so that Hubert, much to his discontent, was fain to remain until the sports in the arena were concluded.

This there was little sign of there being as yet. Almost every variety of exercise that ingenuity or necessity has discovered were displayed there for the amusement of Huoscar—whose calm, never-changing features showed not the slightest trace of amusement or interest.

It was just as Hubert, unable to bear any longer the sense of restless anxiety that was torturing him, had made up his mind, at any risk, to leave the cacique, and endeavour, with his own hand, to effect the deliverance of his master, when there was a commotion amongst the warriors at the entrance to the arena, and slowly opening out into a double line, Hubert saw, to his intense dismay and astonishment, the figure of William of Wyckham, accompanied by no less a person than del Soto, the lieutenant of Pizarro, while behind them marched, in regular order, a dozen of the Spaniards, armed with their muskets, cross-bows, and swords.

"By St. George!" gasped Hubert, "'tis Pizarro's lieutenant, and Will of Wyckham with him. Can it be that he hath turned traitor and left me, only to guide the Spaniards hither, the better to ensure Lord Richard's undoing? But no! that cannot be. Soft—I will hide here and listen. I may chance to hear some word that will guide me to the truth. I shall not be noticed if I keep well back amongst these popinjays."

Concealing himself where the caciques gathered most thickly—behind the throne of the Inca—yet so close, that he would be able to hear the Spaniards when they spoke, Hubert, with his teeth set, and his brows bent in a heavy, ominous frown, waited their approach.

The Spaniard advanced with a slow, haughty step, scarce deigning to cast a glance at the myriad people and the great square, until he was at the very foot of the throne, where he halted, and, with a slight bow to the Inca, turned to the white chief, and spoke to him in Spanish.

"Tell your emperor," he said, in a loud, harsh voice, "the message that I bear from our commander, the noble Pizarro, acting on behalf of his most Catholic Majesty, the King of Castile and Aragon."

Then, handing a scroll of parchment to the white chief, he folded his arms across his breast-plate, and waited, with an air of proud indifference, for William of Wyckham to do his bidding.

But a keen observer might have noticed, beneath all this seeming disregard of the wealth and splendour displayed around him, how the dark eyes of del Soto glared furtively, and sparkled as they lit upon the gold and jewels adorning the caciques, and more especially upon the Devil's Diamond gleaming in the coronet of the Inca.

The scroll which the white chief had to translate into Peruvian for the information of the Inca, was simply an offer of alliance, made by Pizarro, on behalf of the King of Spain, whose power and possessions in the old world were dwelt upon with true Spanish grandiloquence.

"It is well," replied the Inca, when the white chief had concluded. "Let the cacique of the King of Spain know that we accept the offer, and long for his presence, that we may welcome him as a brother."

"Tell the Inca," said del Soto, as soon as this had been translated to him by William of Wyckham, "that the noble Pizarro is but now without the gates, and but awaits the emperor's permission to enter."

"Let him enter at once," said Huoscar, rising; "we ourselves will go forth to welcome him."

A slight smile of sarcastic triumph wreathed the Spaniard's thin lips, and, turning to the musketeers, he made a sign to them.

On the instant they raised their weapons, and putting them upward, fired a volley.

The terrible earthquake, which only a few days' since had razed the city of the plains, did not cause so much consternation amongst the simple Peruvians, as this, to them, awful and inexplicable event. It was as if the gods they worshipped had descended from the sky, armed with thunder and lightning.

The warriors fled, panic-stricken—yells of terror and groans of pain arose from the flying and the fallen, who were trampled ruthlessly under foot by their comrades. Almost before the smoke had cleared away, the great square was empty of all save the crushed and fallen—only a few of the bravest of the caciques remained clustered round the Inca, as if to protect him.

"The craven fools!" muttered del Soto, contemptuously. "But 'tis all the better for our purpose. If the sound alone terrifies them like that, what will it do when accompanied by a hailstorm of bullets? Hark ye, senor interpreter, assure your emperor that yonder was only a signal to let our commander know that all was well, and that we intend no harm to him or his people."

The white chief complied, and, after some time, by dint of threats of vengeance of the Inca, the warriors were reassembled, and del Soto turned to lead his men back to meet Pizarro.

Up to this time Hubert had remained motionless, listening attentively and eagerly to all that passed. As our readers are aware he was but very little acquainted with the Spanish language, but the few words which he did comprehend, taken in conjunction with the familiar terms on which William of Wyckham seemed to be with the Spaniards, convinced him of his old friend's treachery.

e was nearly maddened with rage and grief. Already, in his imagination, he could see his young master writhing in the hands of the tormentors, while Pizarro and Valverde stood by marking his agony. He could bear it no longer, and with a hoarse exclamation of rage, he sprang from his place of concealment, and, rushing on William of Wyckham, seized him by the throat.

"Traitor!" he hissed, between his set teeth; "false to thy friend, and to thy country. Die, renegade!"

The onset had been so sudden and so furious that the white chief was borne headlong to the ground. Hubert, still grasping him by the neck with all his force, fell on him, and, had it not been for del Soto, William of Wyckham's life would have ended there.

But the Spaniard had seen and recognised the free-lance, and, with a cry of exultant malice, he strode forward, and struck the free-lance a tremendous blow on the head with his mailed gauntlet, stunning him instantly.

"Ha!" he cried; "this is indeed a prize, and will be welcome to Pizarro! Ho, there, men! come forward, and bind this English dog!"

The order was instantly executed, and by the time the Spanish spearmen had tightly bound the free-lance with their leathern belts, William of Wyckham arose slowly from the ground with a dazed and bewildered air, for the vice-like pressure of Hubert's grip had nearly strangled him.

"The saints deliver us!" muttered the white chief; "but he hath ruined all my plans. A plague upon his headstrong suspicions. I see it now. He deemed that I was in league with Pizarro; but methinks he might have trusted me."

"Knowest thou this fellow?" demanded del Soto, as he noted the peculiar look—half of sorrow, half of pity—which William of Wyckham cast upon the prostrate form of Hubert.

"Not I," returned the white chief, with affected roughness. "To the gallows with him, for a murdering hound. By St. Jago, he hath well-nigh broken my neck."

"Fear not," replied del Soto. "His own shall pay the penalty. He is an enemy of our noble commander, Pizarro, who will well requite the misdeeds laid to his charge. But how shall he be bestowed for the present? I must haste to meet Pizarro, and conduct him to the presence of the Inca."

"Leave that to me, said the white chief. "I warrant that he will be safe in my custody."

"Be it so," replied del Soto. "But have a care that he escape thee not; he hath the cunning as a whole tribe of monkeys."

"Be assured, senor," replied William of Wyckham, overjoyed that Hubert had been committed to his charge; and, fearful lest the wily and suspicious Spaniard should change his mind, he called around him a few of the Peruvian warriors, and bade them lift the still insensible form of the free-lance, and bear it out of the arena.

"This may prove fortunate, after all," thought William of Wyckham. "If I can but change the warriors who now guard young Lord Richard for a body of my own men, their escape may yet be effected. The saints grant that it prove so; but time will tell."

And so, onward through the crowded square—the throngs of people making way everywhere before the stalwart form of the white chief—Hubert of Chertsey was borne towards the palace where his loved young master was a prisoner.

* * * *

The entry of Pizarro into Caxamalca was made with as much of the pride, pomp, and circumstance of military display and discipline as his limited numbers and means allowed.

He himself, attired in full armour, rode at the head of his little squadron of horsemen. The foot soldiers followed, marching in two compact bodies with muskets loaded and spears carried at the charge. On either flank were the two field pieces, loaded to the muzzle, each with an artilleryman at the breech, bearing a lighted port-fire.

They were a mere handful in comparison with the hundreds of thousands of Peruvians who thronged to gaze with curious eyes upon the dread and mysterious strangers, but their discipline, the superiority of their arms, and their confidence in the indomitable will and courage of their leader, made them more than a match for the untrained irregular forces of the Peruvians.

Slowly and steadily the Spaniards advanced through the golden gates of the city, unmoved, to all appearance, by the strange sights around them. But this indifference, as in the case of del Soto, was only assumed—the greed of gold was already burning in the breast of every one, in none more fiercely than in that of Pizarro.

"Well," he said, in a low tone, as del Soto advanced to meet him, "what hast thou seen. Is all favourable to our project?"

"That is it, noble Pizarro," replied del Soto. "Never saw I anything approaching such prodigality of wealth and magnificence. Even now thou may'st see displayed in the great square enough gold to send our galleons, laden bulwark-deep, back to Spain; while the Inca hath set in his crown a diamond of such size and brilliancy as the world doth not contain its like!"

"And shows he no signs of fear or jealousy at our advance into his kingdom?"

"None, noble Pizarro," returned del Soto. "He is even as a man who clasps a naked sword to his bosom, and finds not his mistake until it hath pierced him to the heart!"

"Heaven hath delivered the heathen and their spoils into our hands," here said Valverde. "Forward, noble Pizarro; the sons of the true church are eager to behold the rich reward of their valour and devotion."

Passing along the broad causeway which led from the gates to the great square, Pizarro and his men soon came in view of the magnificent sight which had so impressed del Soto.

Pizarro had sternly commanded his men to refrain from any expression of astonishment or admiration, no matter what they might see that was strange and novel; but they could not repress an involuntary exclamation of greed and joy at the sight of such wealth as they had never yet beheld even in their dreams.

The Inca, with his splendid following of caciques, and his guard of picked warriors, now advanced at a slow and dignified pace towards the stranger.

Pizarro dismounted, and, attended by Valverde and his lieutenants, halted his troops, and marched towards the Inca.

When they were about twenty paces from each other, Pizarro drew his sword, and flashed it in the air.

The signal was instantly obeyed—the cannon thundered forth their dreadful sound, mingled with the sharper, rattling report of the muskets.

The effect upon the Peruvians was scarcely less startling than it had been on the first occasion. Thousands of the inhabitants, and the warriors, too, fled panic-stricken—others cast themselves down upon their faces, and even the Inca, who regarded himself as a divinity, and invulnerable, trembled before what seemed the more than mortal power of these strangers.

A few words from the white chief, who had placed Hubert in safety, and returned to do his office of interpreter, reassured Hnoscar; but it was evident that the impression made upon him was very deep, and that from that hour forth the Spaniards were virtually his masters.

A signal from the Inca, and a train of more than a hundred slaves came forward, each labouring under the weight of huge flagons, dishes, ornaments, and armour, every piece composed of the precious metal, and cast their burden down upon the ground before Pizarro.

The Spaniards gazed with covetous eyes, for there, in that glittering heap of gold, was the ransom of a dozen emperors.

CHAPTER XXII.

A GLIMPSE AT THE WEALTH OF PERU—ITS EFFECT UPON THE SPANIARDS—HUBERT IN CAPTIVITY—PIZARRO'S VISIT—A LAST CHANCE OF ESCAPE.

STERNLY and strongly as he endeavoured to repress his feelings, Pizarro could not control the flush of greed which rose redly to his cheeks, or keep the covetous glitter from lighting up his eyes.

Del Soto, and even the crafty Valverde, were no less moved, while, as for the soldiers, only the habitual fear they entertained for their captain prevented them from dashing forward and seizing the treasures lying there within their reach.

The Inca noted, with the quickness natural to his race, the covetous looks of the Spaniards, and for an instant a slightly contemptuous smile curved the corners of his delicate mouth.

Then he spoke again.

"Let my white brothers take what they choose. The hand of Huoscar and all that he hath is open to them. Let the great cacique of the Spaniards ask for what he will, and it shall not be denied him."

"Heard'st thou that, noble Pizarro," whispered the priest. "See'st thou that jewel flaming in his coronet? Demand that of him; 'tis a prize worth a hundred such heaps of gold."

"Nay, nay, Valverde," returned Pizarro, in the same tone. "'Twill not be wise to seem too covetous at first. Let us be content for the nonce with the present he offers for our acceptance; as it is, I fear much for the effect of such wealth upon the discipline of my soldiers. They will be clamouring to return to Spain to spend the gold that will fall to their share, and so baulk my enterprise before it a half completed."

Valverde was silent, but in his own mind he had resolved that the priceless jewel should ere long pass from the Inca's possession—by persuasion if possible, by force if the milder form failed.

The interview was soon cut short after the ceremony of making the present was over.

A few expressions of good will and desires for a friendly alliance on the part of the Inca, answered by protestations of unchanging devotion from Pizarro, and then the commander, accepting the Inca's proffer to quarter the Spanish troops in the vast buildings of the palace, embraced the emperor, after the Spanish fashion, and, guided by the white chief and attended by a body guard of the emperor's chosen troops, moved on towards his quarters.

"By St. Jago," said Pizarro to his lieutenant, "but this is rare good fortune, del Soto! There is no need to set spring or spread net, for the prey hath delivered himself into our hands."

"'Tis indeed fortunate," replied del Soto. "For had those Peruvians been suspicious of our intent, and forced us to betake ourselves to our weapons, many a good man and true of thy spearmen would have bit the dust ere we obtained such foothold in the city. They outnumbered us by a thousand to one."

"Were they ten times as many," said Pizarro, contemptuously, "they would scatter like autumn leaves before the thunder of our cannon and the charge of our spearmen. Even now look about thee, and note at what a distance they keep themselves, and how they stare at us like timid children at a wild beast."

"It was well to be cautious, though, noble Pizarro," urged del Soto. "What are we but a handful against a multitude?"

"And what," added Pizarro, "is a rock compared with the waste of waters which sweep around it? Yet the waves dash themselves into harmless spray against the stubborn mass, moving it not an inch from its prison base. Such a rock are we, del Soto, and these Peruvians will have as little power to prevail against us as the waves to which I compared them but now."

Up to this time del Soto, absorbed in the interview with the Inca, had forgotten to tell Pizarro of the capture he had effected that day; but as they came in sight of the massive granite palace, he was minded of his mission, and reported it accordingly.

"Sayest thou so?" exclaimed Pizarro, while the light of gratified malice and revenge glittered in his eyes. "Art thou sure, del Soto?"

"'Tis beyond doubt. I stunned the dog with my own hand, the while he had the senor interpreter here by the throat, strangling the life out of him."

"Ha!" said Pizarro, bending his dark brows upon the white chief—"thou knowest him, too!"

"That do I not," replied William of Wyckham, doggedly.

"How comes it, then, that he is an enemy of thine?" demanded Pizarro, suspiciously.

"Again I must answer that I know not. He must be demented, noble senor; all that I can tell is that he sprang upon me like a wild cat, and would, certes, have squeezed the breath out of my body had it not been for this gentleman."

"'Tis even as the senor interpreter says," said del Soto, in confirmation; "and I incline to the belief that the fellow hath gone mad. Now I bethink me, there was a wild glare in his eyes which savoured strongly of a disordered intellect."

"It may be so," replied Pizarro, thoughtfully; "he was much attached to that headstrong English cub, Richard of the Raven's Crest, and he may have lost his senses through grief. But he dies, were he ten times a madman!"

Ever since the unexpected and unwelcome arrival of the Spaniards, the white chief had in vain been racking his thoughts to hit upon some possible means of extricating Lord Richard and Hubert from the fate which threatened them.

As yet, of course, Pizarro was unaware of the capture of our hero, but that ignorance would not last long. The Inca would surely, in a day at furthest, exhibit to his new ally so important a prisoner, and then all chance of escape would be gone. Pizarro, he felt certain, would himself watch his young enemy jealously while he was led to torture and to death.

Only twelve short hours lay before him in which he had not only to plan but to execute his schemes, but even that time was not his own. He had been appointed specially to wait upon Pizarro, and act as his interpreter, so that, until the Spaniards retired to rest, he could do nothing.

And then again a fresh danger menaced him. Pizarro had signified his intention of visiting the prisoner. What if Hubert, in his wrath at his friend's supposed treachery, should reveal the true nature of their acquaintance. The white chief did not reflect for the moment that Hubert would speak in English—a language of which Pizarro comprehended little or nothing.

"The saints aid me! I shall go mad," muttered William of Wyckham, stamping desperately on the marble floor of the courtyard which he was traversing on his way to give some orders respecting the entertainment of the Inca's guests. "A pestilence light upon Pizarro and his crew of Spanish desperadoes, say I. They will bring absolute destruction upon us all; and plague seize me, if I can devise aught to avert it."

Two hours after, when the Spaniards had refreshed themselves with the hospitality of the unsuspecting Inca, whose generosity they designed to reward with cruel treachery, Pizarro demanded to be led to the prison where Hubert was confined.

With a show of readiness which he was far from feeling, the white chief preceded Pizarro, Valverde, and del Soto to a small but secure chamber, which he was glad to think now was far removed from the place where Richard of the Raven's Crest was confined.

The free-lance was seated in a corner, still bound, as he had been by command of del Soto; but, at the sound of the heavy tramp of Pizarro and his companions, he looked quickly up, but only for an instant; then he resolutely bent his gaze downwards again.

"Now the saints be praised," muttered the white chief. "He is in a sullen mood, and will not speak, though he were put to the torture."

William of Wyckham was right. To all the questions Pizarro put to him—as to how he had escaped being swallowed up by the earthquake, or drowned in the flood, and by what apparently supernatural means he had contrived to make his way to Caxamalca—the free-lance remained obstinately silent.

"The foul fiend must have aided him," said Valverde—"the evil spirit who hath deserted him now, and fled before the presence of even so humble a minister of our holy church as I."

"'Tis well said, padre," returned Pizarro, with a grim smile. "He must be in league with the powers of evil, and, by St. Jago, he shall be tried for heresy and witchcraft, and if he be found guilty, adjudged to the flames!"

Still, even this terrible threat failed to move Hubert, or win from him as much as a movement of his head. The dogged Anglo-Saxon nature was aroused, and if though an utterance of a single spoken word would have saved him from the cruellest of tortures, that word would have remained unspoken.

"Silent, still," said Pizarro, grimly. "Well, be it so; but the time will come, and that ere another sun sets, when this English hound will howl for mercy like a whipped cur. Enough of him, padre. Let us depart, for I am weary, and the sight of one who hath dealings with the foul fiend is not good for the eyes of christian men to look upon."

All this time William of Wyckham had been in an agony of suspense lest the taunting words of Pizarro should wring a reply from the free-lance. He kept himself, too, as much in the background as was possible, lest Hubert, enraged at the sight of the man whom he thought so basely treacherous, should say something which would arouse the wily Spaniard's suspicion.

He breathed a deep sigh of relief when, at length, Pizarro proposed to depart; but his next words filled the white chief with dismay.

"Hark ye, senor interpreter," he said—"in order that better watch and ward be kept over yonder sullen dog, I will leave here some half dozen of my best spearmen."

"There is no need, noble Pizarro," said the white thief, hastily. "My warriors are so keen of eye and quick of ear, that not a mouse could escape their vigilance in the dark."

"It may be so," returned Pizarro, drily. "But yonder fellow hath the strength of a bull, and, should he by chance loosen his bonds, the strong arms of my spearmen would be sorely needed. Those painted boys yonder, whom thou call'st warriors, would be but as a handful of reeds or feathers in his grip."

To have argued the point, to have attempted to oppose Pizarro's will, would most certainly have aroused the suspicions of the crafty Spaniard, and William of Wyckham had to submit to see this strongest of all links rivetted to the chain which already bound Hubert in captivity.

"His doom is sealed," muttered the white chief.

"'Tis out of my power now to aid him, unless heaven itself sends a miracle to his assistance!"

In this state of mingled doubt and dread, William of Wyckham was too disturbed to give the case that calm and cool consideration which it demanded.

He could think only of the danger, but not of the means by which it was to be averted; and so hour after hour passed on. Night came on, and only the sentinels and the guards about the prisoners were awake.

"My own tribe," thought the white chief, "which I have so often led to victory, would surely follow me if I commanded. But what are they against the overwhelming force of Huoscar, backed by the might of the Spaniards? By these means I may yet save Lord Richard, and—— Ha! dolt that I was not to think of it before. The drug—the mezcal berry! 'Tis not yet too late."

The eyes of the white chief were lit up with the sudden light of hope, as this thought passed through his mind; and, with a noiseless tread, he made his way into the inner portion of the palace.

The path was intricate and quite dark, but the white chief traversed the long corridors with the ease of one perfectly familiar with the place.

He had walked fast at first, but after some ten minutes he slackened his pace, and finally halted at the corner of a passage, down which there streamed a clear, steady light, like that from an oil lamp.

There he listened intently, but not the slightest sound disturbed the silence of midnight; and, treading noiselessly with his sandalled feet, he moved on towards the light.

It was streaming through the aperture left between the partly-drawn curtains closing the entrance to some chamber.

The white chief advanced, listening, with his keen ears, for the faintest noise. But there was none, and, with a cautious hand, he drew aside the curtains, and entered the apartment.

It was clearly, but not brilliantly, lit by the golden lamp, which in burning emitted a perfume not unlike that of musk, but so powerful, that the white chief felt himself turning faint and giddy as he inhaled it.

All round the apartment, which was small by comparison with the other vast chambers in the palace, were ranged on shelves a number of flagons and curiously-shaped vessels, some of gold, some of silver, some of earthenware; while quite by themselves, and enclosed in a case of filagree work, were some few crystal phials, carved with a marvellous delicacy of design and workmanship.

"And it is here," thought the white chief, as he glanced around him, "that the priests of the temple keep the drugged wines and the subtle liquors with which they stir themselves up to a maddened frenzy when they feign the gift of prophecy, or when it is expedient to send an enemy out of the world. This must be the place, and these the instruments which I have heard obscurely hinted at. Now, heaven guide me in my choice, and lead me to select aright."

The white chief advanced, and took two of the largest of the golden jars or flagons, placing them near the entrance. Then, lifting the filagree cover, he selected two of the crystal phials, and hid them in the belt of feather cloth which girt his waist.

"Now," he thought, "for the last chance. 'Tis a desperate one at best, but were there a hundred times the danger, I must essay it."

Then, raising his heavy burden, he parted the curtains, and passed once more into the corridor—to save his friends, or die with them.

———

CHAPTER XXIII.

THE DRUGGED WINE—THE SPANISH SENTRY RE-FUSES THE GOBLET—NOT SO THE PERUVIANS—THE TOAST — ESCAPE OF RICHARD OF THE RAVEN'S CREST.

WITH the same caution that he had before observed, the white chief made his way out of the interior of the palace, stopping to listen at every few steps, for he knew that to have been caught in the sacred precincts of the palace by any of the priests, would not only have ruined his plan, but would have entailed a horrible lingering death upon himself, favourite though he was of the Inca.

But when he stepped once more into the silent courtyard, he paused, and uttered a deep sigh of relief—one peril was past. It remained to be seen whether he would be equally fortunate in overcoming the others.

Then, setting down the golden jars, he poured into each the contents of one of the crystal phials, and then, with all his strength, hurled the empty flasks far over the high walls into the moat which lay beyond.

He listened for the faint echo of the splash, and then, nerving himself for his dangerous enterprise, he raised the jars of drugged wine, and moved, with a firm quick step, towards Hubert's prison.

The white chief was yet some paces distant when he saw glimmering in the starlight the steel morion of one of Pizarro's men, and almost at the same moment the hoarse challenge rang out—

"Quien es?"

"Amigo!" replied William of Wyckham, approaching the sentry.

"Stand there!" said the sentry, as the heavy butt of his musquetoon rang with a crash upon the granite pavement; "and return from whence you came, amigo, with what speed you may. 'Tis the commander's order that no one passes my post to-night, save himself."

The white chief muttered a hearty curse upon the untoward vigilance of Pizarro, but he still ventured to urge his point.

"See here, comrade," he went on, "there is light enough for you to note the glitter on the sides of these flagons. They are of solid gold, and contain wine that is even yet more precious. I desire not to pass your post, or cause you to betray your duty, but I will leave the wine here, a deep draught of it will cheer the solitude of your watch."

"Away with the wine, and thyself, too!" growled the Spanish sentry. "I tell thee 'tis more than my life is worth to touch a stoup of wine while at my post; and, by St. Jago, I hazard it even while I stand here parleying! Begone I say, or, muerto de dios, thou shalt become acquainted with an iron bullet from my musquetoon!"

"Be not hasty, amigo," said the white chief, as he retired slowly and reluctantly. "I can find a more hearty welcome for my hospitality than thou seemest disposed to give. Adios."

And, inwardly burning with rage and despair, the white chief made his way heavily across the courtyard.

He was powerless. William of Wyckham had indeed thought for a moment of rushing upon the sentry, wresting his weapon from him, and making the attempt to rescue his old friend single handed.

But there were two solid reasons against this course, which weighed with the white chief even in his desperate mood. First, the hopelessness of contending with a dozen heavily-armed Spaniards, and freeing Hubert from his bonds at one and the same time; and, secondly, the certainty that the alarm would be given, and all hope of rescuing Richard of the Raven's Crest be gone for ever.

"It goes sorely against the grain to leave Hubert," muttered the white chief, bitterly; "but there is no help for it. There is yet a chance of rescuing his noble master, and, once free, his readier wit may devise a plan ere yet it is too late."

It was with a much greater degree of confidence that the white chief approached that portion of the palace in which our hero was confined.

There, he knew, were none but Peruvians, whose lax discipline would readily allow them to drink the drugged wine.

"But a score of them are in the inner court," thought the white chief. "The drugged wine will dispose of them, and all those who guard the outer court are mine own warriors, who will not hesitate to obey my will."

William of Wyckham was soon able to test the accuracy of his calculation, so he passed into the inner court, and saw, as he had guessed, some twenty warriors ranged in a semi-circle around the sleeping form of Richard of the Raven's Crest.

They were all on the alert though, and many an arrow was fitted to its bow-string, and many a lance poised as the white chief entered.

But he was recognised in an instant, and saluted as one who had a right to be there, and the dark eyes of the warriors flashed with expectation as the chief set the heavy flagons down with a clang, and uttered a few words in the Peruvian language.

"By command of the mighty Inca," said the white chief, "at the sound of whose voice the whole world trembles and obeys, I have brought his faithful servants wine from the imperial store-hold wherewith to refresh the tedium of the watch. Bring your goblets hither one by one, and I will fill them, but let no man drink before I give the pledge."

In rapid succession the goblets were filled, and our readers will easily divine the reason which impelled William of Wyckham to command that no one man should drink before another. He was totally unaware of the action of the drugs he had taken, and knew not whether those who drank would fall lifeless or insensible at once, or whether the subtle fluid would be slow of operation.

The white chief raised his own goblet, which, it is needless to say, was empty, and uttered the single word—

"Huoscar!"

The twenty goblets were uplifted at the same instant, the wine was drained, the warriors' lips were opened to echo the name of the Inca, when, without a cry or groan, each man sank insensible to the ground, the metal goblets giving out a sound like a death-knell, as they clanged against the pavement.

A pang of remorse pierced the white chief's bosom like the barb of an arrow as he thought that the poisonous drug had killed them, but the life of Richard of the Raven's Crest—one of his own countrymen—was in question, and he had no time to waste in sympathy or pity.

As we have before said our hero was asleep, but the crash of the falling goblets and the dull thud of a score of bodies tumbling simultaneously to the ground awoke him with a start.

"Hush!" said the white chief, springing to his side. "Up and away. Thy life and mine depend upon the swiftness of our motions."

Richard had been asleep—unfettered and untethered as he came from the arena—pillowing his head upon the glossy neck of his noble charger; but, with the quickness of comprehension of a man accustomed to expect and confront danger at a moment's notice, he sprang up, and stood ready.

"Bid thy horse follow thee, noble Richard, if thou canst," whispered the white chief. "My warriors are posted in the outer court. Follow me, but softly, as thou valuest thy life."

Life was dear to Richard, as it is to all who are young and strong and full of hope, and making a gesture of assent to the white chief, he pulled gently at White Thunderbolt's right ear, and gave a soft low whistle.

In an instant the noble horse, which seemed to

have as keen a comprehension of the danger as its master, rose noiselessly to its feet, and thrust its soft muzzle into Richard's hand.

It was just then that our hero espied his dress, armour, and, above all, his trusty sword, lying not far from the place where he had been sleeping. It took him but a moment to secure these and bind them on the back of his horse, when William of Wyckham re-appeared with a light and joyful countenance.

"Is all well?" whispered our hero.

"Ay," replied the white chief, in the same tone. "But haste, Lord Richard! I know not how long the influence of that drug may last, or how soon some wakeful and intruding Spaniard might prowl into these precincts."

"First let me muffle Thunderbolt's hoofs," said Richard, and with a few handfuls of the long dry tough grass, which had formed his couch, he soon rendered the hoof strokes of his steed as noiseless as his own.

William of Wyckham had calculated truly upon the ready obedience of his tribe. For a long time he had been in chief command of the Inca's army —second only to Huoscar himself—and now when he asked them to follow, they obeyed at once, without even caring to think for what object they were led.

Our hero had now mounted his noble charger, and though he was naked as he had been when contending with the Patagonian in the arena, his sword was by his side, and it would have gone hard with anyone who attempted to stay him then.

But the city was like a city of the dead—no lights relieved the gloomy perspective of the broad streets; only the glimmer of the stars shone faintly on the golden gates.

No guard had been set, for Huoscar deemed such a precaution unnecessary. He had triumphed over his rival, Atahualpa—Pizarro was his ally—what then had he to fear?

With utmost precaution, though, the white chief ordered the massive bars to be unhinged, the chains unfastened, and the huge gates swung back.

"Free!" murmured our hero, drawing a deep full breath.

"So far—yes," added the white chief, dubiously. "But there yet remains a peril direr and deeper to run if you would save the life of your esquire, the free-lance."

"Heaven forgive me!" exclaimed Richard, regretfully. "Here have I been content to march out free without bestowing a thought on my faithful Hubert. Where is he? Hast thou dared?——"

"That have I," replied the white chief. "To-morrow, Hubert of Chertsey—mine ancient comrade—will be condemned by the Spaniards for heresy, and you know, noble Richard, that the slightest punishment inflicted by the Inquisition is death by fire at the stake."

"Never!" exclaimed our hero, tempestuously. "Not while there remains a drop of blood in the veins of Richard of the Raven's Crest."

"Hush!" said the white chief. "Parley in a lower tone, noble Richard, or we may be suspected. If you will list to my plan and design, to be guided by it, we shall yet save him."

"I will," replied Richard, in a low fervent voice, as he pressed the cross hilt of his sword to his lips. "I know naught of thee 'tis true, but instinct tells me that thou art a true man."

"I risk more in this emprize than you can dream of. But to my plot, for day will break ere long."

And bidding Richard stoop his stately head, the white chief whispered long and earnestly.

Then a few last words to the Peruvians as he saluted twelve of the most trusty, and bade them follow him, and the white chief waved his hand to our hero, and disappeared silently as a spectre in the darkness of the night.

CHAPTER XXIV.

THE MORNING OF THE DAY OF EXECUTION—THE BUILDING OF THE SCAFFOLD—THE DEATH-KNELL—THE FIRING OF THE PILE—RICHARD OF THE RAVEN'S CREST TO THE RESCUE.

THE bright sun rose, flooding the city of the Incas with dazzling golden beams, until the plates of precious metal adorning the huge gates of the emperor's palace, and many another building, imposing in the massive simplicity of their architecture, were painful for the eye to gaze upon.

Ere yet it had darted its first rays, a party of Spaniards, attended by some fifty slaves, marched into the great square, the latter laden with planks, and some rude instruments of carpentry.

The sun rose higher—slowly and majestically—and the sharp sound of axes, and the duller thud of hammers mingled with the murmuring hum of the people of the city, who gathered curiously round.

The sun was in the meridian, and its noon-tide beams streamed vertically down upon a scaffold.

Yes—the scaffold where the brave and trusty Hubert was to die the horrible lingering death of being roasted alive!

Death on such a morning as that seemed a hideous impossibility. Where could gloomy Death be lurking while the golden sunshine lit up the beautiful city and the landscape that lay beyond?— while the balmy air was filled with the cries of the jewel-plumaged birds, the hum of insects, the rustle of the odorous plants and trees. Everything told of healthy, vigorous, joyous life—nothing of death.

Save only where that gloomy scaffold upreared itself in the centre of the great square, the stout pole, ready with the chain about it wherewith the prisoner was to be bound, and the piles of faggots and dried grass heaped in readiness.

The Spanish soldiers, who had aided in its construction, stood about in knots, laughing and jesting carelessly, for their rough lives had deprived them of all such womanish sentiments as pity or remorse. The crowd of Indians grew denser and denser, choking the great square, when suddenly the sound of a bell clanged out deep and solemn.

"The trial is over," said one of the Spaniards; "and the English heretic is condemned to the flames. Ha! see, yonder they come."

At the eastern corner of the square the crowd was giving way like water before the prow of some powerful ship, and Pizarro, with his lieutenants, came on with their strong martial stride. Behind them was a compact body of Spaniards, with Hubert of Chertsey in their midst, and by his side Padre Valverde; while, to close up the funereal procession, the white chief, with a strange, pale, anxious expression, headed a body of Peruvian warriors.

"All goes well, so far," muttered the white chief. "The Spaniards' horses have been secured, and guided by the secret way to the outside of the city. The charges of the cannons and the musquetoons have been right well damped, and at the sixth stroke of the death-knell Lord Richard is to ride hither to the rescue. Our Lady grant that all fall out well, and that these murdering Spaniards be cheated of their prey."

Again the mournful clang of the huge bell rang out over the city a third time, and the foot of the scaffold was reached.

Then Hubert passed, and glanced proudly around him. Terrible as was the death prepared for him, he was ready to confront it without flinching.

It was only when his glance alighted upon the figure of his old friend that a spasm of scorn and hatred shook his stalwart frame, for he still believed that the white chief was the traitor who had betrayed his young master and himself.

The escape of Richard had not yet been discovered, for, as our readers know, Pizarro was quite unaware that he was a captive; while the Inca was awaiting the arrival of a solemn festival before he put his white prisoner to death, which would not be for three days yet to come.

"'Fore George!" muttered Hubert, as he ascended the rude steps of the scaffold, slowly, but steadily. "'Tis a gruesome death to die, and I would fain have fallen in a well-fought field, with a bullet through my brain, or six inches of steel in my heart; but, since it must be as it is, I will show them how an English soldier can die!"

The fourth knell pealed out as two of the Spaniards led Hubert to the stake and roughly fastened him to it.

The veteran set his teeth hard, and strained himself to compose every nerve and muscle. There would only be a few brief minutes of agony—ten at most, he thought—but they would be terrible indeed.

The cruel and crafty inquisitor, however, had no intention of letting Hubert die so easily. The faggots and other fuel were so arranged that the flames would not go sufficiently near to burn, but only to scorch. The free-lance was to be roasted alive!

Clang! The fifth stroke of the death-bell vibrated on the air. Valverde raised his hand as a signal, and four soldiers approaching with torches, applied the flame to the four corners of the pile.

The fuel quickly catches, for then wreaths of smoke ascend into the air, and the yellow flames play like serpents in and out the bundles of dry wood and grass.

Clang! the sixth stroke sounds; the white chief presses more closely towards the scaffold; the flames rise higher; but, suddenly, high above the crackling of the burning wood and the shouts of the populace, rings out the battle cry of Richard of the Raven's Crest.

Pizarro heard it, and turned, with the dazed look of a man just awakened from a dream, towards our hero, speeding towards him with the swiftness of light.

What followed passed in an instant, and, as it seemed to the astonished Spaniards, by the aid of magic. With one bound, Richard's horse had leapt upon the scaffold. A stroke of his good sword, and Hubert was free; then, throwing him across the crupper, our hero leapt his horse into the very midst of the bewildered Spaniards, and was speeding away, shouting his battle cry, and closely followed by the white chief mounted on Pizarro's own charger.

"Muerte de Dios!" yelled the Spanish commander, getting up from the ground where he had been dashed with considerable force by Richard's charger. "Where are your musquetoons, ye knaves? Train the field-pieces! They are yet well within range. Ho! bring the horses, some of ye, and quick, or your heads shall answer it. Ha! as I live, yonder goes one fellow mounted on mine own especial charger. There is treachery here!"

And, snatching a musquetoon from a soldier, Pizarro took aim, and fired at the fast retreating fugitives.

The weapon flashed in the pan, and Pizarro, with a furious oath, dashed it to the ground.

"The cannon!" he said. "Quick! they have not yet reached the gates. Here, train them low—so. Now the port-fire."

Pizarro's own hand applied the light; but the powder on the touch-holes of both cannon flashed, and that was all.

The wrath of the Spanish commander was terrible; and so awful was the look he bent upon those around him, that even Valverde drew back.

"There is treachery here!" he said, in a breathless voice. "When I discover him, let him look to it, for were he my own brother, he should die the most lingering and cruel death it is possible for a devil to conceive. But ho! the horses there! We can at least pursue these English hounds."

A grey moustached, bronzed Spaniard, who bore the reputation of being the most reckless of the whole band, fearing neither man nor fiend, had just returned, and now stood trembling like a schoolboy, as he stammered out that the horses too were gone.

For a moment it seemed as though Pizarro was about to give way to some mighty outburst of wrath; but, checking himself by an almost superhuman effort, he strode hastily away towards the palace, accompanied by Valverde, leaving del Soto and Ferdinand to discover in what manner the guns had been tampered with, and, if possible, whether any of the soldiers were in the conspiracy.

Pizarro acted with his usual promptitude and decision. A number of Peruvians were sent out to track the course taken by our hero and his friends, whilst he and Valverde searched the palace, guided by one of the Inca's chamberlains, to discover by what means the horses had been spirited away.

"I marvel much," said Pizarro, "how this cub, Richard of the Raven's Crest, came to be in this city, at our very elbows, and we not to know of it. By St. Jago I begin to suspect that the Inca himself hath had a hand in the rescue. Now I bethink me, I noticed a troop of these Peruvians following closely in the English boy's rear, as he rode off. What think ye, Valverde."

"My suspicions, noble Pizarro," replied the priest, "fall in quite another direction. Rememberest thou the fellow who acted as interpreter between thyself and the Inca, on thy arrival."

"Ay," said Pizarro. "A swarthy, bearded fellow, who spoke Spanish with a strong Cordovan twang."

"The same," rejoined the priest. "He is the traitor."

"Ha! Madre de Dios!" ejaculated Pizarro, "thou art right, Valverde—I see it now. Hence his readiness to take charge of the English cub's esquire when he was captured. But said del Soto naught of a struggle between them, wherein this white chief, as they call him, was well-nigh mauled to death."

"Ay, he did speak of such a matter, noble Pizarro," said Valverde; "but that was a ruse—devised to blind us as to his real motives. Believe me, 'tis he who hath worked all this mischief."

"But not alone, Valverde," returned the Spanish commander. "He must have had confederates, and yet I would not readily believe any of my well-tried veterans guilty of treachery to their captain. Still, how could one man, in a single night, have captured our horses from under the very noses of those in charge, and rendered useless the charges of the musquetoons and cannon?"

"I grant 'twas done with marvellous cunning," said Valverde, "and I doubt not but that the magic art, in which these heathens are said to excel, hath been called in aid."

"Let me but once lay hands upon him," said Pizarro, bitterly, "and we shall see if his magic will save him from a roasting. By St. Jago, it makes my blood boil to think that I, who have grown grey in the council and the camp, should be braved and outwitted by a beardless mozo." *

"They have escaped but for a time," said Valverde. "Remember, Pizarro, the whole country is subject to Huoscar, now that he has conquered, and holds captive, his brother Atahualpa, and that he has but to send forth messengers, with the expression of his will, and this Richard of the

---

* **Boy.**

Raven's Crest and his companions will be in thy hands again."

"Thy scheme seems a likely one," returned Pizarro, more hopefully; "but I swear, by my good sword, that I will not rest until I have wreaked my vengeance on mine enemy, who hath thwarted me and crossed my path ever since I set foot in Peru. I cannot rest, I tell thee, Valverde, until I see him lying dead at my feet. With the others thou mayst do as thou wilt—Richard of the Raven's Crest must die by my hand!"

"With all my heart," echoed Valverde. "He is an enemy to the true cause, and deserves a worse fate than to fall by the hand of so noble a champion. But see, Pizarro, yonder approach some messengers from the Inca, and in haste. Doubtless, we shall learn more of this mystery than is yet known to us. Is it your pleasure that we attend them?"

Pizarro nodded assent, and Valverde, after hearing the message through the interpreter—which was, in fact, what he had anticipated—motioned to the messengers to lead the way, while he and the angry and baffled Pizarro followed, meditating fresh schemes of vengeance.

CHAPTER XXV.

OUT OF THE TOILS—THE BURIAL PLACE OF THE HIGH PRIESTS OF THE TEMPLE OF THE SUN—HUBERT AND WILLIAM OF WYCKHAM EXPLAIN MATTERS—THE COUNCIL—THE WHITE CHIEF PUTS A STRANGE QUESTION, AND INDULGES IN STRANGER CONDUCT.

WITH a wild, ringing cheer, in which his whole soul seemed to go forth, Richard of the Raven's Crest spurred his fleet charger down the broad causeway towards the golden gates of the city.

The white chief was close at his heels, mounted on Pizarro's powerful black war-horse, an Andalusian charger of immense strength and bone, well adapted for carrying such a weight as that of Pizarro when accoutred in full panoply of steel.

They heard the hoarse shouts of the Spaniards—the fierce commands of Pizarro; and, turning in their saddles, they saw the musketeers levelling their pieces and the cannon being dragged into position.

"Faster! good William," said Richard, as he saw these preparations. "A ball from one of those field-pieces may wound our horses, if not ourselves, and then we should indeed be in a perilous state."

"Have no fear, Lord Richard," said the white chief, with a grim smile. "I wetted their iron throats with a full quart apiece of good wine this morning. 'Twas a sad waste, but I had no time to seek for water."

"'Twas a good thought of thine," said Richard, approvingly. "But see, here are the gates, and open. Take thou the lead, and show the way, good William."

It was many a long year since William of Wyckham had bestrode a horse, but he had forgotten none of his old skill, and managed the powerful charger he rode as easily as Pizarro himself could have done.

Forcing the pace a little, he galloped ahead, and turned into the rocky defile, where still remained the body of Peruvian warriors who had so faithfully followed the fortunes of the white chief.

William of Wyckham reined in his horse so suddenly as to throw the powerful animal upon its haunches, and dismounting while it still reared and plunged, madly dragging at the bridle, tethered it to a dwarf mimosa and invited our hero to do the same.

"Our movements must be quick, noble sir," he said; "for the spies will be presently upon our track. How fares it with Hubert?"

The veteran had received a severe blow on the head from the pummel of Richard's saddle as he was hastily dragged from the scaffold, and had not yet recovered his senses.

"He will come to anon," replied our hero, as he lifted Hubert from the saddle, and placed him gently on the ground. "But why do we tarry here, good William? I can see naught around us but inhospitable rocks."

"The rougher the outside, the warmer the welcome within, Lord Richard," responded the white chief. "Will it please you to walk this way, and I will show you a secret which now is known but to one person besides myself."

But our hero had met already with so many wonders in this strange land, that he was prepared for almost anything, natural or supernatural.

There was nothing very unearthly, or partaking of the nature of magic, though, in the white chief's actions. He made his devious way amongst the huge blocks and boulders that cumbered the path, until it terminated abruptly in front of a mighty mass of granite—a very mountain in itself.

On the right of the path was a curious pear-shaped block of the same stone, balanced on its smaller end, and with a smooth round hole, of the diameter of a shilling, in its side.

To this hole, the white chief applied his mouth, and, collecting all his breath, as if for a great effort, blew into it, until Richard thought that no human lungs could bear such a strain.

At last he took his lips away, and, touching Richard on the arm, pointed to the granite mountain.

It had seemed to him compact, firm, in one vast mass ever since the time, long ages ago, when some mighty convulsion of nature had upheaved it; but, looking steadily at it now, Richard became aware that a portion of it was moving outwards, like a vast door swinging on hinges from within.

It was large enough to have formed the portal to the Ark, and as Richard gazed into the gloomy depths beyond, as they were gradually revealed, he shuddered involuntarily as he thought how powerless anyone engulfed in that gloomy tomb would be, if he had but his hands wherewith to beat down the door of his prison.

"Enter," said the white chief, motioning to his warriors to advance. Then he added to our hero, "In a quarter of an hour yonder granite door will close of itself as securely as it was but a moment ago."

"And is there none other means of quitting the cavern?"

"None," replied the white chief. "And the secret, as I told you, noble Richard, is one which Rimac, the High Priest of the Temple of the Sun, is alone supposed to have in his keeping."

"Rimac," repeated Richard. "I know him. Did he not follow the fortunes of Atahualpa—the true Inca?"

"Whether true or false, I know not," replied the white chief, bluntly. "I am a rough man, like skilled in the nice laws of heritage. I ever fought for the hand that paid me best."

"Spoken like a true free-lance," laughed Richard; and then, as the Peruvians were all gone in, and the massive door had begun to close itself as silently and mysteriously as it had opened, our hero and William, bearing Hubert between them, passed the gloomy portal of the cavern.

The Peruvians had already lit some torches. Their manner of procuring light resembled that which was common in this enlightened country less than half a century ago—id est, the flint and steel; the Peruvians employing, instead of iron (a metal of which they were ignorant), a hard, semi-metallic stone, and instead of tinder, the pith of a kind of reed, or very fine grass.

A huge fire was soon blazing in the centre of the rocky chasm, and Richard, casting his eyes around with natural curiosity, saw that it was of vast dimensions, and lined all round with tier upon tier of shelves, nearly every one being occupied by ranges of earthen jars, with curious hieroglyphics moulded or painted on them.

"It is fortunate," said the white chief in a low voice, "that these warriors of mine do not know where they are."

"And why?" asked Richard.

"For this reason, noble sir. Every one of those jars contains the ashes of a High Priest of the Temple. When he is dying, the high priest communicates the secret to his successor, who, in the most profound and solemn secrecy, burns the body with his own hands, putting the ashes in one of those funereal urns, inscribing it with the particular hieroglyphic belonging to his name, and deposits it in its place on one of the shelves. The secret is in its last hands now, for Rimac, the high priest, will die with it unrevealed."

"'Tis a strange land, and a strange people," mused Richard as he looked thoughtfully down upon the pale face of his faithful Hubert, whose forehead he was laving with cool water brought from an inner cavern. "I myself have seen more sights of gramarye* than ever I heard minstrel chant."

"I shall be glad to hear them anon," said the white chief. "'Twill relieve the gravity of the councils we must hold as to our future. But first, I will fetch a stoup of wine for Hubert's refreshment. Methinks he looks less pale."

The wine was brought, and some dried fruits and cakes of meal for Richard's refreshment.

The stimulant soon produced the desired effect, and Hubert, after gulping down a mouthful or two of the sweet, but powerful liquor, sat up and gazed wonderingly around him.

At first, he was unaware of the presence of his master and the white chief, for both were behind him, and Hubert began to move and grumble in his usual fashion.

"Why, what a plague is this?" he muttered. "It seemed but now that I was tied up to be comfortably roasted, and now—— How came I here? and where, in the name of all the saints, is this cave of St. Anthony?"

"I had a vision, too," he went on, slowly stroking his moustache to aid his thoughts, "of young Lord Richard charging down upon the scaffold; methinks even now I can hear the battle cry ringing in mine ears."

"St. George for Merrie England!"

There was nothing visionary about that cry, for our hero, stooping down, shouted it so closely to the free-lance's head, as almost to deafen him.

Hubert sprang to his feet, and the next minute held our hero in a grip like the hug of a bear, the while he mumbled incoherently blessings and congratulatory questions and answers, in a fashion that the most eminent lunatic in Bethlehem Hospital could not surpass.

"Steady! Hubert! Easy with those great arms of thine," said Richard of the Raven's Crest. "Remember that I, too, have been a prisoner, and am still somewhat tender, by reason of the cords that cut into my naked limbs."

"Remember, Lord Richard?" scowled Hubert. "Ay, I remember well enough, and when that false caitiff, William of Wyckham, and I meet again, he will have no cause to complain of my want of memory."

"Truly, I hope not, Hubert," said William of Wyckham himself, advancing from out the shadow and stepping into the full blaze of the fire.

"What!" gasped Hubert. "Is't possible? Thou art not a traitor, then!"

"Thou deserved'st to be called so for thinking basely of me, Hubert."

*Gramarye: Witchcraft—the work of supernatural powers.

"Had it not been for Will of Wyckham," said Richard of the Raven's Crest, gravely, "thou, Hubert, would'st have been naught but a heap of mouldering ashes, left for the idle winds to scatter in the air; and, as for me, I should have shared the same, or, perchance, a worse fate. Beg his pardon, on thy knees, man, for having doubted the bravest and truest man that ever claimed England for his country."

It would be difficult to picture a man with a more sheepish and contrite expression than Hubert wore as he glanced uneasily at his old friend, not in the least knowing how to express his shame and sorrow—until William of Wyckham put an end to his embarrassment by thrusting out his own horny palm, which Hubert took and squeezed with a grateful vigour that sent all the blood to the very finger tips.

During the whole of that evening he was remarkably quiet and subdued, much to William of Wyckham's inward amazement, for he saw that it was remorse, for having suspected a friend of treachery while that friend was perilling his life to save him, that troubled him.

"It will do him good," said Richard aside to the white chief. "He is a little apt to presume upon his experience and knowledge of war. Let us see, when we hold our council to-night, whether the experience of to-day will curb his forwardness."

William of Wyckham, with the skill of an old campaigner, had well victualled the caverns—for there were several, opening out into one another. In two of the inner ones the warriors were stationed, while the outer was reserved for the apartment of Richard of the Raven's Crest, Hubert, and the white chief.

It was here that the council was held, and with as much security from all danger as if they had been thousands of miles away from the crafty and vindictive Pizarro.

"'Tis strange to think," laughed our hero, "that even now, at this moment, my bitter enemy may be within a few yards of us."

"It may well be so," replied William of Wyckham, "but his scent must be keener than a bloodhound's, and his power more than mortal, ere he unearths us from our stronghold."

"But," added our hero, "surely it consorts as little with thy inclination as mine, to stay here, like a badger in his hole, until the hounds come to draw him?"

"True, Lord Richard," replied William of Wyckham. "I am as little disposed as you to stay here in idleness and inactivity, but, saving your honour's presence, we must determine what we have to do before we do it."

"I spoke in haste, as usual," said Richard, with a smile. "Say on, Will. Let thy older head advise my green experience."

"Nay, faith," returned the white chief, with some hesitation, "'tis for me to listen to you, Lord Richard, and obey."

"Tush, man. Think not that I am such a vain fool as to despise the counsel of those who are more experienced than myself. Say on, man, and fear not."

"Well, then, if I must hazard a speech," said the white chief, "may I ask if it is your purpose to seek the coast, and so quit the country, or——"

"By St. George—no!" exclaimed Richard, almost fiercely. "I swear not to quit Peru until I have humbled Pizarro, and thwarted every villanous scheme his brain may hatch. Besides——"

"Ay, my lord?" queried the white chief, as our hero paused for an instant.

"I was thinking of the prophecy of Rimac, the High Priest of the Temple of the Sun, and of what he said concerning me and the mystic diamond."

"Will it please you to tell us the story, noble sir," said the white chief. "I may be able to interpret some parts which might seem strange to you."

WITH A BOUND, RICHARD WAS IN THEIR MIDST, SCATTERING THEM LIKE CHAFF.

Then, to the intense wonder of Hubert, who listened, open eyed and mouthed, Richard told of the strange adventures which had befallen him after his leap into the abyss; which we need not repeat here, as they are all detailed in the first part of this faithful chronicle.

William of Wyckham was silent and grave for a few minutes after Richard had concluded. Then he spoke—

"Certes, noble sir, I confess that you have puzzled me, and given my wits a problem to solve far beyond their powers."

"What part of my story is it that puzzles thee, good William?"

"The legend of the lost jewel of the Inca—the Devil's Diamond," replied the white chief. "I remember now to have heard the priests speaking of the prophecy, and of some stranger, mightier than the sons of men, who was by its aid to restore the glory of the empire of Peru. But I regarded it as an idle tale until now, when you have so strangely confirmed it."

"'Tis as yet but a poor fulfilment of the prophecy," said our hero, with a sombre smile. "I am little better than a prisoner, for I am not free to go where I will. Pizarro lords it in the great city yonder, the rightful Inca has lost his throne, and the diamond, by which I was to work such wonders, is gone from me."

"A month, a week, a day even, may change all that, and give you the upper hand again, noble Richard. Yours is not a spirit to cower before the first blast of evil fortune."

"Heaven forfend," replied Richard, his handsome features flushing with the thought; "but my blood boils when I think how insolently this swaggering Spaniard lords it over all in yonder city, and how I—cooped up here, like a timid girl in a nunnery—dare not go forth because of my unequal force. If I were but sure of getting one good blow at him, I care little what might happen after; but 'tis an hundred chances to one that ere I get near Pizarro, my path would be blocked, my retreat cut off, and I doomed to endure his taunts and revilements."

"If thou hadst but stolen Pizarro's cannon as well as his horses, old comrade," said Hubert, breaking into the conversation for the first time, "we might defy them all."

"I have thought of the matter," replied the white chief, "and I have a question to put to thy master, Hubert, which, I trust, he will not deem me over bold for asking."

"Say on, man," responded our hero, moodily; "ask what thou wilt."

"I have heard Hubert, in the brief speech we have had together concerning you, noble sir, say that you were learned in the subtler sciences."

"Then Hubert's tongue outran discretion," said Richard, with a good-natured smile. "My knowledge of science is but as a grain of sand on the sea shore."

"But, noble sir, know you aught of chemistry—the science of Friar Bacon and the alchemists?"

"Truly," replied Richard, as if partly ashamed of his knowledge. "I did begin the study of the great Arcanum, and had made some progress in the projection of the metals, but 'twas a fitter occupation for monks than soldiers, and I soon tired of it. It liked me better to turn steel into gold upon the battle-field than to transmute lead into the precious metal in the seven-times heated furnace of an alchemist's laboratory."

"And, during those studies, noble sir," continued the white chief, "did you ever learn the secret of the composition of gunpowder?"

"Ay! now I remember me, I have seen it many a time," replied Richard. "But why, man! what thought hast thou in thy head?"

"Pardon, noble sir; but till you have answered my question my thought is useless."

"I cannot remember now the exact proportions, but the ingredients are sulphur, saltpetre, and charcoal."

The white chief leaped to his feet with a joyous cry.

"We can defy Pizarro, then," he said, exultantly. "Sulphur and saltpetre exist in immense quantities in the mountains—the charcoal we can burn—with a little trouble we can find out the proportions for ourselves, and make gunpowder enough to blow Pizarro back to Spain."

Both the manner and the substance of the speech seemed so wild and strange, that Richard of the Raven's Crest and Hubert looked at the white chief as if they feared he had lost his senses.

CHAPTER XXVI.

THE WHITE CHIEF'S PLAN—THE MARCH TO THE PLAINS OF THE DESERT — THE SYMBOL OF DANGER—THE FIERY ARROW IN THE AIR.

THE white chief's proposition was of so startling a character, that his hearers might well have been excused for thinking him distraught.

The manufacture of gunpowder was then still in its infancy, and was still a secret known only to a few alchemists, each of whom pretended to prepare the "villanous saltpetre" in a way known only to himself, and the method of which was jealously guarded.

"What maggot hast thou in thy brain now, Will?" growled Hubert.

"One that will enable us to triumph over Pizarro and his horde of Spaniards," replied the white chief, "if Lord Richard will but listen to counsel."

"That will I readily enough," replied our hero; "but, in good sooth, this plan of thine, Will, seems a wild one."

"And why?" asked the white chief, calmly.

"Supposing," returned Richard, "that we succeed even in compounding the powder, which we are little likely to do, seeing that our means are more limited than our knowledge, of what use will it be without musquetoons or cannon?"

"Perchance, Will hath some notable plan in his head whereby he will make us these weapons too, it may be," laughed Hubert.

"Peace, man, and let William of Wyckham speak," said Richard, somewhat sternly; "this is not a matter for idle jesting."

"Leave the use to me, Lord Richard," said the white chief, with the same air of calm confidence. "I warrant me, and will pledge my life and honour, that if your knowledge of the subtle science enables us to compound the powder, we shall be speedily rid of our enemies."

"Be it so," said Richard; "but I warn thee, Will, that I care to spend but little time in inaction. My blood already tingles in my veins with the desire to set foot in stirrup and ride out to meet Pizarro."

"With what result, Lord Richard?" said the white chief. "Certain defeat, which would be worse than death to you."

"The race of which I come," returned our hero, proudly, "never look upon defeat as a possibility."

"Pizarro," continued the white chief, in the same unmoved tone, "is too cautious to be surprised again. Say, that you and Hubert and I, at the head of my warriors, charged his encampment; well, his sentries would give the alarm, one discharge of their musquetoons and cannon would rout or dismay those Peruvians, and we then should be left to encounter not only the Spaniards but Huoscar's myriads, encouraged by the belief they hold that they are led by demi-gods."

"But we have their horses, good William," said Richard of the Raven's Crest; "thou hast forgotten that. What's easier than to charge down boldly upon the Spaniards, break their line, and kill or capture Pizarro. Remember but yesterday, when

Hubert was snatched from the very jaws of death by such a device."

"And remember, too, Lord Richard," replied the white chief, "that by stratagem the Spaniards' cannon were silenced, else had the result been different. As for the horses, Pizarro will not be long without a fresh supply. Hubert hath told me of the encampment he left at St. Michael's, and doubtless he hath already sent thither."

"Ha!" ejaculated Richard—"I thought not of that. The more reason why we should act, and quickly, too. There will be scant time for thy madbrained experiments, good William. We had better trust to strong arms and stout hearts than to the devices of alchemy."

"I ask but a day, Lord Richard," said the white chief. "But one day, and such advice as your knowledge of the compounding of the powder can give me."

"'Tis well," replied our hero. "One day can matter little. But after that I can no more delay my impulse to meet Pizarro face to face."

"Enough, Lord Richard," responded the white chief, joyfully. "I ask no more, but that I be allowed to begin my work at once."

That request was of course conceded, and the white chief, causing the massive portal of rock to open by the same simple means he had adopted from without, sent forth a few of the warriors as spies.

Returning soon, they reported the mountain passes clear; for, indeed, Pizarro had sullenly and reluctantly given up the search, believing that our hero and his allies had ridden far away into the country, with the object of gaining the sea shore; and as his horses were gone, pursuit was hopeless.

"I expected no less," said the white chief, exultantly. "We will march at once, noble Richard, an' it please you. Ere morning breaks we can reach the destined spot, and begin the work which shall lay Pizarro's power low for ever."

"Amen to that, with all my heart," said Hubert. "But 'twill be with our sharp swords, and not with thy mountebank tricks I wot, good Will, that the deed will be done."

"Spare thy censure till I fail, Hubert," replied William of Wyckham, curtly; and then turning to the warriors, he gave them their orders, which were at once and promptly executed, and they all filed out of the cavern with the regularity of trained soldiers and the noiselessness of spectres.

"Take you all your men?" asked Richard.

"Ay—'twill be as well, in case of a surprise; and, again, the more men we have the more quickly will the work be done."

"The compounding of the powder, Will?" asked Hubert.

"Ay—of what else should I speak."

"'Twill be indeed then of a goodly strength," laughed the free-lance, "if it requires nigh on a thousand men for its preparation."

"Laugh on, old friend," retorted the white chief. "Thou wert ever the readiest to laugh at what thou could'st not comprehend. Let us see if thou wilt be so merry at my expense a short two days hence."

"Heed him not," said Richard, as he bounded into the saddle, "but mount and away. Take we the spare horses with us, good William?"

"Ay, noble Richard. They will serve to bear the powder."

"One ass could well carry all the powder thou wilt produce," growled the free-lance, who, though he dearly cherished his old friend, yet used a friend's utmost license, and criticised him more unmercifully than if he had been a mortal enemy.

It was night when our hero and his followers issued forth from the gloomy portals of that vast tomb. A dense mist had spread itself over the mountain side, and, gradually descending, had enwrapped the whole landscape in its inpenetrable veil.

To proceed along such a rocky path seemed impracticable, but to the white chief not an inch of the country was unknown. He could have traversed it blindfold, and now, moving easily at the head of the Peruvians, and with our hero and Hubert on either hand, he rode forward as confidently as if it had been broad daylight.

It was a cold, chilling mist, which hung about the adventurers like a shroud, and made them shiver in spite of themselves. It was a strange and unpleasant contrast to the genial warmth which they had experienced since their landing in Peru.

"Ugh!" muttered Hubert, "there is some deadly marsh-fever or ague in this mist, Master Will. My old bones feel as chilled as if they had been steeped for hours in ice."

"'Tis but the mountain mist," replied the white chief. "Take a stoup of wine, man—that will cure the ague which thou dreadest."

"Thy old trick," laughed Hubert. "The winecup was ever thy medicine for all the ills and aches that afflict poor humanity."

"Better the cure than the cause," retorted the white chief. "How many a head-ache hast thou owed, in the days gone by, to too deep a carouse of old October or sack, Hubert?"

"Thou hast a keen memory for my peccadilloes," added Hubert. "But mind'st thou the time, good Will, when the watch put thee in the stocks at Guildford Fair, and I knocked the warden o'er the mazzard and released thee, when thou wert even then so drunk, that I had to heave thee across my shoulders, like a dead buck, and carry thee home?"

"A truce—a truce!" cried Richard of the Raven's Crest. "'Faith, my men, an' ye dig up more recollections of these mad pranks, we shall have you presently by the ears again."

"'Twere best to be silent," added the white chief, in a lower tone, "for the night is dark, and spies may be lurking."

So silence came again over the little band. They had already marched nigh on an hour, and yet another passed, ere the white chief reined in his horse, and uttered a low, clear hissing sound, which instantly brought the Peruvian warriors to a halt.

"Is this the place?" said Richard of the Raven's Crest.

"It is, noble sir."

Our hero looked around him, but the mist was still so dense, that it was impossible to see for more than a few yards in any direction. But this seemed in no degree to hamper the movements of the white chief, who, to all appearance, could see as well in that blinding, chilling mist, as in broad daylight.

"Methinks, friend Will," growled the free-lance, "that we should have done better to have stayed in yonder cavern. There at least we were warm, and had shelter, while here, it seems to me, we are like to die of ague before morning."

"Say you so?" replied the white chief. "Is that the way in which the hardy free-lance, the veteran of a hundred hard-fought fields, speaks? But you shall have warmth and shelter enough, never fear man. See yonder!"

Almost as he spoke, some half dozen fires, raged in a semicircle and at a distance of about thirty yards from each other, burst into light with a pleasant crackle.

This had been done so quietly and dexterously by the Peruvian warriors, that it seemed the effect of magic; and when, a few minutes later, the blaze, gaining strength, the light fell upon two small, but snug looking tents of feather cloth, Hubert was fain to give a surly grunt of approval.

"Thou hast the art of well training thy men, good William," said our hero.

"I am pleased that they deserve your praise, noble sir," replied the white chief. "If I cannot claim for them that they will face our own countrymen, or even the Spaniards in battle, and that they are easily daunted by strange sights and sounds, yet they have the dog-like merit of fidelity to their leader, and will obey me to the death."

By this time the tents were reached. One was destined for our hero, the other was to be tenanted by Hubert and the white chief.

The ground had been thickly strewn with dried grass, and, for a couch, a quantity of prepared skins of the llama and the jaguar promised our hero such comfort as he had little looked for in that desolate spot.

"'Fore George, good William," he said, "you will enervate me with these luxuries. I looked but to stretch my limbs on the hard ground, with, perhaps, my good horse's neck for a pillow, and you provide me with a tent fit for the repose of a king."

"'Tis but a soldier's fare, noble sir," replied the white chief; "let but our expedition succeed against Pizarro, and you shall see what luxuries the empire of Peru can boast."

Then, with a military salute, he passed on to post the sentries at the watch fires, leaving our hero and Hubert standing at the entrance to the tent.

"What think you of all this, Hubert?" asked Richard, after a few minutes' silence.

"Of what, Lord Richard?"

"Of this plan of thine ancient comrade, William of Wyckham."

"'Faith, I know not. 'Tis too deep for me."

"And yet he spoke plainly enough."

"Ay, did he. A man's words may be plain, and yet his meaning difficult to understand—even as a riddle."

"Then you think he is trifling with us—that he is not honest?"

"I will venture for his honesty and truth as for mine own," said the free-lance vehemently.

"Well, well, I think so too," said our hero thoughtfully. "A short day will decide whether he hath really brought us to this spot for the purpose he indicated, or for some other design. Ha, Hubert, see yonder! What is the meaning of that?"

CHAPTER XXVII.

PIZARRO AND PADRE VALVERDE HOLD A CON-
SULTATION—THE RESOLUTION—THE FESTIVAL
IN THE GREAT SQUARE — THE SPANIARD'S
TREACHERY—A COURAGEOUS STROKE—PIZARRO
SECURES THE DEVIL'S DIAMOND—THE WARNING
AT MIDNIGHT.

THE most important loss which Pizarro had sustained by the white chief's bold and well executed plan, was the loss of his horses.

Without these he was comparatively powerless, especially in his grand object, the pursuit and capture of our hero and his companions; and to have effected that, Pizarro would have given five years of his life; for revenge was as powerful a passion with the Spaniard as ambition or avarice.

Prompt of resource, though, he had acted as the white chief had surmised that he would, and sent his brother Ferdinand, with a dozen men, back to the little garrison at St. Michael, with orders to return instantly with what horses they could find.

"Perchance by this time," said the Spanish commander to Valverde, "the reinforcements have arrived. If so, let this English cub and his esquire look to it."

"But why?" urged the priest—"why waste further time on this idle pursuit? Why suffer your desire for revenge to baulk the great object

with which we landed in this country, and which, so far, heaven hath seen fit to prosper so wonderfully?"

"You ask me why?" ejaculated Pizarro, almost fiercely. "Hath not this Richard of the Raven's Crest crossed my path and baulked me at every turn? Know you not, full well, that while he, and that stubborn English mastiff he calls his 'squire, live, our lives are not safe. There is nothing, I tell you, Valverde, that they deem impossible."

"What have we to fear?" replied Valverde, calmly. "Are not we the stronger party, a hundred to one; not counting the barbarous hordes of the Inca. Trust me, Pizarro—wait; and this headstrong young Englishman will run his own neck into the noose. In the meantime, let our legitimate purpose —the annexation of these fair lands to the dominions of our royal master, King of Castile and Aragon—proceed."

"You speak wisely, Valverde," replied Pizarro, thoughtfully. "I own that of late I have let my feeling of hatred and anger against this rebellious thwarter of our plans, interfere with our great project; but it shall be so no longer."

"Well said, noble Pizarro," exclaimed the priest, and his sallow features were coloured with a slight flush of triumph.

"Even such a bold stroke as Cortes played for the possession of Mexico, will I adventure now. On the morrow, Valverde, the Inca, Huoscar, holds a solemn festival, to which we are invited. 'Twill then be time to seize upon him, and accuse him of having conspired with this Richard of the Raven's Crest, against our lives."

"Santa Maria!" ejaculated Valverde, "a notable scheme, illustrious Pizarro; especially seeing that this white chief, as he was called—one of the Inca's chosen leaders—was active in aiding young Richard."

"That was he," added Pizarro, with a stern satisfaction; "and if he be not in the city, or ready to answer the accusation brought against him, who shall doubt his guilt, and what more probable than that he acted under the instructions of the Inca, his master."

"But caution is necessary," said Valverde. "Forget not, Pizarro, that these barbarians look upon their monarchs as divinities, and are likely— much as they hold us in awe—to offer resistance if we show violence to Huoscar."

"Sangre de Dios," growled Pizarro, from under his heavy moustache. "Let one of them but lift a finger, and we will crush them like the worms they are. The swords of my men are getting rusted for want of use," he added, with a diabolical laugh. "If these Peruvians give them an opportunity of putting them to use, I shall not cry off the hawks from the prey."

"And even as it seemeth best to your wisdom, illustrious Pizarro," said Valverde, with affected humility. "It is not for me to counsel bloodshed when the words of peace and mercy may prevail."

"Neither peace nor mercy shall we have, padre," said Pizarro, "unless it be such as we make with our good swords. Yonder fellows swarm too thickly, and it needs to teach them a sharp lesson now and again."

Then the conversation ended, and the two men, of such opposite professions, yet so similar in character, in craft, in greed, separated for the night, to think over, and, perchance, dream of, the scheme of villany that they had just been planning.

The morning came, and with its earliest dawn Pizarro had been astir making his preparations.

His forces had been weakened by the expedition he had sent to the garrison at St. Michael in search of horses, but he had retained all his musketeers and his most tried veterans; while he had planted his two cannon so as to cover the square with a cross fire.

To the loading, not only of the cannon but of the musquetoons, he had seen himself, remembering too well, as he did, the trick that had been played him by the white chief, and he had so arranged his little band of troops that they could act in different directions or concentrate themselves upon one point as necessity should determine.

The festival was to commence with the rising of the sun, when the priests of the temple were to perform a solemn service in honour of the deity they worshipped.

These the Spaniards suffered to pass unmolested, though they cast many a covetous glance at the gold ornaments and jewels of the priests; but for these they could afford to wait until they had seized the Inca, and the empire itself was in their grasp.

The moment so anxiously waited for by the Spaniards came at last. The trumpets rung out their salute, the populace prostrated themselves on either side of the way to be traversed by the Inca, and then Huoscar himself appeared, surrounded by his caciques.

He seemed to be more splendidly dressed than even on the first occasion when Pizarro had seen him. His garments were literally ablaze with jewels, and the costumes of the nobles of the empire seemed scarcely less rich. But, far out-ining these all, in lustre and brilliancy, gleamed the Devil's Diamond in the coronet of the Inca.

Little suspecting the treacherous thoughts that lurked in the bosom of his new ally, Huoscar, as soon as he saw Pizarro, waved a greeting to him from the window of the palanquin in which he was being borne.

At the signal, Pizarro advanced, his soldiers advancing too, but preserving strictly their order until the two parties were within speaking distance.

It was then that Pizarro halted, and, calling one of his interpreters, bade him charge the Inca with having attempted and conspired against the life of his guests, the Spaniards, on the occasion when they were about to execute justice upon a traitor.

The Peruvian interpreter, with much fear and trembling, presented himself before the Inca, and delivered Pizarro's message, softening its harshness as much as possible.

The Inca looked at the interpreter and at Pizarro alternately, in angry astonishment. It was sacrilege for anyone to address a descendant of Manco Copac in such terms.

What could it mean? Had these strangers, whom he had treated with the courtesy of familiars, dared to insult him in the face of his own people. He fancied, for the moment, that he could not have heard aright, but a glance at the angry, alarmed faces of his caciques, who, too, had heard the message, convinced him that he was not mistaken.

With a gesture of inexpressible dignity, the Inca signed for his palanquin to be taken back, but scarcely had the bearers made a step to turn, than Pizarro, drawing his sword, rushed forward, and seized the Inca roughly by the arm.

An instantaneous shout of "sacrilege" was raised by the caciques who attended upon their monarch, as they beheld his sacred person thus rudely assailed, and, with chivalrous devotion, though they were unarmed, they crowded about the palanquin, and endeavoured to dislodge Pizarro.

But the Spanish commander, never quitting his hold of the Inca, dragged him from his shelter, and, with half a dozen strokes and thrusts of his big Spanish sword, cut his way clear back to Valverde.

"Now," cried Pizarro, waving his sword exultantly in the air, "down with the barbarians! Fire, musketeers, and cross-bowmen. See that the cannons be well served. Ha! that ploughed a lane amongst the heathen. But fire lower, until the square be cleared. Be ready, men, with the pike and sword!"

But the pike and the sword were not needed. The awful explosion of the two field pieces, the rattle of the musketry, the dreadful and inexplicable havoc which followed the flash and report of these strange weapons, were quite enough for the simple Peruvians.

With cries of terror, they fled; and, with hoarse shouts of fiendish gratification, the Spanish soldiery followed, killing, with sword and pike, butt-end of musquetoon, and cross-bow, the unoffending, terrified Indians, who offered no resistance.

They outnumbered the Spaniards by five hundred to one; yet such was the terror which these strangers had inspired with their mysterious weapons, that they fled panic-stricken, as before the wrath of an offended deity.

Mad with the lust of blood and gold, the Spaniards followed, smote and spared not. Thousands were ruthlessly slaughtered, not one of whom offered resistance to his murderer, or even saw the weapon by which he died.

The horrid carnage lasted till, through sheer fatigue, the soldiers could no longer wield their weapons. Then they trooped back in knots of twos and threes towards the great square, besmeared and reeking with blood; but there was not one who had not secured a plunder of gold and precious stones, which in Spain would have made him wealthy for life.

What an orgie the murderous revellers held over their booty that night! while from the streets beyond there went up to heaven a cry of wailing and lamentation from the widow and the orphan—a cry for vengeance upon the merciless assassins.

But little recked the ruthless Pizarro of that. His subtle brain was turning with a thousand plots to draw advantage from his seizure of the Inca, and his dark eyes glittered with triumph, as, seated in his tent with Valverde, he discussed the subject.

"Seest thou not, padre," he said, "that 'twill be better—far better—to let the Inca live, than to burn him for heresy and treason as thou would'st have it."

Valverde shook his head—a little sullenly.

"Sangre de Dios, man!" said Pizarro, impatiently. "What hath dulled thy wits? They were sharp enough e'en now. Ha! I have it. Thou art jealous because my plan deprives thee of the pleasure of roasting an emperor. Ha, ha! Is't not so, Valverde?"

There was no ring of merriment, though, in the harsh laugh, and a moment after Pizarro resumed—

"Hark ye, padre!—and I will put the case before thee in a few words. While I have the Inca under my hand, he shall still be treated with all the respect due to his station. Those shall have access to him whom he chooses to admit, and, in short, he will, to all appearance, be free. He is as timid as a child in my presence, and it will be easy to force him to give his people whatsoever orders I choose; thus shall I be the actual ruler of Peru!"

Valverde's brows over bent a little, and he nodded.

"With absolute power in my hands, and with the aid of the reinforcements that must soon arrive, the flag of Spain will float triumphant from one end of the empire to the other."

"And then hail, Francisco Pizarro—vice-king of the Golden Americas!" said del Soto, who had entered the tent unperceived.

"Ha! 'tis thou?" said Pizarro, not unpleased at the title which his lieutenant had bestowed upon him in advance. "What news, gallant Soto?"

"Little enough, commendatore—except that I have found it a hard matter to pick half a dozen men sober enough to mount guard."

"Souse the villains with water," good Soto; "drench them from head to foot—that will sober them, I warrant me. A plague upon them! they are mad with drink and greed to-night."

"If the Indians rallied, and had but courage to to attack us," said del Soto, "it would go hard with us."

"Little danger of that," returned Pizarro; "but barricade the entrances into the square, and train the cannon so as to command the path."

"I will see to it, Senor Pizarro—a holy night to you. Reverend padre, your blessing," replied del Soto, bending one knee before the monk.

"Benedicite mi fili," muttered the priest, as he touched del Soto's bowed head with the tips of his fingers; and so the lieutenant passed away.

"It hath been a day, glorious indeed for Spain, and for holy church," said Valverde, thoughtfully.

"True. Not one of my soldiers but is rich enough to purchase a patent of nobility, and become an hidalgo."

"Riches breed rebellion, saith the proverb."

"I have my men too well disciplined; but if they all deserted me, and I had to seek the camp barefoot, I should still be as wealthy as the richest king in Europe."

"How, sayest thou?"

"Rememberest thou that diamond that sparkled in the Inca's coronet, when first we entered the city?"

"Remember it?" said the priest, his own eyes lighting up with a strange fire. "Ay, that do I. Hast thou secured it, Pizarro?"

For answer, the Spanish commander opened a little ebony box, wherein lay the beautiful incomparable diamond.

"'Tis the price of a kingdom," said Valverde.

"And that will be the reward I shall ask from the king in exchange for this jewel," said Pizarro. "'Tis but an empty honour I ask from him, in exchange for a diamond that would make a priest barter his soul for the possession."

"Hold, Pizarro," exclaimed Valverde. "Thou art irreverent, and insult my priestly office."

"I meant no harm, reverend padre," said Pizarro, as he closed the box. "And now, good night; for, truth to tell, I am somewhat weary."

An hour later, and, except del Soto and the few sentries, all were asleep. The cries of woe and lamentation were hushed, and captor and captured alike were hushed in repose.

Pizarro's sleep, though, seemed troubled. He tossed and moaned, until suddenly he sprang up into a sitting posture, and glanced wildly, almost fearfully, around him.

The tent had been perfectly dark but a moment ago, now it was irradiated with a clear pale light; and, glancing at the little table by his bedside, Pizarro saw that the light streamed from the Devil's Diamond!

While yet he looked in wonder at this, something luminous, indefinable in form, hovered above the diamond, and at length took the shape of a human hand, its forefinger pointing to the diamond.

The Fiery Hand had come to warn or to threaten, Pizarro—which, we shall see.

CHAPTER XXVIII.

THE TWO WARNINGS—THE MYSTERY OF THE BURNING ARROW, AND THE PROTEST OF THE FIERY HAND—PIZARRO'S ATTACK—THE SPECTRAL HAND—THE SPANIARD LOSES THE DEVIL'S DIAMOND.

THE sight which had attracted our hero's attention, and caused him to utter that exclamation, was a bright meteor-like spark, which, suddenly making itself visible through the dense mist, described a graceful curve in the air, and, assuming the shape of a fiery arrow, fell noiselessly close to the feet of Richard of the Raven's Crest and his faithful Hubert.

Richard darted forward to the spot where the quivering light had seemed to strike the ground; but there was no trace of it—not a spark; not a smouldering ember.

"Get a brand from the watch-fire, Hubert!" said our hero; "this may be some signal—some warning."

The free-lance strode away, and in a few minutes returned with two flaming sticks of cedar wood, which cast a light upon the earth for yards round.

But still no trace of the fiery arrow could be found. Our hero was certain that he had marked the very spot where it had fallen; but neither his keen eyes, nor those of Hubert, could see aught but the bare earth.

"'Tis passing strange, Hubert," said our hero, "It must have been some exhalation of the mist, such as we have oft seen hovering over the rank-grown quags, or unwholesome marshes, in our own land."

"Nay," said Hubert, "more than once have I seen St. Elmo's fire and the witches' lantern, but this was none of them. Marked you not its shape, and how swiftly it sped through the air? Certes, Lord Richard, 'twas no will-o'-the-wisp or jack-o' lantern that settled there."

"Thine ancient comrade will be here anon," said Richard; "perchance he will be able to solve the mystery. Ha! here he comes."

Just then the stalwart form of the white chief appeared—ghost like—gliding through the mist towards them.

"What, Lord Richard!" he said, "still up and stirring. I thought by this time that ye had been soundly sleeping, preparing by a good refreshing slumber for the morning's toil.

"And so had I been, good William," returned our hero, "but for something strange that hath befallen us. Hearken, and interpret if thou canst!"

In a few words, Richard told of the mysterious appearance of the fiery arrow, and how the closest search had failed to discover any trace of it.

Even in the dim misty light our hero could see that a sudden change came over the countenance of the white chief—an expression of awe, almost of fear—while an involuntary shudder shook his powerful form.

"What is it, man? What ails thee?" demanded Richard. "What is there in the mystery of this fiery arrow to daunt thy stout heart."

"Alas, I know not," replied the white chief in faltering tones, "or if —— "

"Or if what, man?" said Richard, impatiently. "Are we children, to be frightened by some juggler's trick or phantasy of nature?"

"'Twas neither, noble Richard," said the white chief, in a low voice, as if he feared some unknown listener.

"What then, man? Speak!" said our hero, his own impetuosity chilled a little by the evident alarm of the white chief.

"It is a warning of danger, deep and deadly," he replied, solemnly. "From whence it comes, I know not; but it is familiar in the traditions of the Peruvians. Twice myself have I seen it, and each time some calamity, heavy and crushing, hath fallen on me."

"Is this so?" said our hero, slowly. His natural high courage led him to put little faith in tales of superstition and witchcraft; but he had himself seen things that he could not comprehend, and the grave and solemn manner of the white chief impressed him more deeply than he thought possible.

"Bah!" growled Hubert, aside—always as ready to oppose a friend in argument as an enemy in combat—"some old woman's tale, I warrant me. Old Will hath lived with these bare-legged, beardless Indians till he is little better than a school girl himself."

But neither Richard nor the white chief heeded

his words, if, indeed, they even heard them. Both were silent for a few minutes, and then our hero said—

"Be the omen for evil or good, Will, we flinch not from our duty. 'Twill but serve to make us the more vigilant—the more watchful. It shall ne'er be said that a sign from the powers of evil caused the cheek of Richard of the Raven's Crest to blanch, or his hand to falter."

"Gra'mercy! Well said, Lord Richard!" exclaimed Hubert. "A plague upon all old women's tales, say I, and the tellers, too."

"Silence, Hubert," said our hero, almost angrily. "William of Wyckham is as brave a man as thou art, and hath, no doubt, good reason for what he hath said."

"Doubt it not, noble sir," added the white chief, eagerly. "That danger threatens us, be sure; but be also confident that when it comes, Will of Wyckham will take his part as should a good man, true born, and bred on English soil."

"I will not gainsay thee there," said Hubert. "To do thee justice, Will, thou wert ever ready to give or take a cracked crown, since thou wert as high as my knee. But in those days there was no crying out of, 'Danger, danger; look to it!' if e'er a sheet of summer lightning flashed across the sky."

"Peace, Hubert, I say," cried Richard of the Raven's Crest, in that stern tone, which the freelance knew he must obey. "Get thee to thy tent, and prepare for the work thou wilt have to share at sunrise."

Hubert obeyed without a murmur, and, as he disappeared into the tent, the white chief spoke—

"His tongue is as rough as of old, noble Richard, but his heart is still as brave and faithful as his sword."

"Ay, that is it!" replied our hero, heartily. "But now, good William, if thy sentinels are to be depended on, let us rest, for I am weary, and would fain sleep."

"You may sleep soundly, noble sir," replied the white chief. "My Peruvians have the ears of cats and the noses of deer. Have no fear but that if any ordinary danger threaten us they will give the alarm in time."

"Good night then, Will; a safe and holy night to thee."

"And to thee, noble Richard, peace and safety," replied the white chief, as he returned our hero's hearty grip of the hand.

A quarter of an hour after the camp was wrapped in deep and tranquil slumber, save where the Indian sentries stood at their posts, motionless as statues, but vigilant as Argus the hundred-eyed.

* * * *

And how fared it with Pizarro, alone there in his tent—the solemn stillness of the night around him—the darkness illumed by the ghastly light of that mysterious hand, which, seemingly without substance, was yet so awfully visible to his strained eyes?

"This is some trick," he muttered—"some juggling, wherewith the false priests of the Inca think to fright me into restoring their monarch to freedom; but they shall see if Francisco Pizarro is the man to be fooled by a stale piece of mummery."

He leaped from his bed as he spoke, grasping his sword, which ever stood by his couch ready to his hand, unsheathed it, and dealt a tremendous blow at the apparition.

The effect was as strange as unexpected. Pizarro's sword—a Toledo blade, of the finest temper—was shivered to the hilt, and the Spanish commander was himself hurled so violently backward by some unseen force as to be almost deprived of sense.

Then, as in a vision, he saw the fiery hand lift the diamond—still blazing with its supernatural light—from the casket, hold it for a moment as it

were in triumph in the air, and then like a breath it was gone.

Pizarro remained for a moment half stunned and unable to arise from the corner where he had been hurled, but when he recovered the use of his limbs, and, loudly calling for lights, dashed forward and seized the casket, it was empty.

The diamond, worth the ransom of an emperor, had vanished!

———

CHAPTER XXIX.

RICHARD RECOVERS THE DIAMOND—THE SEARCH FOR THE "VILLANOUS SALTPETRE"—FOILED— RICHARD, BEWARE OF A TRAITOR!

OUR hero's slumber was short, but deep and dreamless as that of a little child.

Long ere the sun had sent his first ray darting from the east to dispel the chilling mist that covered the earth, Richard of the Raven's Crest awoke, strong and refreshed.

Yet he thought that he had slept long and was a laggard, for, gleaming through the tent was a brilliant ray, like that of a sunbeam, reflected from his casque, and darting its many-hued brightness a hundred different ways.

With a muttered imprecation upon himself for his tardiness, our hero leaped from his couch, and drew aside the curtained entrance to his tent.

To his amazement all was yet dark, and only the faintest glimmer in the east betokened the coming of the dawn.

With an exclamation of wonder and astonishment, Richard dropped the curtain and glanced once more within. The ray of light was as bright and beautiful as ever; but now it seemed to him to proceed *from* his casque, and not merely to be reflected *by* it.

In wonder and amaze, he stepped forward and lifted his casque from the ground, and there, by its side, contrasting strangely with the dark hue of the raven's plume, was the lost diamond.

Richard could scarce believe himself awake. He took the blazing jewel in his hand, and suffered the casque to drop with a crash to the ground.

"It is real," he said, half aloud. "I am awake and not dreaming. But how came this jewel here? Who could have placed it in my tent? Who could have wrested it from the power of the Inca or Pizarro?—who, by this time had, no doubt, claimed it as a prize. Hubert? No, that were impossible. The white chief? That could hardly be. He is not given to deceit, and had he the diamond he would have restored it to me openly."

Richard flung himself upon his couch again, the diamond still in his hand, and tried to think out the puzzle; but the more he strove, the less able was he to solve the mystery, until there flashed across his recollection the vision of the burning arrow.

"It is that mystic demon that guarded the treasure and first confided it to me who hath restored it to my hands," he exclaimed, starting to his feet. "Well, be it so; I accept the charge, and let him who next tries to wrest it from me beware."

But little, or we might say, no doubts existed in Richard's mind now as to the manner in which the jewel had been restored to him.

The recollection of his first meeting with the demon, the subsequent exhibition of its awful power upon the slave, had convinced him that some power more than mortal dwelt in or watched over the jewel.

There was no goldsmith or handicraftsman near, to set the jewel in our hero's casque, but he wrapped the diamond carefully in a piece of lining torn from his cloak, and placed the treasure in his doublet.

Then he essayed to sleep again, his right hand clasped tightly over the jewel, and when the white chief came to arouse him, he found him lying so, with a smile of calm content upon his face.

"Your slumbers are light, noble sir," said the white chief, as Richard started from the couch even at the tread of his almost noiseless footsteps; "I trust they have been as happy."

"Ay, marry have they, Will," responded our hero, cheerfully, as he buckled on his corslet, with Hubert's assistance, who had just entered the tent to wait upon his young master. "I have had dreams, good Will, that are better than reality, and a reality that would surpass all that thou ever dreamed of."

"'Tis a riddle, noble Richard," said the white chief, "and my dull brains might well addle themselves over the simplest, ere I guessed it."

"And thou, Hubert," said our hero, laughingly, "can'st thou not divine?"

The veteran free-lance only scratched his head surlily, but not a word spoke he.

"Well, I will leave the dream out of the riddle," said Richard of the Raven's Crest, "and show ye the reality, of which I told ye anon."

So saying, he drew the little package from his doublet, and, unfolding it, revealed the mystic diamond, in all its splendour. The rays of the rising sun were streaming through the opening of the tent, and lit up the jewel; but Richard thought that it had gleamed with equal beauty in the cold darkness of the night.

Both the men recognised it, as indeed any one who had ever seen it could not fail to do.

"The lost jewel of the Incas!" they exclaimed together.

"Ay," said Richard, "the lost jewel—the Devil's Diamond—buried for ages in a cavern, far beneath the earth, given to me by its demon guardian, wrested from me by the usurper, Huoscar, and now returned to me by——"

"By whom?" said Hubert and the white chief, in a breath.

"I'faith, I know not. But I shrewdly suspect it must have been brought hither by the same polite gentleman who first bestowed it on me."

"Hist, Master Richard," said Hubert, in alarm. "Speak not so of the evil one."

"And why not, 'faith?" laughed our hero. "Doth not the old rhyme say that the 'Devil is a gentleman?'"

"I love not to trifle with things holy or profane," grumbled Hubert, in a lower tone, as he withdrew himself further from the dangerous vicinity of the diamond; "and, as for that jewel, a murrain seize me if I would touch it, were it a hundred times as large and lustrous!"

"It seems to me, noble Richard," said the white chief, gravely, "that a great destiny, for good or ill, lies before you, as the possessor of that diamond. Whether you have done wisely in accepting it, coming, as it does, from the spirit of evil, you are the better judge. It is not for me to question your right to decide."

"For good or ill," replied our hero, firmly, "the stone is mine. I remember well the conditions which the demon guardian imposed; and, if I keep them not, may the curse he uttered light upon me. I know not yet the full power of the diamond—sure am I that it is undeveloped—and that, so long as my heart is pure, and my actions just, no harm can fall upon me."

"That is plain enough, without the aid of the evil one as interpreter," growled Hubert.

"Will thou never learn to check that wayward tongue of thine?" said Richard, sternly. "I' faith, thou deservest to share a cucking-stool with some old sheep."

"Pardon, noble master," stammered Hubert, growing crimson in the face at this rebuke; "I never thought to live in thy service all these years, and end by being likened to a village gossip."

"Then learn to control that unruly member, and

keep it 'twixt those old teeth of thine till thou art called upon to speak," said Richard, in a far sterner tone than he commonly used towards his favourite and faithful follower. "These are subjects upon which thy scurril jests are unseemly and unwelcome."

The free-lance said no more, but, like a mastiff that has been chastised by its master, he retired to a corner of the tent, there to await some sign or word that he had regained our hero's favour.

But Richard of the Raven's Crest had already forgotten the few sharp words that had passed between him and Hubert. The white chief quitted the tent to marshal his warriors for the expedition to the mountain caves, where he thought to find the saltpetre and the sulphur he required.

To save time—which, in their then condition, was precious—the men were divided into three parties, two under the command of experienced warriors who knew the district as well as the white chief, and the third under the orders of William of Wyckham himself.

One party was despatched to the plains some few miles beyond the spur of the mountain in search of wood fit to burn into charcoal; a second was instructed to ascend the sides of an extinct volcano, which reared its towering height immediately in front, to gather the sulphur which was present in immense quantities in the old craters; while the third, led by the white chief, sought out the saltpetre caves, the most difficult and dangerous task.

Of this last band our hero and Hubert formed part. Their way lay along the base of the mountain. Will asserted that he knew of the presence of saltpetre in the caves, and in masses weighing many hundredweights and even tons.

"Gra'mercy, Will," said Richard, "if what thou sayest proves true, we shall indeed be able to blow Pizarro and his band back to Spain with a more than royal salute."

"You laugh, noble Richard," said the white chief, gravely, "and, perchance, you are right; but my turn will come. This is no idle dream which hath taken my wits captive. I have had the thought in my head this many a year that I would teach the Peruvians the use of Friar Bacon's powder; but when the opportunity came I lacked time, and when I had time I lacked the opportunity, and so my resolution went for naught."

The path was now both difficult and dangerous to traverse, for winding spirally up the base of the mountain, and being encumbered with huge boulders and granite rocks, each man had enough to do to look to his footing, and conversation ceased, save when the white chief, who led the way, gave some caution or direction to our hero and Hubert, who were immediately behind.

Although they seemed to have ascended the mountain but to a comparatively small height, there yawned a fearful chasm on the left side of the path, if such it could be called.

More than once the united strength of the three Englishmen was required to hurl into the precipice some monstrous crag which blocked the path, and before they had proceeded half a mile, their hands and knees were torn and bleeding from contact with the rocks and boulders over which they had to climb.

"'Tis the earthquake that hath done this," said the white chief, halting to wipe the profuse perspiration from his brow. "When last I traversed it the path was as clear as the plains below."

"'Tis pity thou had'st not advised thyself of it, then, old comrade," growled Hubert, "and I for one would have been content to stay in camp and tend our cattle. 'Fore George, I have left a cloth yard measure of good English skin upon the craggy points of these rocks. A plague upon them, and on those who brought us here."

At this moment an exclamation of anger and disappointment broke from the white chief's lips, and he came to a sudden halt.

"What, good William," said our hero, "a fresh obstacle?"

"Ay, and an impassable one, Lord Richard," he replied bitterly. "The earthquake hath rent the pass in twain, and there yawns before us a gulf, which nothing but a miracle can bridge."

Our hero and Hubert approached as nearly as they could, for at that point, the pass only admitted of the passage of one traveller at a time, and, looking out beyond, saw that the path terminated in a tremendous precipice.

"What is to be done?" said Richard, breaking the silence after a few moments.

"There is nothing to be done but to turn back," replied the white chief. "By the saints, I would have rather lost a hundred marks in gold, than the time we have wasted here."

"And I," growled Hubert, "would rather have given two hundred than have lost the skin of my hands and knees. I'faith if those Indians are cannibals, I am ready flayed for roasting, and they can truss me for supper."

"Peace! Hubert, peace! Will that malapert tongue of thine never cease to wag against all reason or order? Well, good William," he added, turning to the white chief, "since better may not be, we must return. Give thy men the word of command. See, they are swarming up, and will push us over the precipice, else."

Reluctantly enough the word was given, and, in reversed order, the party marched—or, to speak more truthfully, scrambled back again.

It was a silent and melancholy journey enough, relieved only by the grumblings of Hubert, who failed not, upon every opportunity, to indulge himself by heaping anathemas upon the boulders, the sharp-pointed rocks, the white chief, and everything and everybody.

He was now unchecked by Richard, for our hero's thoughts were deeply occupied with his future. Since he had recovered possession of the diamond, a strong feeling of hope and confidence had sprung up within his breast—it was as if he had drunk strong wine—his courage and his strength seemed to increase.

When they reached the camp, they found that the other parties had returned successful—the one laden with logs of wood, admirably adapted for conversion into charcoal—the other burdened with huge masses of the crystallised sulphur.

"If thy fortune had been as good," said our hero with a smile, "we might have made this wonderful experiment, whereby Pizarro was to be blown into the sea."

"As it is," growled Hubert, "we went on a fool's errand and have got fools' pay."

"I am not beaten yet," returned William of Wyckham. "Yonder was but one of many places where saltpetre abounds; but it was the nearest and easiest of access."

"Be advised, good William," said our hero. "Give up this mad adventure. Let us ride back to the city and confront Pizarro as Englishmen should, with a defiance on our lips and our swords in our hands."

"You promised me the day, noble Richard," pleaded the white chief. "If, ere the sun sets, success reward not my efforts, then will I follow you whithersoever and wheresoever you list."

"Be it so," said Richard. "I gave thee my word; but do thy best in the time, for no earthly power shall induce me to extend it."

With a brightened and more hopeful countenance, the white chief tendered his thanks to our hero, and issued his orders in rapid succession.

He called forth twenty of his most tried and trusty warriors; nineteen answered, but Pincatl, the twentieth, came not forward to the call.

"Where is he? Where is Pincatl?" said the white chief, anxiously. "I have need of him, for he alone—besides myself—knows the way to the caves."

Messengers were sent through the camp in search of him. The air resounded with his name, but the Peruvian came not.

"This is passing strange," said the white chief, thoughtfully. "But an hour agone he was close by my side, as we descended the mountain."

"I'faith," growled Hubert, "it's easy now to tell where the poor Indian hath gone; he descended the mountain a little quicker than we did by tumbling over the edge."

"Thy tale may be the true one," said the white chief; "but if it is, surely some of those with him must have seen him fall. I will put the question."

Each one of the band who had accompanied the white chief on that fruitless expedition was questioned. Some few of them had seen him; the rest had not. He had disappeared from amongst them suddenly, but how or where none could tell.

This fresh mystery damped for a time the spirits of the leader; but what would they have thought and said had they known that Pincatl was a traitor, and, that instead of lying crushed into a shapeless mass at the bottom of the precipice, he was even then speeding towards Pizarro as fast as his false feet would take him.

CHAPTER XXX.
BETRAYED!

MEANWHILE the white chief pushed on his preparations with as much rapidity as possible, for he knew that with the utmost diligence he could hardly hope to achieve the task by sunset.

"The path is an easier and pleasanter one this time," said the white chief.

"'Fore George! it need be," said Hubert, "or the plague catch me if I travel by it."

"Yonder," continued the chief, pointing to a narrow mountain gorge, "it lies. 'Tis a stream which flows through the very heart of the mountain, almost to the gates of the city."

"Excellent," said Richard of the Raven's Crest, with a quiet smile. "Then, Will, if thou fail for the second time in gathering the precious saltpetre, we can e'en sail on, and meet our enemy."

"'Tis easy to say sail on," commented Hubert; "but, I warrant me, that Will of Wyckham hath no galleon wherewith to sail."

"Hold thy fears, old croaker," returned the white chief, angrily. "There are other means for traversing the waters besides the galleons against which thy addled pate is knocking itself."

"Ay, we can stick a spear shaft atween our legs, and swim on that, even as Gammer Sanders was seen to ride to the moon with a broomstick between her hams."

"How propose you going then, Will?" asked our hero.

"A raft will answer our need, noble Richard," replied the white chief. "'Tis but the cutting down of a few young trees, and the bursting of a few llianas, to serve as rope, and we are fitted."

"And how many of thy men intendest thou to take with thee?"

"None, noble Richard. The raft will be so laden with the saltpetre, that I propose to take none with me save—well, save Hubert; but he hath grown so cross grained, that I care not to ask him."

"'Twould be labour wasted," growled the freelance, who was uncommonly ill-tempered. "My hose and jerkin are torn to shreds now, and I feel as if I had been flayed."

"Then will I be your companion, Will," said Richard; "and as for thee, Hubert, doff thy jerkin and hose, and don the white chief's tunic and sandals; for the nonce thou hast changed places."

"If I do," began Hubert, surlily, "may I——"

"Obey!" said Richard, in that low, stern voice which had, ere that, made many a man quail before him. And, without another word, the free-lance submitted.

A few of the logs, which had been gathered for such a different purpose, were collected, and, under the white chief's directions, formed into a light, yet strong raft, upon the borders of the mountain torrent which they were to descend.

Their equipment was light. A long pole, to steer the raft, and for arms Richard's good sword and a cross-bow, many of which they had found attached to the saddle bows of the captured horses.

The hearty English hurrah cheered them as they pushed out into the stream. The Peruvians were not given to such emotional observances, and, as for Hubert, he was sulky, and uttered nothing more audible than a growled-out anathema upon the whole affair, his master alone excepted.

"And even he," mumbled the free-lance, as he looked down upon his stalwart limbs—bare, save for the slight feather-cloth tunic and the skin sandals—"methinks Lord Richard might have made a merrier jest than to have stripped his old follower of his christian garments, and dressed him out like a mummer or a Jack Pudding."

But thoughts quite different were occupying our hero's mind, as he and the white chief, transformed into the likeness of Hubert, sped slowly but steadily down the lazy current of the mountain stream.

For more than a mile, the stream ran straight, and the craft required no attention from Richard's keen eye or strong hand, but after that the channel became narrow and winding, with sharp curves, which required both skill and courage to encounter.

"We are now nearing the caves," said the white chief, who had been eagerly scouring the landmarks as they slowly flitted by. "Give me the pole, Sir Richard—'twill be safest for me to guide the raft through the darkness of the underground passage."

"Be it as thou wilt, good William," replied our hero; "and what is to be my task?"

"An easy one, good my lord," replied the white chief. "Simply to lie still till I give the word that the goal is reached."

"Well, well," exclaimed our hero, with a laugh, "I have performed more difficult tasks than that in my time, so with thy good leave, Master William, I will snatch half an hour of that repose of which thou robbed me this very morn."

To a young and hardy warrior, such as our hero may well claim to be, a couch of rough uneasy logs affords as delicate a means to slumber as a down bed.

The best proof of this he gave by throwing himself down on the forepart of the raft, and in less than five minutes his deep regular breathing gave token that he slept the deep profound slumber of youth and health.

How long he slept he knew not, but he was roused by a cry from his companion—a cry of alarm and warning.

Richard of the Raven's Crest was awake in an instant, and springing to his feet, felt hastily for the hilt of his sword.

When he had cast himself down to rest, the raft had been at the entrance of the underground taverns, and he had closed his eyes in a darkness as deep as that of the blackest midnight.

Now, however, all was light again, the raft rocked to and fro uneasily on a swift, strong current, and, looking ahead, Richard saw that they were drifting on to a point where were stationed some dozen men armed to the teeth.

It needed but that one glance to tell Richard that the armed men were Pizarro and some of his picked spearmen. That same glance told the white chief that he had been betrayed. The missing warrior, Pincatl, had done his work only too swiftly and too well!

"We are betrayed!" said the white chief, in a breathless voice. "See, noble Richard, if thy strength will prevail against the current for awhile."

Our hero ran to the fore part of the raft, and plunged the pole deep into the turbid current of the stream. For a moment, the way of the raft was checked—it swayed uneasily to and fro, then, with a sharp crack, the pole snapped in two, and the raft was precipitated onwards to its fate!

CHAPTER XXXI.

THE DEFIANCE—THE CHALLENGE ACCEPTED—WILL OF WYCKHAM AT WORK—THE MYSTERIOUS VISIT—THE DUEL TO THE DEATH BETWEEN RICHARD OF THE RAVEN'S CREST AND PIZARRO.

DESTRUCTION seemed inevitable. There were Pizarro, his spearmen, and musketeers waiting quietly for the moment when the raft should strike upon the rock, and deliver its occupants into their power.

Richard drew his sword, and, placing the blade between his teeth, strove hard with the broken fragment of the pole to steer the raft away; but his efforts were of no avail.

The white chief—whom the Spaniards mistook for Hubert, recognising the costume—seized the cross-bow, and a deadly look came over his face as he fitted the quarrel* in its groove.

Just then a voice behind Richard seemed to whisper in his ear—

"Thou art in deadly peril. Essay the power of the diamond."

Our hero started, and turned, but no one was there. He shuddered though, slightly, for he had recognised the voice—it was that of the Demon of the Diamond!

The wish came involuntarily into his mind that the raft might be floated into some place out of Pizarro's reach.

It was hardly half formed in his brain, when a sudden whirl or eddy turned the raft aside, swept it across the stream, and wedged it securely amongst the rocks.

It was only just in time, for already a dozen eager hands were outstretched to grasp the raft.

A bitter curse broke from Pizarro's lips, followed by the hoarse execrations of the soldiers. The channel was there not more then twenty yards wide, and the slightest sound was audible, echoed by the high rocky walls of the stream.

"Ha, Pizarro!" said our hero, tauntingly. "You are foiled again. Treachery ever meets with its just reward."

"And be sure," returned the Spaniard, gnawing his big moustache savagely, and speaking between his clenched teeth, "that thou wilt meet with thine, thou English braggart. Even now thou art in my power; for think not that the width of this narrow stream shall save thee from my wrath."

"I am not in thy power, false Spaniard," said our hero, haughtily. "Now and for ever, I defy thee."

"What! thou darest," exclaimed Pizarro, in a passion of wrath. "I meant, thou English cub, to have taken thee alive, and to have given thee a fair trial before thy peers for the treason and other wrongs thou hast been guilty of; but now, thou and that villain follower of thine, shall surely die, with all thy sins upon thy head."

He waved his hand to his musketeers, who coming to the front, knelt down to take the steadier aim; and our hero, as he stood there erect,

---

* A heavy square-headed iron bolt, used in the strongest kind of cross-bow.

could see the red sparks glow as the Spaniards blew them.

"Down, noble Richard, down!" said the white chief, in a low voice. "Here behind this rock we shall be safe, and I can bring down a few of them with my cross-bow."

But our hero paid no heed to the warning; there he stood, looking the very perfection of manly beauty in the first blush of its healthful spring. There he stood, unflinchingly, regarding his enemies with a scornful smile.

"Say, Richard of the Raven's Crest," said Pizarro; "I will give thee one last chance. If thou wilt yield and submit to me, all things shall be as they were. The past shall be forgotten."

"Never, thou murderous dog!"

That was enough. With a deadly scowl of hate, Pizarro fell back, and gave the word to fire.

There was a moment's pause; three bright jets of flame, three puffs of dense white smoke, which for a moment hid the combatants from each other; three sharp reports, echoed again and again by the rocky walls, until the noise was like that of a distant battle.

The smoke cleared away. Pizarro sprang eagerly forward, certain to see his enemy dead, or writhing in the pangs of dissolution; but no, there he still stood—his arms folded on his breast, a scornful smile wreathing his face and lips.

"Muerte de Dios!" exclaimed Pizarro, as he half drew his sword and turned savagely on the musketeers. "Ye are but old women, to miss such a mark at a score of paces. Load again, ye sons of dogs, and see that ye aim better."

"Spare thy pains, Pizarro," said our hero. "Thou canst not harm me, though I, by lifting my hand, could strike thee dead beyond hope of recall. Now, listen to what I have to say: I know thee to be a brave man, though a bad one. Wilt thou here accept my challenge to meet in combat, three days hence, on the plain in front of the golden gates of Caxamalca? If thou subduest me, I swear by my knightly honour to do thee good suit and service, and to be thy obedient follower in all things. If I prove the conqueror, thou shalt submit to whatsoever terms I shall dictate."

"No!" thundered Pizarro. "I will meet thee, Richard of the Raven's Crest; but it must be a duel to the death. If thou fall, I swear not to spare thy life, though the holy father himself interceded for thee."

"Be it so," replied Richard, calmly; "but beware, Pizarro, of treachery. Though I shall come to the lists with but one, or perchance two followers, I wield a power that thou knowest not of—and now, farewell."

With a vigorous push of his foot, Richard launched the raft once more into the stream, when, to the white chief's intense astonishment, and even awe, it drifted up the current with a steadiness and rapidity that needed neither urging nor guiding.

"A miracle!" exclaimed William of Wyckham.

"Nay, the tide hath but turned—'tis nothing unusual in these mountain streams, Will."

"And the saltpetre, good my lord?"

"Do what thou wilt," replied Richard. "Thou hast three more days in which to do thy work. I will not hinder thee."

* * * *

The time passed away slowly enough for our hero. William of Wyckham had found saltpetre enough for his purpose, and, to his joy, succeeded in his experiment. On the evening of the second day, the warriors under his directions had prepared powder enough to blow up the mountains.

It was on the evening of the second day, too, that a strange circumstance happened to our hero. He had been regretting with Hubert the fact that his armour was not in a fit condition—nor indeed complete enough—to enable him to encounter Pizarro on equal terms; and his sword—good weapon and

true though it was—hardly fitted to parry th blows of Pizarro's huge battle-axe.

When, after sunset he entered his tent and foun upon his couch a complete suit of Milan steel complete to the smallest detail—and a huge two handed sword, his surprise may be imagined, bu it did not last long. The vast power wielded by th possessor of the mystic diamond was just beginnin to dawn upon him.

At last the morning of the third day broke, an when our hero, garbed in his splendid steel armou inlaid with gold, crossed from his tent and spran with a bound into the saddle of his noble whit horse, a tremendous cheer broke forth even from the usually taciturn Peruvians.

It was echoed by a hearty English hurrah from Hubert and the white chief; and as the esquir mounted to follow his master, he said to his ol comrade—

"If Pizarro fall not beneath his sword this day good Will, I will be content to forfeit my hopes o paradise."

"God speed him!" returned the white chief heartily.

And so, in the brilliant sunlight of that beautifu morning, Richard of the Raven's Crest went forth to do battle with the mighty and all-conquerin Pizarro.

———

CHAPTER XXXII.

THE ARRIVAL OF OUR HERO AND HUBERT AT THE GOLDEN GATES OF CAXAMALCA—THE PRELUDE TO THE COMBAT—THE FIGHT ON HORSEBACK—PIZARRO DEFEATED—RICHARD'S GENEROUS CONDUCT—THE DUEL, FOOT TO FOOT AND HAND TO HAND — PIZARRO'S LAST STRATAGEM — OUR HERO'S VICTORY.

FOR some distance, our hero and Hubert rode on in silence, Richard thinking, with "the stern joy that warriors feel, in foemen worthy of their steel," of his approaching encounter with Pizarro.

Hubert's thoughts, too, were similarly occupied. As our hero's esquire, he bore the ponderous two-handed sword balanced on his shoulder, and, as he felt the weight of that mighty weapon, he smiled grimly, and already pictured to himself the Spanish leader lying shattered and bleeding on the ground, and Richard of the Raven's Crest waving the weapon triumphantly above his foe.

Another five miles were passed in the same dull silence, and then Hubert broke it by a loud cough, which was evidently designed to attract the attention of his young master.

"Ha, Hubert," said our hero, turning in hi saddle, without checking his horse, "what wa that, man?"

"Nothing, Lord Richard, except that I was wondering how Pizarro will like one downward stroke of this good sword."

"Wait and see, good Hubert," replied our hero. "The blow hath yet to be delivered."

"True," said Hubert, significantly. "And who can tell whether he will meet you and abide it?"

"Go to, man," replied Richard, a little sharply. "Pizarro is a brave soldier, and hates me too much not to keep his word."

"But if he hate you so much, Lord Richard, that he will *not* keep his word?"

"What mean you, Hubert?" said our hero, checking his steed, so as to allow his esquire to come up with him.

"Why, this simply," replied Hubert, "that Pizarro regards his word as of no more value than the empty breath that utters it, and that, instead of an honourable antagonist, ready to meet you, foot to foot, and sword to sword, you may only encounter a score of desperadoes, each with a dagger for your back, or a musket bullet for your head."

"Enough of that, Hubert," said our hero. "I tell thee I am resolved to meet Pizarro in single combat, and meet me he shall. If he contemplates treachery, I have that in my possession which will shield me from all harm, and bring ruin and confusion down upon him."

The free-lance uttered a half-articulate growl, expressive of his dissatisfaction at his young master's resolve, but he dropped behind again into his place, and spoke no word until the mountain defile was reached, and they were within sight of the golden gates of Caxamalca.

A quick flush rose to the handsome face of Richard of the Raven's Crest, as he saw that such preparations had been made for the tourney as the time and place afforded.

A large circular space had been cleared and levelled, so that no obstructions should cause the horses to stumble, and, enclosing this on one side, were the chosen warriors of Huoscar, now under Pizarro's rule, while on the other was a formidable body of Spaniards, some on horseback, fully equipped, while the foot soldiers, not less than two hundred in number, were heavily armed with spears, cross-bows, and musquetoons.

"By my patron saint," muttered Richard of the Raven's Crest, "Pizarro hath not let his time lie idle. His reinforcements have arrived; but it matters not. Were the whole chivalry of Spain at his back I would defy him."

So saying, he spurred forward, and making his horse execute many a caracole and demi-volte, and a dozen other tricks of the manège, in which the knights of the chivalrous ages were wont to exhibit their dexterity, our hero moved out into the open.

It was evident that he was expected and watched for, as, scarcely had his stately figure been in view a moment, than the Spanish trumpeters sounded a clear defiant blast, which was almost instantly responded to from within the city. The gates were thrown open, and Pizarro appeared, accompanied by his brother and his principal officers.

The stalwart, powerful figure of the Spanish commander was encased in a complete suit of black armour—even the huge battle-axe, which hung at his saddle-bow, was of the same sombre hue. His horse, too, a splendid Andalusian, had not a single white hair to mar the uniform beauty of its jetty coat. Grim and sombre, sitting on his steed upright and motionless as a statue, Pizarro seemed the very personification of Death the destroyer.

Almost at the same moment, Richard and Pizarro entered the lists from opposite sides, and reining in their horses, looked steadily at one another. The Spanish commander kept his visor down, but our hero could *feel* that the dark eyes of his enemy were bent upon him with a steady gaze.

There was a pause for a few moments, and then del Soto, taking upon himself the office of marshal of the lists, dismounted, and, walking into the centre of the ground, spoke in a loud clear voice—

"I call upon Richard Plantaganet, commonly known as Richard of the Raven's Crest, to come forward and justify with his body the challenge he hath given unto Don Francisco Pizarro, a true subject and faithful servant of the most high and mighty Charles, Emperor of Spain."

Our hero's voice, clear and musical as the notes of a silver clarion, rang out in reply, as he dismounted and advanced into the lists—

"I am here," he said, "ready to prove, my body against his, that Francisco Pizarro is a false and disloyal traitor, an assassin and a liar, and in token thereof I throw down my gage."

Then, concluding with the awful and solemn oath, with which it was necessary that the combatants should bind themselves to the truth of their statements, Richard of the Raven's Crest cast his gauntlet down before him, and drew his stately form up to its full height, looking half sternly,

half scornfully at Pizarro, whose turn it was now to utter his defiance.

The marshal of the lists now turned to where he still sat motionless upon his black charger.

"Don Francisco Pizarro, Adelantado* of the Golden Americas, you have heard the defiance of Richard of the Raven's Crest. Do you acknowledge that his accusations are true, or do you take up the gage he hath cast down?"

The sombre figure, hitherto so motionless, became in a moment animate. Despite his heavy armour, Pizarro vaulted easily from his saddle, and, taking up his place by the side of del Soto, raised his right hand heavenward.

"By all that I hold most sacred," he began, in his deep, stern voice—"by the true Cross—by the holy Mother of Him who died upon it—by mine own honour—I swear that Richard of the Raven' Crest hath foully lied, and I here present myself—my body against his on foot or on horseback, to prove that I have spoken the truth, in token whereof I take up his gage, and thus return it."

So saying, Pizarro picked up the gauntlet, held it aloft for a moment, and then hurled it with a contemptuous gesture at our hero's feet.

In taking the oath, Pizarro, according to the rules of the lists, had been obliged to raise his visor, and, while he gave utterance to his defiance, Richard's eyes had not left his countenance for a moment.

It was pale—our hero noted that—the natural swarthy hue of the Spaniard had changed into a dull greenish pallor, but not a muscle of his face twitched or betrayed the least sign of remorse or fear.

"Be it so," said Richard to himself as he turned and walked back to his horse. "He comes to the fight perjured—with a lie upon his lips—to which he has called all that is most holy to bear witness. He will die as he hath lived—accursed."

Hubert was standing by our hero's noble white charger, his veteran cheeks aglow with pride and hope, for he had seen by what had passed—though he understood not the language—that Pizarro had not turned craven at the last moment, and that the combat would take place.

"Ha, Lord Richard!" he said eagerly, "right glad am I that all my prophecy went for naught. Let me look once more to your harness. A loose rivet, or a neglected brace, hath oft caused many a good knight to go down before his weaker enemy."

With practised eye and hand, the veteran tested every joint of his young master's armour, but there was no fault. Gorget, cuirass, and all were perfectly secure, and t played as freely as though they were made of s k.

It was indeed a strange sight to witness the solemn preparations made for that duel to the death, in the heart of a foreign country, in the midst of a strange people.

The Peruvians stood where they had been stationed, leaning on their bows and spears, looking on in silent awe and wonder at these proceedings, so strange and novel to them. The Spaniards were equally silent, for, according to the rules of the lists, it was death to anyone to laugh, groan, cry aloud, or do anything to distract the attention of the combatants after the defiances were exchanged.

And now the supreme moment had arrived at last. The master of the lists, del Soto, retired to the side, and now cried three times at measured intervals.

"Do your devoir,† good knights."

At the third time, both Richard of the Raven's

---

* Adelantado—Lieutenant-Governor—a title equivalent to that of Governor-General of India, for example; but conveying with it almost irresponsible power.

† Devoir. Literally, "duty." It signified in the language of chivalry, that each combatant was to fight his hardest for the cause he thought just.

Crest and Pizarro vaulted lightly into their saddles, encumbered with heavy armour though they were.

Then del Soto lifted Richard's glove—the gage of defiance—above his head, and flung it into the middle of the lists, calling out as he did so—

"Laissez-aller !"*

As if they had been launched simultaneously by some mighty force, the two horses bounded forth into the lists, snorting, tossing their proud heads, and breathing the smoke of battle from their red nostrils. It seemed, indeed, as if they too were inspired by the hate that burned in the bosoms of their riders.

Pizarro came on, his visor down, his huge battle-axe gripped in both hands, to deal one terrible blow that should end the strife at once.

Richard, dropping the reins upon his horse's neck, rested his huge two-handed sword easily upon his left shoulder. His visor was raised, and his bright blue eyes had an ominous glitter in them.

They were within a few yards of one another. The clouds of dust flung up by each horse's hoofs were mingling, when suddenly Pizarro rose in his stirrups, and, swinging the battle-axe high above his head, discharged a terrible blow full upon our hero's crest.

But Richard had seen the movement, quick as it was made. Like unto a flash of lightning his two-handed sword swept round and met Pizarro's blow.

There was a clear metallic ringing sound, like that from some huge anvil stricken by a Titan's hammer, a shower of sparks, and then, when the whirlwind of dust had cleared away, the spectators saw Richard sitting upright, unharmed, upon his noble steed; while Pizarro, half unhorsed by the shock, was clinging to his bridle, and glaring with a look of shame and rage at his useless weapon lying on the ground, its ponderous head shorn off by that good blow of Richard's.

By all the laws of the lists our hero had now a perfect right to have ridden up to Pizarro, and to have slain him without pity or remorse; but such butchery was not for him to do. His foe must be stricken down weapon in hand, on equal terms.

"Give him another battle-axe, or what arm he listeth," cried our hero. "I will not slay a defence-less man; and see, Pizarro, that thou choosest one that will not fail thee, for by God's light my blood is up, and I strike hard and home."

"Fool !" muttered Pizarro, as he leaped from his horse, and glanced over the pile of arms they had brought him; "thou hast thrown away thine only chance. Here is a weapon steel from blade to hilt; let us see if thou canst shred this like an onion. Give the signal, del Soto," he added. "I burn to avenge this insult on yonder smooth-faced cub."

He vaulted into his saddle, and waved the ponderous weapon aloft, notched already in a dozen places. Del Soto gave the signal, and once again our hero and Pizarro swept down upon each other.

This time Richard struck the first blow, but so lightly and carelessly did he appear to deliver it that it seemed as if a child might have parried it.

It was only in appearance though, for as Pizarro raised his axe to ward the blow, it was dashed aside like a reed, and, alighting on Pizarro's helmet, hurled its wearer to the ground.

A second time was the life of his enemy in Richard's hands, and a second time did he spare it. He knew quite well that he was galling his desperate foe to madness, and this was our hero's aim. He would first make him mad with rage, and then laying him at his feet, dictate to him such terms as a conqueror exacts from the vanquished.

Pizarro was perfectly livid with wrath. He looked more like a corpse than a living man, heightened as the effect of his pallor was by the dull blackness of his armour.

* Laissez aller. Literally, "let go." Equivalent to our English military word of command, "Charge."

Again the Spaniards expected to see Richard ride up and dispatch his foe, and again were they wrong in their surmise.

He dismounted, gave his noble charger, who had borne him so gallantly, to Hubert to lead away, and then approaching Pizarro, he said with a touch of mocking sarcasm in his voice—

"Holà, Senor Pizarro. It seems that thy horse is restive, or thy seat in the saddle not so firm as of old. See, I have dismounted. Let us finish this quarrel foot to foot and hand to hand."

"Sangre de Dios !" hissed the Spaniard between his clenched teeth, and his dark eyes seemed literally to blaze with fire as he spoke. "I know not what demon hath aided thee, Richard of the Raven's Crest, but beware, for thou hast raised a devil in my breast, which nothing less than thy life's blood will appease."

"And do thou beware, Pizarro !" replied our hero, sternly. "Twice hath thy life been in my hands since we began this combat; beware the third !"

Then turning away, he retreated a few paces, and leaning on the cross of his two-handed sword, waited while del Soto and Benalcazar re-adjusted his armour and renewed the rivets of the gorget, which our hero's last blow had loosened.

"What ails thee, Pizarro ?" del Soto ventured to ask in a low tone; but his leader only answered by a bitter execration, and bade him hasten.

This time no signal was given to the combatants—none was needed. Richard was ready there in the centre of the lists, calm and relentless as Fate, waiting for Pizarro, as he came slowly forward, crouched like a leopard for its spring.

For now the Spaniard thought he had the advantage: his greater weight, the more firmly-knitted muscles of manhood, and above all his skill in the use of the weapon he wielded, must give him the superiority over his youthful enemy.

But he knew not yet the full strength that lay in those limbs, shapely as Antinous', but strong as Hercules; and above all he forgot the blood that coursed in Richard's veins—one drop of Cœur de Lion's blood would have made a hero of a cripple.

All the art of which he was master he tried this time upon his foe, conceiving that one well-delivered blow would render him the victor; for no armour ever made by mortal hands, could withstand the shock of that steel axe wielded by his arms.

Richard acted entirely on the defensive, anticipating Pizarro's feints by evading a blow wherever it was delivered, with the languid ease of an accomplished boxer who finds himself attacked by a novice.

A very little of this began to tell even upon the Spaniard's hardened frame; the sun was intensely hot, and the weight of his armour and of his weapon began to tell heavily upon him.

He could see, too—and this enraged him most—that Richard was playing with him. It was torturing, maddening to his proud spirit, and urged him to what his cooler judgment would never have allowed him to do.

Advancing by imperceptible degrees till he was almost within range of the terrible two-handed sword, Pizarro set his teeth hard, contracted every muscle of his powerful frame, and collecting all his strength for one supreme effort, whirled the ponderous battle-axe as if it had been a feather, and rained down a shower of blows upon his enemy.

Any one of those, if it had struck our hero full and fairly, would surely have levelled him with the ground, and decided the fate of the combat; but now his lightness of foot and quickness of eye stood him in good stead.

Leaping to one side, he evaded the first tre-mendous down stroke; a second he parried with his sword, but so great was its force that his ward was only partially successful, and the broad blade of the axe dinted his helmet; a third and fourth he parried with more ease, and then a hot flush rose to his temples, and he decided that the time was come to end the combat.

Pizarro's blows still fell, but slow and weak in comparison with his first onslaught. Our hero watched his opportunity, and when Pizarro's axe was raised aloft, his sword flashed out with resistless force, and hurled the weapon from his grasp far out into the field.

Again that mighty sword came down—his helmet was stricken from his head and rolled away into the sand; while there, gasping on the ground, a defeated and disgraced man, lay Pizarro, the mighty conqueror of Peru, with Richard of the Raven's Crest, his conqueror, towering above him like a demi-god!

CHAPTER XXXIII.

RICHARD THE CONQUEROR—THE FIRST FLUSH OF VICTORY—OUR HERO DEMANDS FROM PIZARRO THE FULFILMENT OF THE CONDITIONS—PIZARRO YIELDS—HAIL TO THE NEW GOVERNOR OF PERU!

A LOW murmur, almost inaudible—a sound like the sighing of a gentle breeze amidst branches of a great forest—arose from the spectators as they saw Pizarro fall, and then a breathless awe inspired silence.

Richard stood there for a moment, his sword uplifted, his handsome face flushed with the exertion, but wearing a look of scornful triumph as he looked at Pizarro laid so low at last, and by his hand.

The Spaniards kept their positions still, both officers and men, for so great was the respect entertained for the laws which governed the trial by combat that none interfered, though they could even then have saved Pizarro's life. This only they resolved, that when the blow was struck that ended their leader's career, Richard himself should surely die.

But for the third time, to their intense surprise, our hero lowered the sword, one thrust of which could have rid him for ever of his enemy, and looking towards del Soto, Benalcazar, and Ferdinand, beckoned them to him with his mailed right hand.

They came, wondering what new scene in this tragedy they were to behold.

"Senors," said Richard, with that quiet dignity which sate so well upon him, "there is your leader vanquished by my hand in fair and open fight, as ye have seen. By list and by law his body is mine, to dispose of even as I choose."*

The Spaniards nodded sullenly. They could make no other reply.

"Three times have I spared his life, when I might in justice have taken it as his victor. I have called you to let you hear my reasons. But first get your leader some wine or water and revive him."

"To what end, Senor Englishman?" said del Soto, sullenly. "It is thy intention to dispatch him—do it now ere he wakes to the consciousness of the disgrace that hath befallen him."

"Fetch hither wine or water," said Richard again, in that commanding voice which few men cared to hear and disobey. "Ha! here comes Padre Valverde; he will have some cordial fitted for the purpose."

The wily Valverde had been lingering on the outskirts of the lists, watching the combat, and

* One of the rules governing the practice of trial by battle was that the victor, if his adversary was still living after confessing himself vanquished, should have power to dispose of his enemy as he pleased, even to burning or dismembering him—it being considered that he, as a perjured man, had no claim to mercy either in this world or the next.

calculating how he might best turn the issue to advantage which ever side fortune favoured. Our hero was the victor, and now he cringed before him in humble salutation.

"Benedicite," he murmured softly, as he approached. "Is it the last offices of holy Church you ask for yonder dying man? Alas! I dare not give them. The issue of the fight hath proved that he is perjured. Accursed be he therefore. Anathema maranatha——"

"Hold, sir priest," said Richard, interrupting Valverde; "your offices are desired, but neither for cursing nor blessing. Hast thou about thee any elixir or cordial which will restore Pizarro from this faint?"

Padre Valverde rapidly produced from the bosom of his robe a small phial, which he unstoppered, and held for an instant to Pizarro's nostrils.

The effect was instantaneous. The Spanish leader opened his eyes, raised himself upon his elbow, and glared wildly around him.

"Where am I?" he gasped, feebly. "Is this death? Ha! I remember."

His eyes had rested for a single instant upon the noble form of our hero bending over him, and he sank back with a groan, wrung from him by shame—not pain.

"Thou art here, Pizarro," said Richard—"here, in the lists, where thou hast fallen—conquered by my hand. Dost thou remember our compact?"

Pizarro opened his sunken eyes, and fixed them upon Richard with a look of the deadliest hatred, as he replied, sternly—

"Ay, I remember it. I swore that if the victory was mine, I would show thee no mercy—and I would have kept my word."

"Thou art a rash man to taunt an enemy whose foot is on thy breast, and whose sword point is at thy throat," said our hero, sternly. "But call to thy remembrance, Pizarro, what I said would be thy fate if the victory fell to my lot?"

"Say on," replied Pizarro, sullenly; "or, better still, complete thy work, and end my disgrace and my life at once."

"Such is not my purpose," said Richard of the Raven's Crest. "I spoke at the time when thou most treacherously waylaid me in the mountains, of certain conditions that I should impose. Wilt thou hear them?"

"Ay," replied Pizarro; "but be brief."

"The first condition that I impose upon thee, in return for sparing thy life, and thy soul too, seeing that the reverend padre has refused to perform the last offices of holy Church over thy body, is that thou quittest this country at once."

Pizarro started, and a faint flush of red tinged the deathly pallor of his cheeks, but he made no answer.

"Yes or no—answer quickly," said Richard of the Raven's Crest, raising his sword. "Ha! stand back, senors; if one of you but stir a finger to meddle with my just rights, I will cleave him to the chine. Answer, Pizarro, yes or no."

"Yes, since it must be," was Pizarro's answer, given in a tone so low, as to be scarce audible.

"Secondly," continued our hero, "I require that you depute to me your authority—absolutely, I holding myself responsible only to your master, Charles, Emperor of Spain."

Again the faint voice of the humbled Spaniard expressed assent.

"It is enough!" said our hero, triumphantly. "You have heard, senors. Henceforth, you will obey me as your leader, for hath not Pizarro so spoken, and given his plighted word?"

Conquered and humbled though he was, the words of Pizarro still carried sufficient weight with them to make him obeyed, and, one by one, the officers swore allegiance to Richard of the Raven's Crest on the cross-hilt of his sword.

"It is well," exclaimed our hero. "Rapine and plunder shall no longer desolate this fair land, and the massacre of an innocent people shall no more be the sport of christian men. See Pizarro safely borne to his dwelling, senors. I appoint my esquire, here to be watch and ward over him. What ho, Hubert!"

Hubert came up, leading Thunderbolt, and with an expression of sore discontent upon his face.

"What now, my man? Hast thou no word of gratulation for me?" said Richard, in English. "Thou lookest as unhappy as if thou had'st seen me lose the battle."

"Nay, Lord Richard, that thou could'st not do; but then they are bearing away that caitiff Spaniard, Pizarro, alive, when thou had'st the chance, an hundred times, of sending thy sword a good foot into his midriff."

"Tush, man," said Richard, smiling. "Pizarro is better worth to us alive than dead. Follow his bearers, and keep good watch and ward over him till I come to thee. Let no one approach him. Let no one give him food or wine but thyself. Dost thou hear?"

"Ay, my good lord," replied Hubert, brightening up at the prospect of having his enemy, Pizarro, confided to him as a prisoner. "I will not fail, be sure."

And only waiting until he had seen his young master vault into the saddle, and ride off at full speed to carry the good news to the white chief, Hubert turned towards the golden gates of the city, and soon came up with Pizarro's litter—Pizarro, once his persecutor, now his prisoner!

Three months have passed away since the memorable combat between Richard of the Raven's Crest and Pizarro, and during that time events of no small importance have taken place.

Sternly carrying out to the letter the conditions he had imposed, our hero had in person placed the humbled and disgraced commander on board a galleon, the master of which was an Englishman, with instructions to steer direct for Spain, and to deliver into the emperor's own hands a letter which Richard had written, and bearing also an enormous quantity of gold plate, which the gratitude of Atahualpa, now restored to the throne of his fathers, had insisted on bestowing upon our hero.

The usurper Huoscar had been given into his brother's hands, to be dealt with as he should think fit; but Atahualpa's mild and gentle nature abhorred the idea of putting to death one of his own race, although he was illegitimate; and by the cruel laws of the Peruvians should have been put to the cruellest of deaths for his attempt upon the sovereignty.

In that short time the firm yet wise rule of our hero had proved, even to the covetous Spaniards, that justice and fair dealing with the natives brought them more profit than the bloodthirsty and cruel rapacity of Pizarro.

They had but to ask and have. The gold they so much coveted was offered to them in such abundance, that even the Spaniards began to have a contempt for it. The most fertile parts of the land were apportioned to those who cared to settle down into cultivators of the soil. Many of the soldiers married with the Peruvian women, the marriage ceremonies of both countries being zealously performed, and a second Arcadia seemed to be growing up under the watchful care of the new ruler, when an unhappy event occurred which destroyed at a blow the whole of the edifice of peace and prosperity which had been so carefully built up.

And this was the work of one man. There was a traitor in the camp. Who was he?

CHAPTER XXXIV.

THE TRAITORS IN THE CAMP—SIGNS OF THE COMING MUTINY—RICHARD OF THE RAVEN'S CREST RESOLVES TO CONSULT THE WHITE CHIEF—THE CONFERENCE—THE VISIT TO THE SECRET TOMB OF THE PRIESTS OF THE SUN—THE WHITE CHIEF'S SECRET—THE EXPLOSION IN THE MOUNTAIN.

A TRAITOR! There is something in the very sound of the word which makes a man knit his brows and look suspiciously about him. An open foe—a bold enemy—can be met as openly and boldly; but an unknown, undetected traitor—a creature who, at the very moment he is plotting your destruction, may call you his friend and shake you by the hand—is a thing to shudder at and crush, even as one crushes beneath his heel a poisonous reptile.

The signs of disaffection, the tokens of a coming mutiny, were too apparent to be mistaken, even by the unwilling eyes of our hero. He was still obeyed, but no longer with the ready cheerfulness which the men had displayed when once they had become reconciled to his leadership.

They went sullenly and silently about such duties as were necessary in the armed encampment which Richard maintained in Caxamalca as his capital and centre of government.

From the districts, too, where little knots of the Spaniards had settled down as cultivators of the soil, there began to come rumours of acts of tyranny and oppression, of cruel deeds, and murders committed upon the Indians by their new masters.

It was now that our hero felt the real difficulty of his position. He was virtually alone. He saw now that the subtle influence of treachery was at work, that he could not depend upon the loyalty of a single Spaniard whenever the smouldering embers of revolt burst into flame.

He felt, too, the need of some one with whom to hold counsel, one whose cool judgment and trained experience would have guided and controlled his own more youthful and impetuous course. Hubert was faithful and courageous as a mastiff of the true breed, but Richard felt that it would be useless to advise with him upon so delicate and difficult a subject.

Then there flashed upon his mind the thought of the white chief. Richard had already seen many instances of his readiness of resource, and of his possession of an intellect, clear and profound in emergencies. Above all, he was English in heart and soul, and the thought had no sooner passed through our hero's mind than he resolved to consult him at once.

To William of Wyckham Richard had, despite the evident jealousy of the Spaniards, committed the governorship of the colonies—if we may so call them—which had been established outside the city walls, so that our hero, in visiting him, served a double purpose, for he hoped to get at the truth regarding the atrocities alleged to have been committed by the Spanish.

Attended only by Hubert, he rode forth, little thinking how great the mischief his temporary absence would cause. The presence of his kingly form, the stern glance of his blue eyes, had kept the demon of rebellion in check. Now that he was gone, it uprose and shook itself free from his thrall.

Richard rode on at full speed, the headlong pace of his charger, fleet as it was, being distanced by the bewildering rapidity of the thoughts that crowded on him; but when he drew rein at the encampment he had decided upon no course.

William of Wyckham received his leader standing, and waited respectfully as Richard cast himself upon a couch of llama skins, and, pressing his hands over his eyes, sought to collect his thoughts. After a few moments he rose abruptly, and said—

"William, I have sore need of counsel. There is treachery afoot, stalking in the very light of day before my face, and I know not how to stamp it out."

The white chief, without changing a muscle, said in a low grave tone—

"I have known it long, lord Richard."

"Known it!" exclaimed our hero, starting up, with a dark frown upon his face—"known it, and not told me!"

"You knew, too, lord Richard," replied the white chief, calmly, "and to the full as soon as I did. I have marked, again and again, the look of anger that shaded your brow when your orders were so sullenly obeyed."

"True," said Richard, half despairingly; "I have seen it, good William, but I have been powerless to check it. If the foul plague spot had appeared in one place, I could have cut it out with my sword, and that on the instant, but, like the live lightning, it hath blasted the whole flock at once, and left me powerless."

"Not so, lord Richard," said the white chief. "I did not see the coming storm without preparing, as far as in me lay, to avert it."

"How, good William?" said Richard of the Raven's Crest, impetuously. "Give me but means to check this accursed rebellion before it hath gathered too strong a head, and what reward thou choosest to ask is thine."

"I ask for none, good my lord; it is sufficient for me that I have tried to do my duty," said the white chief. "You have not forgotten, noble Richard, the powder stored in the secret tomb of the Priests of the Sun?"

"I have not," replied Richard; "but of what use is it to us without cannon or muskets when the Spaniards break into revolt?"

"But, if that difficulty hath been provided against?" said the white chief.

"Impossible."

"I will show you, noble Richard," replied William of Wyckham, gravely, "that it is not so impossible as you think. I have not been idle during the past three months, since you honoured me with the governorship of these outlying districts."

"Faithful and true I know thou art," said our hero, earnestly; "thou hast no need to give me further assurance of that."

"If it will please you, noble sir, to accompany me to the mountains, I will then explain, better than I can by words, what I have in my meaning."

"Willingly," said Richard, "and at once, good William, for the time is short."

A draught of wine, a short and hearty meal, and our hero, the white chief, and Hubert, mounted, and sped off at a gallop towards the dark and gloomy mountains, that from their lofty eminence seemed to frown ominously upon them.

As the white chief approached the goal, he called a halt, and, dismounting, approached the rock with as much precaution as if he had been confident that it was environed by a formidable foe.

His experience of Indian warfare had taught him this apparent excess of caution. Apparently it was not needed, for there was no sign of living creatures amongst the rocks.

The huge door swung back upon its invisible hinges, and the three Englishmen entered.

It was illumined by a number of lamps, fed with the secret oil, which, according to the priests, would burn for ever, until looked upon by an unbeliever in their divine worship of the sun—when they entered the lamps would instantly go out.

No such change, however, took place as our hero, Hubert, and the white chief, strode over the rocky floor, and the massive gate shut out the light of day.

"You see, noble Richard," said the white chief, "that I have taken some liberties with the remains of the departed priests of the sun. The saints grant that none of them may die, for, if the sacrilege is discovered, the authors will meet but scant mercy from the knives and poisons of the priesthood."

"What hast thou done then, Will, that thou shouldest dread the vengeance of these fanatics?"

"Only emptied some hundred or so of the jars containing the ashes of the priests, and used them to store my gunpowder in withal."

"Bah, thou hast nothing to fear, man!" replied our hero. "The revolt of two hundred Spaniards is of more consequence, and more to be feared, than the uprising of the whole Peruvian nation."

"Fanatics are ever to be feared, good my lord," said the white chief; "a religious fanatic is a madman, who fears nothing, sticks at nothing when his faith is insulted. But, prithee, come this way, noble Richard; I am a fool to waste time so valuable in idle clatter."

They passed the huge jars, more than a hundred of them, as Will of Wyckham said, filled to the top with dull black powder, very little like the powder of our own times, each irregular polished grain of which looks as perfect as if it had been carefully finished off by a skilled workman.

"One tiny spark in the midst of that," said Richard, "and Pizarro's vengeance would be complete."

"There is no danger," said the white chief. "The lamps are safely guarded, and we have no traitors in our midst."

So they moved on, and not one noticed the lithe figure of Pincatl, the spy and traitor, crouched behind the tall jars.

He had been the white chief's favourite attendant for years, and he knew enough of English to understand most of what had passed. His dark keen eyes glanced at one of the lamps, and an ominous smile curved his thin lips, but he crouched down again and waited.

The white chief led our hero far into the recesses of the cave, and then, rounding a sudden curve, Richard and Hubert saw a sight that made them start, and utter an exclamation of unfeigned astonishment.

For there, in the full light of the lamps, were no less than twenty small cannon, but of such quaint shape and material as at once proclaimed them the work of no European artificer, and just beyond them, tied up in bundles with remarkable regularity, was a quantity of what seemed to be cuttings from some large reeds.

"You seem astonished, noble Richard," said the white chief. "I told you I had not been idle, and yonder lie the means wherewith we shall be able to route the Spaniards and their allies were they a dozen times as numerous."

"By the rood! 'tis a marvel," said Richard, "how thou hast without iron and without artifice contrived these. But how light of weight they are. By the mass, a boy of ten years old might drag one for his go-cart!"

"Little wonder, good my lord," returned the white chief, calmly, "when you consider that they are made of wood."*

"Of wood?" repeated our hero, as he bent to examine the cannon. "'Tis true, by the rood! This is a sorry jest, good William."

"'Tis no jest, noble Richard. Not one of these you see before you but may be more safely used than the cumbersome brass cannon of the Spaniards."

And then in a few brief, but telling sentences he explained how the very wood employed was as hard as iron, and unassailable by any means but fire; how each length had been carefully chosen, and

---

* Cannon of stone, wood, and even leather, hardened by some chemical process, were often used in the early days of the discovery of gunpowder. The wooden cannon were strengthened by being bound after the manner of a cask, with thick hoops of iron.

strengthened by bands of silver and a breech piece of the same metal, that being the commonest, and the only one except gold, in which the Peruvians knew how to work.*

Richard was but half convinced. It seemed to him so incredible a thing that wood should be able to withstand the immense force excited by a full charge of powder.

The white chief's statement, however—which he could not disbelieve, knowing his incorruptible integrity—that every cannon had been tried, removed his last doubt; but he had still another question.

"But, good William, how comes it that the roar of cannon so near the city gave not the alarm to us within? I swear by the rood, though I be as keen of ear as any man, that no report reached my ears."

"And for a simple reason, noble Richard," replied the white chief. "I always made the trials here amongst the mountains, and only when a storm was raging. Your hearing would indeed be keen if you could hear the passing report of a culverin amidst the awful roar of the rolling thunder."

"I am satisfied, good William. And now one question more, and I have done?" said Richard, pointing to the bundles of reeds we have already mentioned.

"That, an' it please you, good my lord," said the white chief, "is my secret until to-night. Will you deign to wait a few hours, until I am ready to disclose it?"

"As long as thou wilt," said Richard. "For it seemeth to me that thou art fitter to be the leader than I. Thou hast been up and doing, while I dreamed."

Up to this time Hubert—who looked upon the culverins with the utmost disgust, when he learned that they were wood—had held his peace; but when his beloved young master, whom he regarded as the first of created beings, began to condemn his own inactivity, and exalt the white chief above him, he grew angry.

"What!" he growled, "and is the safety of christian men to be entrusted to a few wooden cannon, which I could crack with my finger and thumb, and a wooden head, which I have a mind to crack for nothing. Pardie, a goodly venture!"

"What art thou prating about now, Hubert?" demanded our hero, who had only caught a few muttered words of his esquire's uncomplimentary soliloquy.

"Only this, Master Richard," said Hubert, "that when yonder pop-guns are discharged, I may be posted in front to help the ball along, for, by my patron saint, it will never else reach its mark."

"Hold thy prating tongue, Hubert," said Richard, half angry, half amused at the free-lance's impertinent criticism. "Heed him not, William, thou knowest his tongue of old; but, as we go on, advise me as to what thou would'st do when—which the saints avert—the Spaniards break into open revolt."

"Now, good my lord," replied the white chief; "you tax me beyond my powers. When you command I can obey, but I cannot lead."

A moment's thought convinced our hero of the propriety as well as the wisdom of the white chief's words. The means were ready to his hand; he was supreme as yet—at least in name. It was for him to act.

They had now passed from the rocky tomb into the open air, and there Richard of the Raven's Crest halted for a few moments in deep thought.

"If," he said, "the Spaniards are now ripe for revolt, they will seize the opportunity afforded by my absence to raise the standard of rebellion, and close the golden gates against my return."

* It is a well-known fact that at Potosi, and other silver mines in Peru, the veins of the precious metal were found to be absolutely pure, and could be cut out in blocks with a chisel. These mines have been worked for many centuries, and still seem unexhausted.

"Or," suggested the white chief, "you may find the gates open and everything to all appearance in order and tranquillity until you are well within the toils, when you might be surrounded and overpowered by numbers and be made a prisoner."

"A fate ten thousand times worse than death!" said Richard. "I must not risk it."

Then he added, after a short pause—

"William, thou must despatch one of thy warriors whom thou canst trust into the city, to learn whether these rebels are ripe for their traitorous work."

"Good, my lord," said the white chief. "Even I must be your messenger; there are none amongst my warriors who understand the Spanish tongue."

"I am loth to let thee go," said our hero; "yet it must be. But first, good William, we will hie back to the camp, and bring up such of thy warriors as thou hast trained to the use of the cannon, and horses sufficient to bear the ammunition and drag the culverins."

"No need for horses," growled Hubert, in an undertone. "I will undertake to carry a couple of the pop-guns under each arm, and march a dozen miles to boot."

"It shall be done, good my lord," said the white chief. "'Twill be easy for me to enter the city under cover of the night, and by to-morrow at dawn you shall know all that you desire."

"'Tis a dangerous mission, Will," said our hero; "and were there another able to take thy place thou should'st not go."

"Danger! Lord Richard?" repeated the white chief, with a laugh. "It hath been my playfellow from babyhood. Fear not but that all will turn out well."

The words had scarcely left his lips—their steeds had not yet taken their first stride—when there was a strange rumbling sound, proceeding apparently from the very bosom of the mountain.

They had not time to exchange a word or even a look, when the ground seemed to open up before them, a vast sheet of flame shot high into the air, followed by a cloud of dense white smoke and a tremendous report, which seemed to shake the very earth to its foundations, and, blinded, stunned, and breathless, Richard and his companions were hurled violently down the rocky ravine!

CHAPTER XXXV.

AFTER THE EXPLOSION—THE WHITE CHIEF'S SURPRISE—THE DISCOVERY OF THE TRAITOR—THE RETURN TO THE CAMP—RICHARD SUMMONS THE DEMON OF THE DIAMOND—A REVELATION—DESTINY.

THE escape of Richard and his friends was little less than miraculous; for, in addition to the danger they had been in from the force of the explosion, a shower of huge pieces of shattered rock had rained down upon the ravine, almost any one of which would have crushed an elephant.

Of the horses, two were killed. White Thunderbolt alone escaped, and, though he had galloped off directly with fright, returned readily at his master's whistle.

For a moment or two after the first anxious inquiries as to whether either of the three were seriously hurt, there was a deep silence, each one looking towards the vast gap in the mountain side, where, but a few moments ago, had been the secret tomb of the Priests of the Sun.

Then the white chief spoke—

"There has been treachery here, Lord Richard. The sound of the explosion will bring the Spaniards down, like carrion crows, to feast upon the scene of our destruction, and perchance search for our mangled remains. But, ere we go, I would fain know to whom we are indebted."

"Waste not the time," said Richard. "'Twas the result of accident—a spark from the lamps."

"Impossible, good my lord; it could not be. Spare me but a few moments, or ride on, and I will follow."

The next moment he was clambering over the uge rocks, which now obstructed and blocked up he defile, and then he was lost to view, as he tooped to examine the ground.

He had not been absent five minutes, when they saw him again returning, his face pale and stern, and with a dead man's shattered hand held tightly in his grasp.

"See here," he said, pointing to one finger of the hand, on which there was a massive gold ring, engraved with some mystic characters. "This is the hand of Pincatl, whom we supposed to have perished on the mountain. He is the traitor, and it was he who so nearly betrayed us into Pizarro's hands when we were on the raft, and your good genius averted our doom."

"He hath met with a just reward," said Richard, sternly. "So may treachery ever work its own destruction. His blood be upon his own head."

"Amen!" added Hubert and the White Chief, solemnly, and then with one accord they turned their footsteps from the doomed ravine.

Walking and riding by turns, the three companions reached the encampment in a far gloomier state of mind than they had quitted it a few short hours before.

But there was work to be done, and a course of action to be decided on, and they set about the task with a calm resolution which seems peculiar to the English character.

"Now, good William," said our hero, resolutely, "that this unlucky chance hath shattered thy well-laid scheme to pieces, we must shape our plans anew."

"True, noble Richard; even had we time, our enemies would not afford us opportunity to do over again the work of the past three months."

"That being the case, we must consider how best, with the means we have, to shake the rebellion to the dust, and re-establish my authority as ruler."

"Good, my lord," replied the white chief, sorrowfully, "we have none."

"None but our good swords, and strong right hands!" said our hero.

"And we are three against three hundred of the most desperate ruffians in Spain, armed, too, with weapons which will lay us low ere we get near enough to strike one good blow at them."

"Malediction!" said Richard, between his clenched teeth. "Is there no way out of this strait?"

"I see none, my lord. My warriors would have fought, and fought well, if I could have shown them that I, too, had the power of making thunder and lightning—as they call the explosion of fire-arms—at will, and scattering my enemies; but that hope is gone for ever."

There was again a long and deep silence. It had already grown dark, and the watch-fires were glowing redly through the gloom. Suddenly, Richard spoke again—

"Let the night decide," he said. "I am weary, and I have need of rest. Let every light and fire in the camp be extinguished, lest it serve as a guide to our enemies, and by daybreak, good William, come to me, and thou too, Hubert. Now leave me."

When they were gone, Richard closely drew the curtains which screened the entrance to his tent, and took from the breast of his doublet the little packet which contained the diamond, and slowly unfolded it, while his thoughts possessed the wish for the presence of its Demon guardian.

The light, which the priceless jewel gave out, flashed more brightly, and fell upon the dark shadowy form of the Demon standing motionless in the centre of the tent.

"I am here," it said, in a voice which was like an echo, or, like a sound heard in a dream. "What wouldst thou?"

"This," said Richard, who, brave as he was, could not repress an involuntary shudder at the sight of the shadowy being who seemed to be the arbiter of his destiny; "give me the means to quell these daring rebels, and to restore order and peace amongst these unhappy people."

The Demon shook its head with a slight gesture of dissent.

"It cannot be!" it said. "The destiny of this empire is in the hands of one mightier than I. Thou hast fulfilled the prophecy. The true Inca hath been restored to his throne, and peace and prosperity have once more smiled upon it. If the rude hands of Pizarro and his followers again stir up strife and dissension, thou hast naught to do with it. Henceforth, thy destiny and his lie wide apart!"

"Not so!" exclaimed Richard, impetuously. "I will spend the best years of my life, and the best blood in my veins to thwart his evil courses."

"It may not be!" said the Demon. "Thou hast accepted the diamond, Richard Plantagenet, and with it thou must take——"

"What?" demanded our hero, as the Demon paused with that mocking smile still upon its face.

"Thy destiny!"

A low sardonic laugh echoed through the tent, —the Demon vanished as the light of the diamond paled out. Richard stood for a moment, breathing heavily; then, everything seemed to whirl around him, and, staggering forward, he fell upon his couch —insensible!

* * * *

When the day broke, and the white chief and Hubert sought their leader's tent, they found him lying on his couch, his face marked with a hectic glow on either cheek, his eyes bright with the light of fever, and his lips giving utterance to the wildest ravings.

"He is poisoned! Holy mother, have mercy on him! This is some foul trick of his enemies; they have crept upon him in the night," exclaimed Hubert.

"Not so, old comrade," said the white chief. "'Tis a fever, and a malignant one. See here, too," he added, "what is this?"

There was a small piece of parchment lying on the settle by the side of the couch, on which were traced a few lines in Richard's handwriting.

They ran thus—

"When the fever, which I feel burning in my veins, attacks me, bear me at once to the sea coast and ship for England. Use thine own discretion as to whether thou wilt accompany me."

"And is that," said Hubert, in a low tone, "my master's wish?"

"See for thyself, man," replied the white chief, holding out the parchment; "the writing is clear enough."

"Nay, thou knowest I am no clerk,"* said Hubert; "but as it be as thou sayest, let us about the matter at once."

The white chief's first act was to search for certain herbs, the value of which he well knew, and from them compound a draught, which he administered to Richard. The fever was almost instantly allayed, but he still remained unconscious to all that was passing around him.

"Four horses will be enough," said the white

---

* Clerk. A term used during the middle ages to designate all holding of the priestly office, who were then about the only persons able to read and write. Even in our own days, in all legal documents, a clergyman of the Established Church was described as a Clerke. So greatly was learning esteemed in those dark ages, that a person accused of any crime—even murder—could, if he were able to read and write, plead "benefit of clergy," and claim his acquittal.

chief. "I have had a litter made for Lord Richard, on which he will lie as easily as in a tent. A second will carry stores enough for our use, and the other two thou and I will ride."

"And is my young master no better? Doth he not mend?"

"Better; ay, that is he," replied the white chief. "Else had I put off the journey. The draught I gave him acted like a charm."

"Hath he spoken?" demanded the free-lance, eagerly. "Will he know me, think ye, Will?"

"Nay; and not perchance for many a day," replied the white chief. "When the fever hath left him he will be weak as a little child, and must not be harassed, as thou would'st do, with talk and questions."

"And I tell thee, Will," replied Hubert, doggedly, "that it will go ill with the man who stands between me and Master Richard once the plaguing fever hath left him, and he able to know me and call me by my name."

"Nay, but Hubert ——"

"Nay me no nays," interrupted the obstinate esquire. "I may not be so skilled in leechcraft as thou, Will; but this I know, that the sight of a friendly face is better to a sick man than all the 'pothecaries drugs' in Europe."

"Never fear, man, thou shalt be satisfied; and now see that the horses are brought up. I have seen that the packing and the litter is as soft and easy as the king's couch."

As tenderly as if he had been a sleeping babe, our hero's stalwart form was placed on the litter, the curtains carefully drawn, and so the little cavalcade slowly began its march towards the distant sea-coast.

Ten days were passed before the vast ocean lay stretched out before them, and, to the white chief's astonishment, Richard still remained unconscious, and could not be brought to speak or even recognise his friends by so much as a look.

Yet his pulse was full and firm, his breathing regular, and the glow of health had returned to his cheeks.

Neither the white chief nor Hubert could understand this strange malady, neither could the learned leech,* whom they found at the little colony of San Miguel, where they fell in with a galleon about to be despatched to Spain for fresh supplies.

What would they have said had they known that the letter they had read was none of Richard's, but prepared by the art of the Demon of the Diamond, and that the stupor under which our hero then lay was a spell cast upon him by the same powerful hands?

But what was the destiny to which the mysterious influence of the diamond was forcing him with irresistible power? There was the riddle. How could it be solved?

It was fortunate that, at the little colony of San Miguel, there was no one who was acquainted personally with our hero or his esquire. The few soldiers stationed there—if such lawless adventurers deserved the name—were newly arrived from Spain, and had, as yet, heard nothing of the defeat and deposition of Pizarro.

"We are fortunate in choosing this place," said he white chief. "In a few hours the galleon will stretch her sails to the breeze, and, unless our good fortune desert us, and our enemies have followed close in our wake, nothing can prevent the escape of thy noble master and thyself."

"And thou, William?" said Hubert; "thou forgettest thyself."

"My way lies thither," replied the white chief, with something of sadness in his tones, as he

turned and waved his right hand towards the shadowy outline of the Andes, which reared their majestic peaks high into the cloudless heavens.

"Nay, nay, man," said Hubert; "that would not be my master's wish, an' he were able to speak and tell it thee."

"It would, Hubert, for it is my duty. What, thinkest thou, will become of my warriors, who have been so long faithful to thy master's cause? The Spaniards will turn upon them without mercy. Not one of them will be spared, unless I am there to guide and counsel them."

Hubert consented ruefully enough to this view of the case, for he was a firm advocate for the strict performance of duty himself.

"But, good Will," he added, after a pause, "it is not thy intention to pass thy whole life here? It is no place for an honest man, now that these thieving, murdering, swarthy-visaged Spaniards have settled, like locusts, on everything."

"True enough, Hubert. I feel as thou dost, and fain would I lay my old bones to rest in our own fair land. I see too clearly that the footing Pizarro and the others have obtained will be made good, if not by them, at least by their successors. The empire of the Incas is doomed. It is the will of God, and nothing can avert it."

"If that be so," said Hubert, "and even my dull brain can see that thy prophecy is a truthful one, why stay to avert the inevitable? Thinkest thou that my noble young master would have decided on this step if there had been a shadow of hope remaining? Come with us, then—pluck up a cheerful heart, and shout, as thou hast often done, 'Hey for Merrie England!' Why, man, the very name should make thy old blood dance in thy veins, and make thee as sprightly as a lad of twenty!"

"Thou forgettest, Hubert, that I have a promise to perform, a duty to fulfil, ere I can turn my back on this land. Thy duty is to follow and serve thy master—mine is to save my warriors, if I can, from the fangs of those Spanish ban-dogs. That duty done——"

"Ay, and then, Will?"

"Why, I care not how soon I turn my back on this land, and cross the seas to set eyes once again on our own dear country."

"A bargain!" cried Hubert, extending his own huge palm. "Thy hand upon it, Will."

"There, man," said the white chief, giving the veteran free-lance a grip that made his fingers tingle again.

"Good. Now, hast thou the tools of the scrivener's trade—pen and ink-horn—about thee?"

"Nay. What occasion have I for them? What wouldst thou have me write?"

"A note, good Will, of the place where thou may'st at all times hear of us when the saints speed thee to England."

"Tell it me, Hubert. My memory hath but little to burden it, and I warrant me I forget not a syllable."

"Listen, then. 'Tis Master William Reddeler, at the sign of the Angel, in the Chepe, London. Wilt thou remember that?"

"Ay, were it ten times as long; and now the time comes when we must say farewell for many a long day, old comrade. See, a shallop is putting off for the shore, and the sailors are climbing like cats amongst the rigging. One more God-speed to thy master, Hubert—would that he could understand me—and then farewell."

The white chief parted the curtains of the litter, laid his hand gently on the forehead of our hero, and, with a softly-muttered prayer, withdrew.

Then came the bustle of the last preparations for departure, the hearty farewell of Hubert, shouted by his stentorian lungs from the shallop, and then again from the sides of the galleon, until she spread her white wings to the breeze, and

---

* The term by which professors of the medical science were then known. Surgery was for a long time allied to the barber's trade, and the Honourable Company of Barber Surgeons is yet in existence, with power to issue diplomas to its members.

steadily sailed away towards the blue mist of the horizon.

The white chief stood there—a silent, solitary figure—until the galleon was nothing to his sight but a speck upon the water. What was that cold chill that crept slowly over his brave heart, seeming to freeze his very blood? What was that feeling of unutterable sadness that oppressed his mind? Was it only the natural grief one feels at parting with a dearly-loved friend? or was it a presentiment warning him that he would never see them more, and that he was going back to Death?

CHAPTER XXXVI.

THE RETURN OF THE WHITE CHIEF TO THE PERUVIAN CAMP—THE SPREAD OF THE REVOLT —THE CHIEF'S COUNSEL—ALAXA'S PETITION— THE BAND OF PATRIOTS—THE RIDE TO CAXA-MALCA—THE NIGHT WATCH—THE SURPRISE.

THE white chief's return was eagerly looked for at the camp, and if ever for a moment on his way back he had regretted not having gone on board the galleon and sailed for England, that feeling would have been dissipated by the eager and trustful welcome the Peruvians gave him.

There was indeed need for his presence and for prompt action, for from the chief whom he had named as leader in his absence he learned that no less than three small parties of the outlying Spaniards had attacked the camp, demanding in the first instance, with all the insolent authority of conquerors, all the gold that was in the tents, and, when this was refused, endeavouring to force an entrance.

All of these, however, had been repulsed by the Peruvians, who, thanks to the training of the white chief, had lost much of their superstitious terror of the Spaniards.

"Well done, my brave Alaxa," said William of Wyckham. "You have bravely and well defended the trust I gave into your keeping. But the loss on our side—how many? These Spanish wolves visit not the fold without reaching some amongst the flock."

"There are twelve killed and twenty wounded—nearly all dangerously," replied Alaxa. "More would have fallen, but only a few had muskets."

"Ha!" said the white chief, as a thoughtful frown compressed his handsome war-worn features. "We must be up and stirring, Alaxa. One or two of the hornets are crawling round the camp; but in a little while we shall have the whole swarm about our ears."

"Let them come," said Alaxa, defiantly, as he shook his spear in the air. "Now that we know that they are mortal like ourselves, and not the descendants of the gods, we care not for them."

"Nay, Alaxa," replied the white chief, sadly. "With only too much gladness would I lead you against your foes, if we were only certain of taking one life of theirs for every ten that fell on our side. But that would be useless, even the sacrifice of the lives of a thousand brave men."

"Try us, noble chief," said Alaxa.

"It would be useless, I tell you," replied Will of Wyckham, "unless I could animate the whole of your countrymen with such a brave soul as beats in your bosom. Ere now, I tell you, the tale hath reached Spain that gold is to be found here as abundantly as pebbles on the sea shore, and that jewels of inestimable price are to be had for the bartering of a few beads and bits of brass. The mere tale will bring hither thousands upon thousands of idle, needy, unscrupulous adventurers, without a single virtue except courage. Take my word for it, Alaxa, they will sweep on resistless as the sea, and engulf mercilessly all that comes within their reach."

"The words of our noble chief are words of wisdom. When he speaks, we all listen and obey; but will he in his greatness hear Alaxa speak?"

"Say what you will. My ears are open."

"Then," began Alaxa—drawing his lithe form up to its full height, while his handsome features flushed beneath the dusky skin with pride and anger—"my prayer to our chief is that he will lead us against these insolent Spaniards. If our bodies are too weak, and our weapons too feeble to sweep them from off our land, let us at least show them that our hearts are strong. Better to die in defence of our country, and let our bones mingle with its dust, than live on to be the slaves of those who despoil and dishonour us."

"Well said, Alaxa," said the white chief, gravely. "What you have asked for is your right, and if your comrades are with you, I will not fail, be sure of that."

"They are, noble chief—to a man. While you were absent we spoke of it again and again. I have been through the camp, illustrious leader, and there is not one who is not staunch and true."

"Remember," added the white chief, "that in this enterprise every man's life no longer belongs to himself—he devotes it to his country."

"They know it, noble chief," replied Alaxa. "Each warrior will gladly die, if in giving his life he but takes a Spanish one in exchange."

"Good, then," replied Will of Wyckham, upon whose features an expression of hopeless, calm despair had settled. He knew now what Fate had in store for him—he knew what boded the presentiment he had felt when he parted from Richard and Hubert.

"I am a doomed man," he thought; "but I shall die at least doing my duty—defending the country of my adoption against the ravenous Spaniards. But it is hard. I should have dearly liked to have set my foot once more upon the green sward of old England, and to have heard the merry voice of the lark sounding again within these ears. But away with such thoughts, they will unman me; and all the heart and strength that I have is sorely wanted now."

He strode hastily back to his tent, and, casting himself upon the couch, buried his face in his hands, and sunk into profound thought.

For more than half an hour he remained thus. Then he arose, and with a calm, composed face, and a slow, majestic step, he passed out of the tent, and summoned Alaxa to him.

"Alaxa," he said, "although the very nature of our purpose dooms us to death, yet our first course should be to make our memory feared, if not respected, by these Spaniards."

"Ay, noble chief," said Alaxa, "they hate us now—to make them fear us would indeed be a triumph."

"We must not act like desperate men, who rush bare-breasted upon the swords of their enemies. I mean, Alaxa, to sell every life in this camp so dearly, that the Spaniards shall rue the name of the white chief as long as they have tongues to tell the story."

"You promise us indeed a glut of vengeance," said Alaxa, his dark eyes sparkling with a fierce joy.

"But it must be secured, Alaxa, not by mere fiery courage—that would destroy us and our hopes of vengeance. We must be cunning as the panther —silent as the snake. Do you comprehend me?"

"Ay, noble chief, that do I," replied Alaxa. "To start upon them when they have besotted themselves with the fiery spirit they distil from plants and trees, and creep up in the night so silently that their dull sense shall not detect a sound, and thus, uttering our war-cry, leap up and deal death amongst them."

"Even so, Alaxa," said the white chief; "as they have dealt with you, so deal with them.

Falsehood, treachery, cruelty—these have been their watch-words. We will hurl them back in their teeth, and teach them to dread the wrath of an oppressed people."

"Your words fill my heart with fire," said Alaxa, in a suppressed voice. "Speak, noble chief; what are your wishes?"

"Where are the twelve young warriors whom I trained to speak the Spanish tongue?"

"Alas!" returned Alaxa, "six of them will never speak more—their tongues are silent. The Sun God hath received them into his bosom?"

"Dead?"

"Ay. They were the foremost when the Spaniards attacked us—the foremost and the fiercest."

"'Tis pity, for I had need of them," said the white chief. "Send the rest hither, Alaxa."

They came, and the orders given to them were short and stern. Each one, proceeding in a different direction, was to visit a certain number of the detached settlements of the Spaniards, and find out what preparations were being made to avenge the repulse of the attack upon the camp.

"As for yourself, Alaxa," said the white chief, "you will remain here, and take the command during my absence. I go to Caxamalca this night."

"To Caxamalca!" ejaculated the Peruvian, his swarthy skin seeming actually to grow paler as he heard the words.

"Ay, to Caxamalca," repeated the white chief, steadily. "What is there in that to frighten you or I?"

"'Tis venturing into the bear's den, naked and unarmed," cried Alaxa. "Do not go, illustrious chief; upon you depends the success of our purpose."

"Its success depends, Alaxa, upon obedience to my orders," replied the white chief, sternly. "I go to Caxamalca, because there is none other who can do the work I have to do. See that my horse and arms are in readiness for me the moment the sun sets."

Alaxa was silent beneath his chief's rebuke. He bowed low, and retired, and William of Wyckham, with a deep sigh, as it seemed, of weariness, passed again into his tent, and remained there, in meditation, till the deep shadows gathering round warned him that the hour of his departure was nigh.

Alaxa led up the powerful charger at the very moment when the white chief emerged from his tent.

"'Tis well," he said, in the deep, grave voice which he had assumed since his parting with our hero and Hubert; "you are punctual, Alaxa."

Carefully his practised eye and hand tested the girths and the bridle, and noted that his weapons were fit and ready. Then he leaped into the saddle, waved his hand to Alaxa, uttered a few words of adieu, and rode away at full speed towards the city of Caxamalca.

CHAPTER XXXVII.

IN WHICH THE STORY OF OUR HERO AND OF THE DEVIL'S DIAMOND DRAWS TO ITS END.

THE white chief knew that he was riding to almost certain death when he undertook to play the spy upon the Spaniards at Caxamalca; yet he never flinched, even in thought, from his duty—no, not for a single instant.

He knew that, keen as were his eyes, and quick his ears, there were thousands quick and keen as he amongst the Peruvians, ready to hunt him down, and betray him to their haughty masters.

The white chief would have done better to have gone on foot, for he had learnt, during his sojourn with the Indians, to glide noiselessly as a snake, even through a forest glade, strewn deep with the rustling leaves of autumn.

He well remembered this, and had considered it, but he would have to deal not alone with fleet-footed Peruvians, but with the Spaniards, and they, mounted on their powerful Andulasian barbs, would soon run him down upon the open plains.

At every furlong that he traversed, the instinct of the warrior seemed to be aroused to quicker life within him; and, with head bent forward, eyes straining to pierce the dense gloom of the starless night, and ever ready to catch the faintest sound, he rode slowly onward.

"Ha! what was that glimmer to the left? The white chief checks his horse with an almost imperceptible touch upon the bridle. There again, in the same spot! The white chief looked and listened, as men only can whose lives depend upon their vigilance. But the glimmer, if glimmer it were, and his eyes had not deceived him, was gone. "'Twas but the flash of a fire-fly," he said.

With a whispered word, and a shake of the rein, he urged his horse on again, when a shadowy figure crossed his path—then another and another, to the right, to the left, behind, before—while suddenly, in the very spot where he had seen the glimmer, the light of a great fire shot up, and shone upon the arms and armour of at least a hundred Spaniards.

Despite all his care and skill he had been led into an ambush.

Swift as lightning he glanced around—the Peruvians, to the number of many thousands, were closing in upon him in a circle. To break through such a host would be well nigh impossible—he and his horse would be riddled with arrows; but amongst the Spaniards in the centre he recognised del Soto, the treacherous priest, Valverde, and Pizarro's brother, upon them he would avenge himself and his lost friends—Richard of the Raven's Crest and Hubert.

Already showers of darts and arrows began to fall about him; some few scratched him, but the majority were ill-aimed, and passed him by.

The Spaniards now were preparing their muskets, and the white chief knew that it was time to act.

He swung himself suddenly from his saddle, and supporting himself thereon by the sheer muscular power of one knee, sheltered himself completely behind the body of his horse, which he urged into a fierce gallop around the fire.

He had his bow and arrows ready—a shaft was fitted to the string, and discharged with lightning rapidity.

It struck del Soto full upon the breast, but the stout leather was impenetrable as steel to all save the force of a bullet, and the missile glanced off harmlessly.

A second shivered to splinters upon the steel morion of the younger Pizarro; but a third did its work better, and wetted its feathers in the life blood of Padre Valverde.

"One at least," muttered the white chief—"but it is a sorry trifle while the others live. Fool that I was not to have armed myself with sword or axe. I could even now dash in and give a good account of two or three before I fell. Ha!"

As the exclamation left his lips his horse bounded high into the air, dashing its rider to the earth, and then falling upon him, crushed him into insensibility.

*   *   *   *

Again the curtain rises upon the great square of the city of Caxamalca—again does the mid-day sun blaze down upon the many head dresses of the Peruvians, the gold and jewelled ornaments of the caciques, and upon the Inca himself, who, though still outwardly the ruler of his empire, is but the slave and prisoner of the Spaniards.

For there in the place of honour sits the younger Pizarro, assuming the governorship till the hoped for return of his more warlike and unscrupulous brother from Spain, and about him are groped his most trusted officers, men upon whom he can rely to the death.

Only one well-known face and form was absent. The cruel, crafty face of Padre Valverde is not there, and never again will that cunning brain plot against the peace of mankind, for he lies stark and stiff, pierced to the heart by the white chief's arrow.

And for that William of Wyckham has to die that day. It is to see him suffer that all this preparation has been made—to witness his last agonies that tens of thousands have assembled here in the bright noon-tide.

The hour is at hand; for now the blare of a trumpet rises high above the hoarse roaring of the crowd, and some dozen slaves enter the guarded space in the centre of the square, leading amongst them four beautiful horses, each of which is girt with a broad, strong surcingle.

Another blare of the harsh-voiced trumpet, and the white chief, bound hand and foot, is borne into the square, and carried close to where the group of Spaniards sit upon their raised seats.

Here his ankles are unbound sufficiently to allow of his standing, but the guards still keep their hold, and menace him with their lance points, for they remember, and fear, his prowess in the field.

"Dog of a heretic," began del Soto, bending his black brows upon the white chief, "double spy and double trait or—for thou hast not only rebelled against our lawful authority, but against that of thy acknowledged master, the Inca—thou art justly adjudged to die; but yet, so great is our desire to be merciful, even to so great a villain as thou art, that we are ready to change thy sentence to the more merciful one of perpetual imprisonment in the mines, but only on two conditions."

"I can readily guess it," said the white chief, "but say on."

"It is, that you deliver into our hands, or disclose the secret hiding-place of the false and traitorous Englishman known as Richard of the Raven's Crest, and his esquire, Hubert of Chertsey."

"Were my arms free, thou lying Spaniard, with a heart as dark and evil as thy face, I would give thee such an answer as would last thy life. But, since that may not be, know that William of Wyckham spits at thy offer, and leaves his dying curse for thee and thy traitorous brood."

"Away with him," thundered the Spaniard, livid with wrath. "Slit his foul tongue. Ho, there, ye slaves, bring up the horses, and see that ye bind him fast, or ye shall share his fate."

To be torn in pieces by four maddened horses ! It was an awful death—a death the bare mention of which is enough to make a strong man shudder. Yet, save that his bronzed cheek was a shade paler, and that the solemn light which comes to men who stand upon the brink of eternity, was in his eyes, his manner was as calm and composed as if the dreadful scene about to be enacted was but some trifling sport of no moment to him.

He suffered the fatal cords to be bound to his limbs without a murmur. Only, when all was ready, and the slaves waited with their cruel whips for the last signal, his lips parted, and a murmured prayer went up to Heaven for our hero and his old comrade, Hubert.

*   *   *

So died the white chief—brave, true, and loyal to the last—a victim offered up upon the altar of Spanish pride and cruelty. A true Englishman,

his last thought was of his duty, his last words a prayer to God to bless his friends.

And what now of our gallant hero, brave Richard of the Raven's Crest, and of his faithful follower, Hubert. Let us briefly, as the story draws to a close, trace some portion of their career.

Richard did not recover his senses until the galleon was safe within the port of Cadiz, and Hubert, with a jealous care, had conveyed him to a handsome lodging hard by the Puerta del Sol, in company with the mass of treasure—not the spoil of conquest—but the free gift of the grateful Inca.

The greatest treasure of all—the Diamond—Richard had kept within his bosom during the whole voyage, the fingers of his right hand clasped about it as if even in his trance he knew its value.

When he first recovered and found that he had been so strangely conveyed away, he refused to believe the explanation offered, deeming that it was a trick of Hubert's to induce him to quit a place so full of danger; and in the heat of his resentment he dismissed the veteran from his service, and embarked on board a galleon bound for the New World.

It never reached its destination. When only four days' sail away from Cadiz, it was wrecked, and only some half dozen of the living freight were saved, including Richard.

Nothing daunted, he tried again and again, but each time some dire disaster overtook the vessel, and the superstitious Spaniards—not without good reason—began to look upon him as dangerous, and not even the heavy bribes he offered would induce one to sail with him.

Tired at last of his vain efforts, and convinced that it was folly to struggle further with the will of the strange being who had so constituted himself the guardian of the Diamond and the controller of his destiny, our hero plunged at once into the midst of the bright and joyous pleasures which the splendid court of the Spanish Emperor offered to the rich and noble.

And here again the watchful vigilance of the friendly demon stood him in good stead. Many a gay gallant—many a wily courtier envied and feared the handsome, dauntless young Englishman, for whom the smiles of beauty were so plentifully lavished, and whose wealth seemed boundless as the ocean.

Bravos were hired to stab him; but they never lived to tell the tale of their failure to their masters. Subtle poisons were mingled with the wine he drank at some brilliant banquet—Richard always pledged the perfidious host as he quaffed the bumper, the poison harmed him not—but the next morning the would-be poisoner was always found dead in his bed, with a look of unutterable horror on his face.

After a while, however, Richard began to long for one more view of the white cliffs, and sweeping meadow land of his dear native country; and, in company with Hubert, he bade farewell to the gay capital of Spain; and, as rapidly as the tardy means of those days permitted, made his way to Calais, where he took ship for England, in company with the ever-faithful Hubert, whom he had soon traced out, and amply recompensed for his unreasoning anger.

And here we will leave our hero, happy in the possession of youth, health, and a wealth "beyond the dreams of avarice." At some future time, it may be our province to record the further fortunes of Richard of the Raven's Crest; but now, for the present at least, we drop the curtain upon the Devil's Diamond, and write—

www.ingramcontent.com/pod-product-compliance
Lightning Source LLC
Chambersburg PA
CBHW081214170626

46811CB00010B/3288